AN EXCITING NEW MYSTERY SERIES
A GREAT NEW DETECTIVE
A TERRIFIC NEW AUTHOR
DEAD TIME

"AN AUSPICIOUS DEBUT . . . Bland handles the evolving relationship between Marti and a white male partner unsure of a woman's place in the police world with sensitivity and humor, while evoking with chilling reality the plight of endangered children and the mentally ill."
—*Publishers Weekly*

"MARTI MACALISTER IS A MOST WELCOME addition to crime fiction. Thoughtful, professional, and fully human, she brings a complexity to the personal side of police work seldom presented in fiction. Eleanor Bland has created a great supporting cast, too, in MacAlister's sympathetically drawn partner, and a crew of street kids living in the margins of modern America."
—Sara Paretsky, author of *Guardian Angel*

"MARTI MacALISTER IS A TOUGH COP WITH A TENDER HEART. Eleanor Bland has a fine, sensitive eye for society's invisible people. Read this one!"
—Barbara D'Amato, author of *Hardball*

"ELEANOR TAYLOR BLAND IS A PERCEPTIVE AND COMPELLING WRITER. The characters are so real you worry about them, their secrets so intriguing you won't be able to stop reading. It's a book you won't forget soon. And after you've read it, there are people you'll never again view in the same way."
—Susan Dunlop, author of *Death and Taxes*

"AN AUSPICIOUS BEGINNING FOR MRS. BLAND."
—*Alfred Hitchcock Mystery Magazine*

DEAD TIME

Eleanor Taylor Bland

A SIGNET BOOK

SIGNET
Published by the Penguin Group
Penguin Books USA Inc., 375 Hudson Street,
New York, New York 10014, U.S.A.
Penguin Books Ltd, 27 Wrights Lane,
London W8 5TZ, England
Penguin Books Australia Ltd, Ringwood,
Victoria, Australia
Penguin Books Canada Ltd, 10 Alcorn Avenue,
Toronto, Ontario, Canada M4V 3B2
Penguin Books (N.Z.) Ltd, 182–190 Wairau Road,
Auckland 10, New Zealand

Penguin Books Ltd, Registered Offices:
Harmondsworth, Middlesex, England

Published by Signet, an imprint of New American Library, a division of Penguin Books USA Inc. This is an authorized reprint of a hardcover edition published by St. Martin's Press.

First Signet Printing, November, 1993
10 9 8 7 6 5 4 3 2 1

PUBLISHER'S NOTE
This is a work of fiction. Names, characters, places, and incidents either are the product of the author's imagination or are used fictitiously, and any resemblance to actual persons, living or dead, events, or locales is entirely coincidental.

For Elaine Riley,
my half sister,
wherever you are.

For technical assistance, I'd like to acknowledge Kevin Bland; Keith Corbin, Esq.; Elliott Dunn, Esq.; Eunice Fikso; Curtis Gentry, ex-Bear; Russ Peterson, Dean of Instruction, College of Lake County; Jerry Pietrzak, Ph.D.; Lucy Rawn; Anne Savarese; and Ruth Wickert.

Thanks also to Todd and Anthony, Aunt Alice, Barbara, Diane, Dolores, Emily, Janice, Lelia Jo, Katey, Louise, Mildred, Marie, Marianne, Patty, Peetey, Sandra and Selina.

Prologue

When it began snowing Georgie was still half a block away from the Cramer Hotel, holding Padgett by the hand and pulling him along. Padgett was almost as old as he was, close to nine, and it was time he stopped being scared of the dark.

"It's snowin', Georgie. We'd better go back."

Padgett even sounded scared. No matter. He had to learn how to take care of himself. Who knew what would happen once they got to Minneapolis? Wasn't nothing forever. Most things didn't last long at all.

"Trade mittens," Georgie said, knowing Padgett's had holes in the thumbs and not wanting to hear about his hands being cold.

Glass broke and Padgett jumped. "They fightin'," he said, sounding like he was getting ready to cry.

"Drunks," Georgie told him. "Bar on the corner about to close up. We late 'cause you been pokin' along. We was 'sposed to get the stuff from Burger King, come by here for the cookies, and go back. But you had to keep hangin' around there 'cause it's cold. Be cold till spring and maybe still be cold then."

But it wasn't the cold that Padgett didn't like, they were both used to that. It was the dark.

"Come on. And be real quiet."

Instead of going down the alley and through the window like he always did, Georgie decided to go in the front way where there was more light. By the time they reached the big glass front doors two drunks had come out of the bar and were swinging at each other. One slipped and fell.

"I wanna . . ." Padgett began.

"Come on," Georgie said. You'd think Padgett would be used to drunks fighting by now. Grew up with it same as he did. Boy got shakin' scared if he got near someone drunk. Good thing Padgett was good at stealing, 'specially out of stores. Boy would be useless if he couldn't do that.

It wasn't much warmer inside than out. Georgie pointed to his sneakers, lifted his feet. Padgett walked quietly, too. The floor was made out of some kind of swirly pink and white stone that was easy to make noise on. Georgie tiptoed over to the long dark counter that was taller than he was and showed Padgett where he'd carved his initials in the wood. Peeking around, he saw the guard sleeping in the chair. The radio was playing, mostly static. The man mumbled something and his hand moved but he didn't open his eyes.

Padgett wasn't scared of drunks when they were sleeping. He pointed to the radio. Georgie shook his head. No sense stealing nothing that old and beat up. Padgett pointed to the man's pockets. Georgie shook his head again. Maybe when they came back down. Not likely that the man had any money, though.

As they tiptoed away, something went clanking across the floor. Georgie turned and grabbed Padgett by the arm. Leave it to him to find a beer can to kick.

"Hey!" The man behind the desk saw them. "Hey! You kids get out of here."

Georgie yanked Padgett's arm, pulled him down the hall and into a closet. He pushed a bucket with a mop in it against the wall and water sloshed on his Converse.

"Damn kids. Where are you?"

"Shh," Georgie whispered. "He won't come lookin' for us."

"Damn kids," the man said again, sounding farther away.

The closet smelled of dirty water and pee. Georgie opened the door and peeked out. "Come on. And watch where you're walkin' this time."

They kept to the wall and ran up the stairs to the second floor. The light on the landing was out so they propped open the door to the hallway. Then they sat on the step and looked into the bag Georgie's friend at the Burger King had given him after he handed her his fifty-five cents.

Good, a fish sandwich, LaShawna would like that. And two Whoppers. He gave one to Padgett, mostly so he wouldn't complain about not getting it, and left the other one for Jose because he didn't get to come tonight. He took the double cheeseburger and left the two hamburgers for Sissie. She didn't like melted cheese or pickles or bread or too much of anything else except pop, bubble gum, and candy.

The talking, or what Georgie could hear of it, started while they were eating. A man's voice. Not loud, but sounding loud because everything was so quiet and because his voice was so deep.

"Where is it?" Then, "I want it. Now."

Not fighting words but mad sounding.

Padgett started shaking and made a scared sound like a puppy whining.

"Man's not drunk and they're not arguin'," Georgie said, sounding madder than he meant to. He made a big deal of peeking into the hall and motioning to Padgett to follow him on tiptoe. Kid had to learn to do these things.

They were right by the door where the talking was. Usually when he came here on Friday night the lady who stayed there would give him all the quarters in her purse. She'd be wearing them old-timey dresses and singing along with those big, funny-sounding records she played on the wind-up record player. She wasn't singing tonight. There wasn't any music.

"You!" the woman said, sounding as small and as scared as Padgett. "My God. I thought I was crazy. You."

"Who else have you told?" the man asked. His voice made Georgie think of a pit bull growling and he shivered.

"Who else?" The woman said. "I didn't know. Not till now. I didn't know."

"Bitch," the man said. "Crazy, stupid bitch."

Georgie had heard James Arthur talk like that when he was getting ready to hit Momma. He put his hands over his ears, waiting for the man to start beating her. Padgett had dropped what was left of his burger. He was holding on to Georgie's arm so tight and staring so hard at the door, Georgie didn't think he'd be able to get him to move. He tried to pull his arm away but Padgett wouldn't let go.

There was a sound inside the room like something falling on the floor, then drawers opening and closing. The man cussed. The woman didn't say anything. Georgie gave Padgett a look. "See," he whispered. "Told you it was nothin'." He didn't let Padgett see that the way the man sounded had scared him too. He looked at the plate of cookies on the floor down the hall, gave Padgett another nudge.

Padgett stopped sniffling and wiped his nose with the back of his hand. He moved away from the door and began inching his way along the hall, dragging his feet like they were too heavy to lift. The door to the woman's room opened and they both jumped, then stared at the man.

Padgett ran first, to the stairs, up instead of down, toward the light on the third floor. Georgie followed, just as he heard the man coming up behind them, his feet banging on the steps. The man stumbled, cussing when he fell.

"Keep going!" Georgie said.

As Padgett reached the fifth floor Georgie grabbed him. "The door." He pushed Padgett so that he went through the door and landed on the floor in the hallway. Georgie grabbed his arm, half dragging him into a room he'd been in before.

"Get under the bed," Georgie whispered, lifting the sheet and blanket that were mostly on the floor. They crawled under the lumpy place where someone was sleeping, curled up against the wall under the head of the bed, and held their coat sleeves over their mouths so nobody would hear them breathing.

Georgie watched from the place under the bed that the sheet didn't cover and hoped the man wouldn't see them. He could feel his heart beating. He stared at the light from the open door, saw the shadow fall across it, and heard the floor creak. The man's boots were big and heavy. The floor seemed to shake as he came into the room. He was breathing deep and coughed, clearing his throat.

"Whaa ... Hunh ..." the drunk on the bed mumbled. "What the hell?" A half-pint whiskey bottle fell on the floor as he tried to get up. "Damn. What the hell ..."

The man who had been following them backed out of the room.

Georgie waited a long time without moving, then crawled to the door and looked into the hall. No reason for that man to be chasing them. But if he caught them, called the cops ... La-Shawna would be worried if they didn't get back soon.

"Stay here, so's he only catches one of us," Georgie said.

He went down the hall, checked the stairs for two flights, then went back up and got Padgett.

"Scared for nothin'," he told him. "Probably ran for nothin' too. Man's gone. Just some drunk. Bet that wasn't even an argument."

"Was too," Padgett said. He began crying. Georgie saw that he had peed his pants but didn't say anything.

"Where's them mittens?" he asked.

Padgett shook his head. Georgie took off the ones with the holes in the thumbs and tried not to think about his own being lost.

The staircase was real dark when they went back downstairs, but it only seemed scary because Padgett was holding his hand so tight and still crying. When they got to the second floor and nothing happened they began to run. Behind them a door opened and the man was after them again. They ran through the lobby, looking back to see the man still following them.

Outside, Padgett slipped in the snow and landed on his butt.

"Come on," Georgie yelled, yanking at his jacket. Looking up, he saw the lady with the shopping bag who was the singing woman's friend.

Nessa watched as the children ran away. She turned to see what they were running from and saw a man watching from the doorway of the hotel. His scarf was pulled up around his face, a ski cap pulled down low. She felt reassured by the weight of the bowie knife she always carried in a special pocket. He'd get more than he was looking for if he came messing with her. The man turned and walked away, hunched over into the wind that was blowing snow into his face.

She listened for a minute, heard nothing but the wind. She wondered where the two little boys had run off to, glad that the man had gone in the opposite direction.

She'd never seen the kid who fell before. Skin white as the snow; black hair falling over his forehead. She'd seen that other one though, the skinny black kid. She'd seen him a number of times. He was small for his age, had a sweet smile and big sad eyes that made her want to hug him. Out panhandling and stealing from folks at this hour. And almost got caught from the looks of it.

Dorsey gave him money. Should have made him do something to earn it. That quiet, fat guy down the hall left cookies out. And then there were the drunks who came in, left their doors open, and got whatever money they had taken out of their pockets.

No need asking where the kids' parents were. Odds were there wasn't any daddy around and the mother, prostitute maybe, or a junkie or a drunk. Folks wasn't responsible no more, not like when she was comin' up. Nowadays they just dropped 'em like they was part of a litter and left 'em to fend for themselves. Nothing like it was years ago.

The wind was coming strong off Lake Michigan, whipping around the corner of the building. It was colder than it would have been if she'd come out earlier but she didn't go out during the day, too many people out then. She waited until night came, and darkness. She felt safer when she was alone. She ducked her head and shifted the canvas shopping bag she was carrying, Dorsey's supper inside, wrapped in foil and still warm. The light from the front doors of the Cramer Hotel spread out in a dim arc on the sidewalk but didn't quite reach the curb.

She opened the door and went inside, her boots tapping as she crossed the marble foyer and went up the three steps to the lobby. Place was s'posed to be locked up after midnight. Never was. She crossed to the oak desk, old and scarred up with dozens of initials and profanities. Skinny old night man, smelling of sweat and muscatel, sprawled in the overstuffed leather chair that was squeezed between the counter and the wall. He was drooling on the flowered throw that was pulled around him like a blanket. She took the back stairs to the second floor. Elevator hadn't worked in years.

The hallway was almost dark, just one low-watt light bulb dangling from the ceiling about halfway to Dorsey's room. A mouse darted out of her way. Ordinarily she liked quiet but here it just made her jumpy. She hurried along, startled when someone snored, then eased past an open door, looking in to see that the room was empty and hoping she wouldn't bump into whoever was renting it. The toilet at the other end of the hall flushed and she walked faster, stepping over a half-eaten hamburger and taking out

the key. She was in too much of a hurry to notice the door was already unlocked until she
was pushing it open.

She stopped, door half-open, one foot in the
room, hearing her heart beating too fast, shout-
ing warnings. Door shouldn't be open. She
shouldn't be going in. She didn't hear Dorsey's
childlike high-pitched voice call her name. The
cat, Samantha, came in all at once and ran in
worrisome circles around her, meowing, yellow
fur bristling, tail high.

Nessa stood at the threshold and looked inside, saw Dorsey lying on the floor, eyes staring
without seeing anything anymore. Lord, don't
let this be real. She looked up at the ceiling, with
the crumbling plaster and light fixtures that no
longer worked. She followed the streaks down
the faded red flocked wallpaper, past the lighter
squares and rectangles where pictures had once
hung. She listened to her heartbeat, the way she
was breathing as if she'd been running, afraid
to look back at Dorsey. The cat's box had been
changed, the saucer for her food washed and
placed beside the bowl filled with water.

The card table was all set for supper, two
folding chairs pulled up. Tea kettle on the hot
plate, four sugar packets beside the small jar of
coffee. That old junky Victrola they'd found at
the Salvation Army store was in the corner, top
up. A dozen scratchy 78s were in the box underneath. The Andrews Sisters, Nelson Eddy,
Jeanette MacDonald. Dorsey was waiting for
her, same as usual. But not coming to greet her
with that languid drawl and lopsided smile.

Nessa's stomach began churning. She wanted to turn and run out of this place just like the two little boys had.

She looked at the floor instead, followed a path made by the white plastic beads Dorsey almost always wore. They were scattered across the scuffed hardwood floor, from the sink to the metal posts of the bed. Then Nessa looked at Dorsey again, lying in such a little heap on the floor. Dorsey loved to dress up, have tea, pretend. Tonight she was dressed as if it was 1940 and she was going to a high school prom. Coppery red hair teased into puffs, blue eyeshadow, red rouge, pink lipstick, that turquoise taffeta dress so old and shiny. Eyes, such a deep startling brown, open, but not seeing nothing no more.

Nessa put down the shopping bag. She went to her friend, to the only person she had held a conversation with in more years than she could remember, and closed Dorsey's eyes. She saw the bruise and swelling on the side of Dorsey's face that rested against the floor, touched a purple place that was still warm as if that would make it feel better or go away.

Who had done this? And who would care? Just another schizo, just another crazy—that's all poor Dorsey would be. Schizos and drunks, whores and junkies. That's all any of them were who lived here. "Worthless parasite," a social worker had called her a few years ago.

She glanced at the bureau, then looked again. The drawer that wouldn't close all the way unless you made sure it went in straight wasn't

19

flush against the bureau. Dorsey couldn't stand it when things weren't in place. Never would have left the drawer like that. Nessa went over to the closet, not sure why she was on tiptoe. Someone else had looked in here, too. Dorsey's purse was on the floor, right where she always put it. Nessa looked inside. The handkerchief was rumpled, not folded like Dorsey kept it. And the little cloth bag with her makeup inside was unzipped. The money was still in her wallet, but the snap was unfastened. Nessa put the purse back with everything just like she'd found it.

Dorsey's evening gowns, each as fancy and as old as the one she was wearing now, were still hanging up. One lavender sleeve with the velvet nap rubbed off near the cuff rested against a red lace bodice. Not the way Dorsey would have hung them.

Nessa reached to the back of the closet, found the full length raccoon coat and stuck her hand into the pocket. Pushing her hand through the hole and all the way down to the hem, she found the letter and the emerald ring. The person who had killed Dorsey and searched her room must have been looking for these. She forgot about the bag with the food in it until she was standing in the hall, then left it because she could not go back into that room.

She left the door open so somebody would find Dorsey by morning. Samantha followed her out, meowing. Nessa scooped up the cat and tucked her inside her coat. Poor Samantha. The tears came as she tried to comfort her.

1

When Detective Marti MacAlister arrived at the Cramer Hotel a number of elderly residents had sorted themselves into two small groups, one male, one female. Five women huddled together near the massive oak desk. The white-haired woman leaning on a walker spoke in a loud whisper.

"Well, *she* certainly isn't a police officer. I thought they were only letting people in on official business."

A tiny dark-skinned woman with at least five slips hanging below a short, fuzzy blue robe answered.

"Hah. Got cop written all over her. Now ain't that a sight, Betty? Black and a woman and not wearin' no uniform."

"Ain't ladylike lettin' 'em walk around in pants," the first woman said. "Should at least make 'em wear skirts. And I want to see a badge."

Marti nodded as she walked past them but she didn't offer any identification. Four men who looked about as old as the women stood at the stairwell. One took a step toward her and gave her a belligerent stare. She shouldered past him without speaking. At five-ten and a hundred and sixty pounds she was what her mother had called healthy. Her size pleased her, and most people tended to move out of her way.

A uniform came down the stairs. She didn't recognize him by name but he knew who she was. "Jessenovik get here yet?" she asked.

"Yes ma'am."

Vik was her partner. She had been asleep when the call came on this one and she assumed that he had too. "Who's recording?"

"Burdett. He was the first one here, ma'am."

"Terrific." Six months on the force and Burdett thought he knew it all. When she reached the second floor Vik was standing in the hallway yelling at an evidence tech.

"What the hell do you mean we might have some of our own prints in there?"

She couldn't make out the response.

"Routine!" Vik shouted. "Routine!

"Burdett!" he called. His thick, salt-and-pepper eyebrows almost linked in a furious scowl, gray eyes like twin storms gathering over Lake Michigan. "Are you the idiot who thinks this is just routine? Get out here, now, before you screw up something else."

Burdett came out. He was almost as tall as Vik. His dark hair was swept back from a widow's peak in careful waves. His shoes were spit-shined and she was willing to bet he polished his badge every day, too.

"It's just another Jane Doe. DOA on this beat at least once a week. Be lucky to identify her,"

Burdett said, omitting the "sir" that was expected from a rookie.

Marti came up alongside Vik, saw his hands clenched into fists. She couldn't think of any reason to defuse the situation and said nothing.

Vik went into the room. He was tall and thin with graying hair that always looked unkempt. His beaked nose, slightly skewed, added a vulturelike look to his appearance, especially when he looked down at someone with his eyebrows bunched together, which was often. He stopped at the foot of the bed, tapping on the metal frame.

"Just some Jane Doe who checked into the local flophouse and got herself all decked out like Queen Elizabeth and opened her door to the wrong prince."

The anger in Vik's face caused Burdett to bump into Marti as he backed away. Vik jabbed at the air with his index finger as he said, "We are peace officers, boy. We serve and protect. Everyone. We do not pick and choose who's worthy of our attention or our services. We do not discriminate in the way we deal with victims, living or dead. You disturbed my scene of crime. You touched things in this room. You touched her. You may have interrupted my chain of evidence. Having done that, you will now begin pretending that you are a reasonably competent police officer. And stay the hell out of my way, permanently."

Marti knew that Vik was angered by Burdett's attitude toward the deceased. That, as well as Burdett's carelessness, annoyed her too.

Now she'd have to find out what he'd touched, how much disturbance he had caused.

"I need to ask you some questions," she said. It took almost an hour to take Burdett through his movements from the time he entered the room, to determine what he had touched. She didn't hurry, wanting to inconvenience him and hoping it made some impression. Then she got out her camera and shot two rolls of film that included only what had not been disturbed.

"Don't know what the hell they're teaching 'em anymore. Got rookies making field decisions as to which bodies are important enough to warrant preserving evidence," Vik muttered as he came over to her. "Guess we're just supposed to zip this one up in a body bag and go home."

Police work, as far as Vik was concerned, was divided into two categories: man's work, which involved supervising the evidence techs and all other personnel at the scene, and woman's work, interviewing people.

Since her interpretation differed, Marti pulled on a pair of transparent rubber gloves and went over to look at the body. Lauretta Dorsey, according to the janitor who had found the body. That was all they knew about her so far. Red hair arranged in precise waves and curls, natural, no dye, makeup evenly if heavily applied. Marti hadn't seen a taffeta party dress like that one in years, except in old movies from the forties.

The doctor who pronounced her dead said the woman had recently ingested an alcoholic beverage. Marti got close to her mouth, smelled liquor. The body had cooled. There was a large bruise on the side of her face. The area around her eye had begun to swell before she died. Marti examined her hands without removing the plastic bags the doctor had placed there. The middle right index finger had skin scrapings and a broken nail. Ignoring the red nail polish, Marti looked for signs of age, guessed that the woman was in her mid-to-late thirties. Rigor had begun to set in.

She looked about the room, paying less attention to the shabby furnishings than to the orderliness, and her sense that the order had been disturbed. The kitty litter in the cat's box hadn't been used. A small dish had been washed and placed on the floor beside a bowl filled with water. Two glasses in the sink, rinsed but not dried. The old Victrola held her attention. She had seen one once, not long after she joined the force, in an apartment where they found a very old woman dead. The veneer had begun to peel away on this one. Some of the wood was warped, as if it had been in a damp place or gotten wet. Old 78s were stacked in a box that had been pushed beneath the curved mahogany legs.

There was no dust, but she drew her finger along the floor and came up with some yellow cat hair. She told Burdett to look for the cat. When he answered he addressed her as ma'am. Maybe Vik's tirades did work with some people.

A small canvas bag had been left on the floor

near the card table, a plate covered with foil, chicken and dumplings with collard greens inside. Marti sniffed. It smelled just like Momma's would have, just a hint of basil and bay leaf in the chicken broth.

She took more pictures: of the woman, of the packets of sugar stacked beside the instant coffee, of the two glasses, of the bureau drawer not quite aligned, the six pairs of white cotton underpants folded and placed in two rows in the drawer, of the clothes in the closet hung in an order that she didn't recognize at first, red, purple, yellow, green, blue, black. No orange, or brown. She thought of a color wheel and the purple velvet clashed against the red lace. Someone had dumped the contents of the woman's purse on the floor in the closet. Lipstick, mascara, foundation, white cotton handkerchief that hadn't been used. No wallet or identification.

Vik came over, snapping his notebook shut. They stood by the window, watching as the team from the coroner's office removed the body.

"Your nose is damned near twitching, Mac-Alister."

She tried not to bristle at his reference to instinct. "Man's work, policing," he had told her, when she first joined the force here. "We remain calm and detached. We investigate. We don't let anything as unreliable as intuition interfere with common sense and sound judgment." That was over a year ago. She was more tolerant of Vik now, but more because she'd gotten used to him than because his attitude had improved.

"Her face is bruised," Marti said. "Someone hit her. Argument, maybe. The place was tossed, but carefully. The unaligned drawer is an easy miss and I don't think they even thought about the color sequencing of the gowns. Then there's the contents of the purse."

"So, the perp thought he was clever, heard someone coming and panicked."

"I think there was more than one person involved. Someone who knew her pretty well. Someone who didn't. And someone who brought her some supper. Might be the one who closed her eyes."

"This isn't Chicago, MacAlister. The odds on there being a conspiracy to kill a nutcase holed up in a flophouse are slim to none. This is just another mediocre small-town crime. Some guy down the hall probably came on to her and got mad when she turned him down."

She had gotten used to Vik's references to her time on the force in Chicago before she came here. "That remains to be seen, Jessenovik. Living sixty miles from Chicago doesn't exactly put us out in the wilderness."

Her first day on the job Vik had said, "Look kid, I know that when you were in the big city you got to draw your weapon on the least little pretext to keep a situation from getting out of hand because you're a female. Just remember, we're small-town cops here. We're professionals. No illegal weapons concealed on our persons, no questionable tactics or undue force. No breaches of anyone's civil rights." He had taken a long drag on his cigarette and dismissed her ten years of honorable service and four commendations with a flick of his finger as he knocked off the ash.

"Ninety thousand people. Town's not that small," she had answered, certain that crime didn't change much from one place to another. Volume maybe, and to some extent the type of perp. She hadn't expected much else to be different and hadn't been disappointed.

Now she'd worked with Vik long enough to know he was just blowing smoke with his talk about Chicago. She also knew that Vik really wanted Lincoln Prairie to be a small town with small-town problems, the way it was when his father had walked a beat here. Occasionally that worried her. She wondered what would happen when he couldn't think of it that way anymore.

Vik took another look in the closet. "Obsessive-compulsive. With this and the way she's dressed we need to check for a history of mental illness on file somewhere."

"Might as well talk to the janitor now," Marti said.

They stepped into the hallway. The remains of a burger still in its Burger King wrapper had been dropped in the hallway just outside the door. Marti snapped a picture of it.

Arnie Herman, the janitor, was a small, dark-skinned man with close-cropped white hair and tremors in both gnarled hands. His bib overalls didn't quite reach his ankles, his brogans were run down along the outer heels, and something red had been washed with his T-shirt, turning it an uneven pink. He had a musty odor, a combination of dirt, perspiration, and urine. Marti placed his age at somewhere between eighty and ninety.

"I ain't done nothin', Officer sir," he said, voice quaking. "Door was open an' I jes' kinda peeked in."

Vik looked at Marti.

"How long have you worked here?" she asked.

The janitor gave her a surprised look, as if he either hadn't noticed that she was there or didn't think she could talk.

"Ma'am? Shouldn't he be the one askin' the questions?"

"They let me handle that every once in a while."

"Yes ma'am. If you say so." He turned to Vik. "You sure it's okay, her askin' the questions?"

Vik leaned over him with an angry scowl. "She's a cop, isn't she?"

"Yes sir." His voice quavered. "If you sayso."

"What time did you find her?"

"Can't say. No watch. Right before I ran downstairs and the desk clerk called you."

"Did you go into the room, touch anything?"

"No ma'am." He looked at Vik and added "Sir. Didn't go no further than this here." He pointed to the threshold.

"You did touch the door?"

"Oh. Yes. I'm sorry. I didn't know." He looked at Vik as if he was expecting him to produce a rubber hose. "I ain't got no kind of record, sir. Nothin'. Ain't never done nothin' illegal in my life and I'm eighty-four years old. Born in Sheffield, Alabama. Can write my name, too."

Marti took him through his movements again, and explained that he would have to be fingerprinted.

"But sir," he said to Vik. "I ain't done nothin', honest. I ain't killed her. Swear to God." He raised his right hand.

"We have a lot of fingerprints," Marti said. "We need to know who they belong to."

"Ain't never been fingerprinted in my life," he protested. "All I done was tell Wayne that the princess here was dead. That's all I done. Now I'm gonna have a police record. I'm eighty-four years old, ain't never done nothin' illegal in my life. I only knowed she had some money 'cause I heard her tellin' Wayne she was movin' out next month. Swear to God."

"What money?" Marti asked.

"I only overheard her talkin' to Wayne. Ain't seen nothin'. Didn't never see her counting no money when she come home that day in the taxi. Swear to God."

"How much money didn't you see her count?" Marti asked.

"How would I know? I tol' you I ain't never seen it. I just heard . . ."

"Where did the money come from?" Marti persisted.

"You is a real cop, ain't you?"

"Where did she get the money?"

He looked from her to Vik, back at her again.

"Lordy, Lordy. A colored woman cop an' I done got her mad."

"I'm going to get real mad if you don't answer my questions."

"Never talk to her myself. Don' know where she got them hunnurd-dollar bills or how many of 'em she had. Don't know no more'n what I tol' you and never shoulda said that."

Convinced that he didn't have more information, Marti nodded to Vik. It took them another ten minutes to convince him that he was not under arrest and would not have a record.

2

Nine other residents lived on that floor. It was
Saturday and most of them were well into their
weekend binges. One of them couldn't even focus on Marti's badge as he stood swaying in the
doorway, winking with one eye and then the
other as he tried to see what she was holding.
Giving up, he left them standing there, went
over to his bed, and fell on it. Loud snoring
came from the next room; they were unable to
rouse the occupant. Vik used a pass key to get
in. It was a woman.

They spoke with two women and a man who
had no idea who Dorsey was. One man gave
them a bleary-eyed stare and slammed the door.
Dorsey had scratched someone last night, but
they didn't see anyone with scratches on their
face or arms.

An unmarried couple lived three doors down
from Dorsey and across the hall. While they
were not entirely sober, Marti guessed that this
was as close as they were going to get. The
woman opened the door. She and a man in un-
dershorts and a T-shirt were sharing a gallon
jug of muscatel in a room with a view of a brick

wall. The woman brushed at her blue polyester pantsuit wrinkled by too much heat in the dryer and tried to secure stringy strands of gray hair with black hairpins.

"What day did you say this was, honey?"

"Saturday, ma'am."

"Already. You hear that Al, it's Saturday."

The man was old, too. He refilled a juice glass and ignored them.

"What's the date, hon?" the woman asked.

"December ninth." Marti omitted the year and waited.

"See Al, I told you New Year's ain't come yet. That was Thanksgiving a coupla weeks back, wasn't it, hon?"

Marti nodded.

"And it's Saturday, huh. Sounds right. Disability came Monday. Hey Al, we got to pick up our food stamps today."

"Your name, ma'am?" Marti asked.

"Ginnie, hon. Virginia Mae Hepplesten." She waited until Marti wrote that down, made sure her last name was spelled correctly, then said, "Folks just call me Ginnie, hon. Shame about ol' Dorsey, ain't it. Think you know who did it?"

"You knew her?" Marti said.

"Not really. Nice kid but a little . . ." She pointed to the side of her head and made a circular motion with her finger.

"What can you tell me about her?"

"Not much. People here mostly keep to themselves. Sang a lot. She'd wind up that old Victrola and sing songs I ain't heard in years. I was always telling Al here that she wasn't old

33

enough to know some of 'em. Like the Andrews Sisters, stuff we were listenin' to during the war." She looked at Vik. "Second World War, not World War I," she clarified, as if she thought Vik was old enough to have fought in 1914.

"She have any friends?" Marti asked. They had decided not to mention the money the janitor had referred to. "Any visitors that you know of?"

"I think she slept all day, hon. Al and me here, early to bed, early to rise. Didn't hear Dorsey at all till evenin', though. One of them night people I s'pose. Eight, nine o'clock she'd be just a singing away. Sometimes she got all gussied up like somethin' in *Gone With the Wind* and talked to herself for hours. Could tell it was just her. She'd change her voice from a little kid to a grown-up when she answered back, but it was still just her in there. If anyone came to see her, they came real late. After we went to bed. Ain't that right, Al?"

Al still hadn't acknowledged that anyone else was in the room, let alone responded to any of Ginnie's prompts. The woman talked enough for both of them. Marti nodded encouragement and Ginnie went on.

"Course now if somebody did do her in, I'll bet they got in here when them doors downstairs was s'posed to be locked. You see Al, I told you that good for nothin' Wayne Baxter wasn't watchin' nothin' when he's s'posed to be sitting at that desk."

Al poured more wine and kept looking out the window.

"Think you can do somethin' about that, hon? Report him or somethin'? We s'posed to be safe in here at night, though Lord knows someone wants to get you nowadays they'd do it in broad daylight if they had a mind to, wouldn't they Al, honey."

"Did she have a cat?"

"Yeah, old Samantha, fat yellow striped tabby. Wonder where she's gotten herself off to. Dorsey spoiled that cat rotten. Independent little cuss though. I'll make sure she gets fed if I see her wandering in the hall. Good mouser, worth keeping around."

"Coulda been who she was arguin' with," Al said in a deep but whining voice that startled them both.

"Arguin'? Dorsey?" Ginnie said.

"Was it last night?" Marti asked.

"I ain't heard no argument, Al," Ginnie told him. "I ain't never heard Dorsey argue with no one. Sweet little thing, she was. Daft as all hell, but sweet."

"Al," Marti said. "Did you hear an argument last night?"

Al shook his head, ran his fingers through his hair. "Don' know. Sorry. Mighta dreamed it."

He considered his glass, downed the remaining wine and refilled it.

"When do you think you might have heard or dreamed it?"

Al shook his head. "Don' know." His belch signaled the end of the conversation.

"Never heard no arguments," Ginnie insisted.

Marti was convinced she was telling the truth, but was equally certain that Al was, too. She didn't think she was going to hear anything else useful. It took another five minutes to get away.

The only other resident awake, alert, or ambulatory was a short, stocky young man not more then twenty-three or so with small eyes that looked like dark beads in his fat, puffy face.

He gave his name as Lenny Doobee. "I was wondering if you would ever find out," he said. "They were here again last night."

"Who?" Vik asked.

"Foreign agents, of course. The Ayatollah's got KGBs spying on us."

"What do they look like?" Vik asked, glancing at Marti with a quick lift of his eyebrows.

"Oh, I didn't see them," Doobee told them. "But I heard them. They come every Friday night at midnight."

"How many?" Vik asked with more patience than Marti expected.

"Oh, I only hear one. But there are others on the stairs waiting for the all clear."

"Don't they ever get it?" Vik asked.

"Get what, Officer?"

"The all clear."

"Of course not." Doobee did something close to sucking in his belly, which was impossible. His stomach hung over his belt in folds. "I stand guard here all night, sir. The only reason they got through last night is because I wasn't here." He hesitated, looking downcast. "I really wasn't feeling well, sir, so I stayed at the Respite."

The Respite was a short-term facility for the mentally ill. It provided them with shelter for a day or two.

"Did you know Lauretta Dorsey?" Marti asked.

"Oh no," he said, becoming apprehensive. "I don't know anyone. Don't know anyone at all."

"People down the hall say she was friendly."

"No. No," Lenny said. He tried to close the door, but Vik dropped his leather-bound notebook and it fell between door and frame.

"Oh, sorry, kid." He stooped to retrieve it. "You don't have to talk with us, but we need some help with this. We'd sure appreciate it if you would cooperate."

"I didn't know her. I didn't. Honest."

"Of course you didn't," Vik said calmly. "But you lived on the same floor just a couple of doors down. Sometimes an observant person like yourself sees things, knows things without realizing they're important."

"She was so pretty," Lenny said, beginning to relax and look sad. "So pretty. Her hair. Red. Real red. Nice, like her eyes. I didn't hurt her. I would never hurt her. Honest."

Marti could see that Vik was beginning to have one or two doubts about that. So was she.

"Maybe she talked to you."

"No!" Lenny became alarmed again. "No! She never saw me. She never was up in the daytime and at night I had to stand guard so no one would hurt her."

"And you were standing guard last night?" Vik said.

"Yes. But I didn't see her. I got sick. I had to go to the Respite."

"Did you pass her room when you went downstairs?" Vik said. He would have had to.

"No!" Then, "Yes, but her door was closed and she wasn't wearing her blue dress."

"What was she wearing?"

"I didn't see her. I don't know!"

He was becoming hysterical.

"Son," Vik soothed. "She was wearing a blue dress when she died. Turquoise blue. You saw her, didn't you?"

"No, no. She wasn't dead. She was sleeping. She fell down and she was sleeping. She isn't dead. She isn't. You've made a mistake. She'll be playing her music and singing again tonight."

"Son," Vik said. "We need you to come down to the precinct and answer a few more questions. We think you might know something important. Something that might help us."

"I don't know. I have to ask my doctor first."

"We'll let you call him right away," Vik assured him.

"And you won't tell my mother?"

"Not a word," Vik promised.

Mollified, almost childlike, Lenny agreed to go to the precinct.

Burdett was the only uniform in the hallway. "Get your partner," Vik called in a voice less than friendly but not annoyed enough to alarm Lenny.

Burdett's partner was a lanky blond who looked even younger than Burdett. "Lenny is going to try to help us with this investigation," Vik said. "He might possibly have seen something last night that will be useful. Please escort him to the precinct and let him sit with the desk sergeant. He wants to call his doctor. Make sure he does that right away. And no idle conversations, okay?"

Before they questioned Lenny again they would have to talk with the doctor too.

The blond uniform took Lenny by the arm. "This way, sir." He was smart enough to take his cues from Vik. "Have you had breakfast yet? We'll get you some coffee and doughnuts while you're calling your doctor."

Watching them walk down the hall, Vik said, "Thank God, that blond kid knows what he's doing. Needs to be more assertive or Burdett will get them both kicked off the force."

"He saw her with that dress on," Marti said. "Question is, alive or dead?"

"Or while he was helping her go from alive to dead," Vik grunted. "Be nice to wrap this one up quick. A nice simple homicide. One nut case killing another. This kid seems harmless though. One thing we don't need is a phony confession."

"Best to keep him isolated at the precinct where he can't pick up any more details and can only tell us whatever he saw," she agreed. "Shouldn't take that much to get him to talk." Marti shrugged. Maybe they did have their man. "This place is depressing."

"Never used to need places like this. People took care of their own."

39

"Or hid them away in places like the state hospital at Elgin," she countered.

Vik grimaced at that bit of reality and walked ahead of her.

Wayne Baxter, the night clerk, had been roused from sleep. He sat on the edge of a metal frame bed with a soiled mattress and no sheet. The place smelled of spoiled food, probably from the pot on the electric hot plate. A small refrigerator with a noisy motor kicked on as Marti walked into the room. Baxter scratched at his armpits, smelling like he slept on old newspapers.

Not as old as he appeared, Marti decided. Scrawny as a plucked chicken, hair thinning with a bald spot on top and stoop-shouldered, but not old.

"Friday night, you know," he mumbled, rubbing several days' growth of beard. "Who doesn't have a drink or two Friday night? They find out, I'm outta here."

"Was the front door supposed to be locked?" Marti asked again.

He shrugged. "Supposed to be."

"Was it?"

"Maybe not," he admitted, looking anywhere but at Marti and Vik. "People here, they come and go. 'Specially on a Friday. And always losin' their keys. Keep the door locked after midnight, the boss says. What am I supposed to do, I ask him. Can't lock 'em in. Can't tell 'em not to go out. Can't lock 'em out either. Think I'm gonna run back and forth lockin' up and unlockin'? Boss don't care. Too cheap to install a buzzer or somethin'. I mean for three-twenty-five an hour and a place to sleep . . ."

"So the door wasn't locked," she said. He still hadn't looked at her.

"No," Baxter said, annoyed by her persistence.

"Who came in?"

"Hey, like I told you. It's Friday, I had a few drinks. I admit it."

"What time do you think you passed out?"

"Hey lady. Look, I'm no drunk."

"Sure. You just had a few drinks. What time you think you went to sleep?"

Still indignant, Baxter said, "Eleven, maybe twelve."

"Can you pin it down for me?" She pointed to a radio that looked to be of fifties vintage, wondered if it worked.

"Oh," the night clerk said. "Reception wasn't too good last night. Lotta static. Listened to the news though. Heard some of it anyway. Tried to get a little music, this jazz station from Chicago. Too much static, couldn't hear nothin'. Said the hell with it. Cut it off after that. Yeah. Either eleven or twelve. For sure."

Marti couldn't decide if he was talking so much because he always did, because he was nervous, or because there was something he didn't want to say.

"You're sure that's when you went to sleep?"

"Yeah. Like I told you—"

"Eleven or twelve," she interrupted. "You didn't see anyone come in here after that?"

"No."

"You didn't see Lauretta Dorsey last night?"

"No. Like I told you. Dorsey wasn't one to leave her room at night. Didn't never see her hardly unless she was out and didn't come back till I came on at eight and that wasn't very often. Most of the time she . . ."

"Wayne, you're lying," Marti said.

"Now look, I ain't gonna be called no liar by some female who—"

Marti took two steps closer, trying to ignore the body odor. Wayne scooted to the end of the bed.

"Wayne, you're lying to me. A woman was found dead upstairs while you were supposed to be watching who was coming and going. And you're lying."

"Look, I don't know nothin'. Don't know who killed her, don't know who took her money, don't know nothin' about nothin'."

Marti stood in front of him, arms folded. "What money, Wayne?"

He sagged against the metal frame. "Oh, shit."

"Tell me about the money, Wayne."

"I didn't kill her. I didn't kill her. Oh shit. Now you're gonna pin it on me. Shit, shit, shit. Look," he said, licking his lips. "She gave the money to me to hold for her. I didn't take it. She gave it to me."

"Then where is it?" Marti asked.

"Here!" he yelled, jumping up. "Here! Take it! You'll just find it anyway. She gave it to me. I ain't no thief. Ain't never stole nothin' I didn't have comin' to me." He reached into a hole in the mattress, pulled out a blue plastic wallet. "Here. See? Would I give it to you if I stole it?"

Marti didn't even attempt to follow his logic. She held out a plastic bag. "Just drop it in there."

"I don't need her money. Told her I didn't need it. Just keeping it for her, that's all. Oh shit. Women ain't nothin' but trouble." He glared at Marti. "All of 'em."

"We want to talk with you at the precinct, Mr. Baxter."

"Look, I know this doesn't look good but I didn't kill her. I borrowed the money. She didn't have no more use for it. But I didn't kill her. She was already dead."

"We'll talk about this at the precinct," Marti told him.

"My coat! I need my coat!"

She told a uniform to get it. He went to the closet, got a wrinkled olive drab army coat and searched it.

"Found this in the pocket, ma'am." He held out a small pocketknife.

"I forgot it was there! Man's got a right to protect himself, working in a place like this."

Marti read him his rights.

"Wait! Wait! It wasn't me. I didn't kill her. It must have been that guy on the third floor."

"What guy?" Marti asked, acting disinterested.

"John."

"Right." She turned to Vik. "There's a john on the third floor."

"No! No! It must have been John. He lives in 3B. Room in the front."

She watched as the uniform led him away, then turned to Vik.

"Shit," they said in unison and headed for the stairs.

Room 3B was empty. The door wasn't locked; the bed wasn't made, there weren't any clothes hanging in the closet. Coat hangers littered the floor. The top drawer in the bureau hung open at a precarious angle. Dirty socks and underwear had been thrown in a corner.

"Someone could have left in a hurry," she conceded.

"Might have just decided to move out before they got him for not paying his rent."

"We'll have to track this one down. Better get the evidence techs up here. Just in case."

"Right," Vik grumbled. "Damn. Lenny, Wayne, and now we've got a John. I hate it when we start out with more than one suspect. Let's go."

Outside the wind blew cold and bracing off the lake. Marti squinted into the glaring sunlight, released from the oppressiveness she had felt in the Cramer Hotel.

She hesitated before getting into their unmarked car, a silver Dodge Aries that, her daughter insisted, everyone in Lincoln Prairie could identify as a cop car without even seeing the special locks, extra antenna, and handleless back doors.

She entered on the driver's side. It had taken Vik three months and a fractured wrist to agree that she should drive. When they had first started working together the junk hanging from the rearview mirror had been reassuring: purple rabbit's foot, a St. Christopher medal, a four leaf clover, and a medallion commemorating Pope Paul's visit to Chicago. He might not believe in intuition, but he was superstitious.

"Lousy day," Vik grumbled as they drove away.

3

The precinct was in a two-story gray brick building that was part of a city-county municipal complex in the center of town. Wayne Baxter had been escorted to a holding cell, a five-by-seven-foot windowless room with a bunk and a toilet. Marti was in no hurry to interrogate him. She preferred to allow the ambiance of custodial facilities make an impression first.

Lenny was sitting with the desk sergeant. He was wearing a watch cap and a navy peacoat, a size too small, that was buttoned. Sugar from the jelly doughnut he was eating dusted the front of his jacket.

Marti got his doctor's name and phone number and called it. Then she took Vik to one side.

"Psychiatrist. Lenny's real name is Leonard Horvaster. Moderately retarded with a few neuroses and highly unlikely to do anything violent or even defend himself. That was about all I could get out of him. I called the Respite, too. He checked in a little after one this morning. He was shaking and terrified of something, incoherent when asked what was wrong. They figured it was his imagination again. Usually whatever he tells them has only happened inside his head. Social worker there said he's a loner, becomes fearful in almost any situation. No history of violence. Tends to be childlike. Think of him as being about ten to twelve years old, not twenty-three. She thought it would be okay to question him. Said we shouldn't be aggressive."

Lenny clutched a bag of doughnuts as he went with them into the interrogation room. Once inside, he pulled a chair over to the corner and sat there looking at them as if he expected some kind of punishment. That and the social worker's remark about agression had Marti thinking she must seem like one of the monsters in *Where the Wild Things Are*.

"Lenny," she began, "this is the only room we have for questioning people. There's nothing to be afraid of."

"No windows," he said.

"No," she agreed.

"I don't like places with no windows."

Some psychologist had determined that the disgusting shade of pink paint on the walls made people feel calm. Marti hoped it worked.

"I didn't know her. I never talked to her."

Marti looked at Lenny—rolls of fat, a couple of chins hiding his neck, pudgy hands, sausage fingers, little dark eyes that were fearful.

"Who comes on Friday night?" Marti asked, speaking quietly so he wouldn't become more frightened than he was.

"The little people," Doobee said.

"What do they look like?"

47

"I don't know." He tightened his grip on the bag of doughnuts. "I don't see them. I just hear them in the hall. I leave cookies out for them and in the morning they're gone."

"What's gone?" Vik asked.

Lenny gave him a look. "The cookies."

Marti signaled Vik to shut up and said, "Did you see someone in the hall last night?"

"No."

"Did you hear someone?"

He shook his head.

"I think you did."

He was silent for a moment, then burst out, "It wasn't the little people. They wouldn't hurt anyone."

"But you did hear someone."

He nodded, hunching over as if trying to get smaller.

"Did they see or hear you, Lenny?"

He gave a vigorous shake of his head. "No. They never see me. I stay inside my room. I'm afraid to come out."

"But you did see Dorsey, didn't you? You saw her wearing that dress."

He nodded.

"Could she see you?"

Lenny shook his head.

"Could she speak to you?"

He shook his head again. He didn't look up.

"Did you see anyone in the hall?"

"No." It was little more than a whisper.

"Did anyone see you?"

"No."

"Lenny, the officer who brought you here is

48

going to take you back to the hotel. Will you be afraid there?"

He nodded. "I'm always afraid."

"Will you be afraid that the person you heard in the hall will come back and hurt you?"

"No. Nobody saw me. I didn't see them."

He was huddled into his jacket now. Marti didn't know any way to determine if he was just afraid or if he was afraid of something specific. She would call the psychiatrist and explain what had happened. Maybe he could figure it out. Maybe he would share what he figured out with her.

The night clerk was next.

Vik had checked with the evidence techs. "Woman's wallet. A VA Hospital ID card inside, belonged to Dorsey. No make on the finger-prints yet. Lots of money—5,077 bucks. Wonder where she got it."

"And why," Marti added.

She had Wayne Baxter brought in. He seemed to be adequately intimidated by his surround-ings and he had the shakes. His biggest concern was probably whether or not he'd get another drink anytime soon. She intended to charge him with theft. They'd have to get him to the jail infirmary before he went into d.t.'s.

"Tell me about the wallet, Wayne."

"I don't have to tell you nothin'. I want to see a lawyer. Now."

Belligerent drunks annoyed her. "This isn't 'Hill Street Blues,' Wayne. We don't have a cute female attorney waiting around for clients to be brought in. You'll be arraigned Monday morning. A public defender will be appointed then."

"Then I ain't saying nothin'."

Marti stood up. "Fine." She called to the uniform. "Suspicion of murder one, theft over five thousand dollars."

"Hey. Wait a minute. I ain't killed no one."

Marti turned to him and shrugged. "Couldn't say. You're not talking."

"Where they takin' me?"

"Jail."

"The hell they are. I'm an alcoholic. You gotta take me to detox. I ain't got to go to no jail. Not Wayne Baxter."

"They'll put you in the infirmary."

"In jail? Jail's got an infirmary? I got to eat that garbage they call food? I demand to see my lawyer. Now. I'm s'posed to go to detox. I know my rights. You're violatin' my rights as an alcoholic. I'm suing you for this."

"Your lawyer can take it up with the state's attorney," Marti said. "After you talk with him."

She walked out of the room with Vik close behind her. "You think of anything else we can nail him with?"

"I think he'd kill for that money if he had to."

"Probably had some grandiose idea that he was entitled to it."

"No scratches," Vik reminded her.

"Maybe she scratched someone else," Marti snapped, not convinced that Wayne Baxter had done anything more than rob the dead, but wishing he had.

The other teams questioning residents at Cramer came up with seven possible suspects. One had scratches on his face, another on his arms. Three had prior felony convictions involving violence. One of them was a woman. Two had warrants outstanding. Marti and Vik agreed to hold the two with scratches until they determined whether or not they had a match on the tissue found under Dorsey's fingernails. They questioned the others but couldn't even determine whether or not they knew Dorsey. There were no fingerprint matchups.

Lunch was a couple of sandwiches out of a basement vending machine. Then they went upstairs to the corner office they shared with two vice cops. The rest of the floor was divided up and sectioned off with partitions. Detectives got the rooms along the outer wall. It seemed airy and spacious after the cramped interior room where Marti had worked in Chicago. Windows the length of two walls provided a view of the courthouse, construction on the new jail, and, when she had time to notice, transitions from day to night, a glimpse of the weather, and street sounds; a car horn, a siren, a group of secretaries going to lunch, muted sounds but audible.

Someone had put a spider plant on the windowsill. Everyone dumped cold coffee and flat pop into the pot, and a few people ground out cigarettes in the soil. Every few weeks someone remembered to water it. The plant had adapted so well to abuse and neglect that it had begun to reproduce and a dozen babies dangled on long stems that almost reached to the floor.

Posters and pinups were not allowed, but calendars were. Six calendars hung on the walls. One, turned to October, showed a nearly nude model who looked ready to salivate as she gazed with adoration at a two-way radio. Another, turned to April, showed a busty young woman wearing little leather strips over strategic areas who seemed about to mount a Smith & Wesson. Marti had seen more imaginative art work at the precinct in Chicago. The calenders didn't bother her.

Now she sat at her desk, looking out at the snow blowing past the window, calming down. Letting the falling snow soothe her. Winter was her favorite time of year. She wasn't sure why. As a child, she would sit in front of a small kerosene-fueled space heater and imagine fat logs crackling on a hearth where she could toast marshmallows and make popcorn. Now she had a fireplace, but rarely took the time to light it. She thought instead about having to scrape the car windows on her '85 Olds and shivering for five minutes before warm air began blowing through the vents. Still, something of that childhood feeling remained. "The urge to hibernate," her husband Johnny would have said. Her late husband, Johnny.

Her chair gave a small squeak as she leaned back and looked down at her desk, at the sand and cactus terrarium that her nine-year-old son Theo had given her, at the soil- and grass-stained softball she had kept from Joanna's last game of the season. Joanna would be fifteen in January, a winter child like Marti, but Marti didn't want to think of her own birthday yet. She would only be three years short of forty.

Vik came in, sat down with a heavy put-upon sigh and struggled to open his file drawer and extract some report forms. He glanced at yesterday's *News-Times,* tossed it into his IN-basket, sighed again, and gave her a look that suggested she should volunteer to type his reports as he dictated them—something he had hinted at only once.

She took out a legal-sized yellow pad. She preferred to write down her impressions with elaborate detail but in a less formal way, a work habit that annoyed Vik, who thought everyone should be as concise as he was. Looking down at the blank sheet of paper, she said, "We've learned nothing about this woman. Not one damned thing. She lived there a year and a half and nobody knew her. No personal papers. Why not?"

"Only three sets of prints, two partials," Vik said.

"Somebody knew her, Vik. Knew her well enough to be careful when he went through her belongings. Tried to leave everything in place. Maybe he closed her eyes. That's something someone would do if they cared for her."

"Lover's quarrel, maybe," Vik muttered. "Nice, straightforward motive. That money's a good motive too."

"Or whatever they were looking for. Nothing

there. They must have found it. Still leaves us without a suspect."

"Got lots of suspects," Vik said. "Got us a whole hotel filled with crazies, retards, winos, and junkies. Got more suspects than we know what to do with. Even got one who got away. Could be anyone." He pulled his coffee cup over, looked down at it and then at her.

"I've got some instant," she offered.

He looked at his cup again, then he checked his watch. "Wonder if Cowboy's coming in any time soon."

Cowboy made coffee that was as good as her mother's had been.

"Bunch of crazies," Vik went on. "My worst nightmare come true. And if there were a few more idiots like Burdett interviewing them we might never zero in on whoever it was."

"You've got to trust someone," Marti said.

Vik laughed, but there was no humor in it. "No sign of a struggle. Dorsey trusted whoever she let in."

Marti got on the phone. She had to track down the cab driver the janitor had mentioned. There were only two cab companies in town and the dispatcher identified the driver right away. Ten minutes later the driver called. She had picked Dorsey up at the train station; the train was inbound from Chicago. Marti filed that away. It meant nothing at the moment.

There was a knock on the door and a uniform came in. He put a pair of mittens on Vik's desk. "Found them on the back stairs, sir. Second floor of the Cramer Hotel."

"So?" Vik said.

"They're kids' gloves, sir. No children allowed at the Cramer. Couldn't find anyone who had or knew of any kids visiting. And look, they're still damp. Couldn't have been there that long."

Marti stared at the mittens. Blue with a Scottie dog design. Thin. Not what she would buy to keep her kid's hands warm. A kid's mittens. Were children involved somehow too?

4

It was just getting dark when Georgie headed back to the Cramer Hotel on Saturday. Ducking his head, he walked into the wind, wishing that it would hurry up and get warmer or that he'd find a way to get a heavier coat. The snow felt like needles sticking him as it blew against his face. He wasn't sure he should go into the hotel before dark, but his mittens were in there. Padgett dropped them last night and now he was wearing Padgett's but he wanted his own mittens instead. His didn't have holes in the thumbs.

He began coughing and couldn't stop. He ducked into a doorway, hugging himself so his chest wouldn't hurt so bad, and hacked until he spit. At least he wasn't coughing so often anymore. Cold finally must be going away.

He'd told LaShawna that so she wouldn't worry about him so much. Every time she sat there real still with her hands on her stomach she was worrying about something. He tried to stay with her more so she wouldn't worry about him, but then she'd just worry because he had this cold. LaShawna worried about all of them.

When they got to Minneapolis she wouldn't have to worry anymore.

He went past the Greyhound station, saw the man who sold the tickets inside sweeping up and about three people waiting for the bus. Nothing like that big place in Chicago. Smaller than a grocery store. He wished it was bigger so he could figure out a way to get them some bus tickets. But with the seats and the counter and everything right there, there wasn't no way to do nothing without the man seeing him. If he could just get hold of some tickets, LaShawna could read some and write. She'd be able to figure out how they could use them.

The man sweeping didn't even look at him, so he must not remember him walking past there every day this week. He went around to the back, checked the padlock on the iron grating that covered the back door. Saw the tiny window up too high to reach. There must be a burglar alarm too. Someday he'd know how to get into a place with a burglar alarm. But he didn't know how to now and if he got caught, Padgett and Jose and LaShawna and Sissie wouldn't have no one to take care of them, no one to get them to Minneapolis.

He looked at the trash, just two small plastic bags that came out of a wastebasket. He had torn one of them open day before yesterday. Wasn't nothing in there that would do him no good. Wasn't nothing in there now either.

When he came around front the bus to Minneapolis was waiting. LaShawna had a teacher come from there. Sent her a postcard from there last summer that LaShawna had taped to the wall where they was staying. Had a lake with a little house by it and a man and boy fishing from a boat. LaShawna said they would like it there, that it wasn't nothing like St. Louis.

He felt a tickle in his throat, knew he wanted to cough again and walked faster, seeing how long he could go without giving in. He almost made it to the corner.

Two blocks and he was near the Cramer. There was a police car in front and another in the alley. He wouldn't be able to get his mittens today. Maybe after he went to the store and got the fruit and dented cans the man threw out and took them back for supper, maybe he could come back. No, LaShawna wouldn't let him go back out tonight.

Ducking his head deeper into his collar he walked past the big double doors without looking in. Behind him, he heard the doors open. He made believe he had to tie his Converse. Maybe he could find out why the police were there and figure out when they'd be leaving. He really did need his own mittens.

"Lord, chile," he heard a lady say, "a body ain't safe nowheres no more. Lotta good it does us to have a door that locks when we got a fool behind the counter too lazy to lock it."

"Poor chile, getting herself killed like that."

That was them two old ladies he thought must be sisters 'cause they always wore the same color.

"Never did hear of her doin' nothin' to nobody."

"Well, she won't be doin' no singin' no more."

The singing woman. They had to be talking about the singing woman. He began coughing and the ladies came over to him.

"You all right, little boy?" One of them began patting his back.

"Gettin' kinda late for you to be out, ain't it? Be dark soon." This one began dabbing at his face with a Kleenex. When her hand touched his face her fingers felt scratchy and dry. He wanted to push her hand away. Instead he looked up at her.

"Can't go home," he said, sounding real sad.

"Can't go home? Lord chile but you better."

They sounded just alike. Must be sisters.

"Ain't half as cold now as it will be in another hour."

"Can't," he said again.

"Why, little boy?"

"Mikey, ma'am."

"And so well mannered. Why can't a nice little boy like you go home?"

"My momma's gonna whip me. Gave me five dollars to get milk and bread and I done lost it. See?" He held up his mittens, showed them the holes in the thumbs. "Must fell outta here. I got to find it."

"Lord, chile. I know your momma wouldn't want you coming home all sick over no five dollars."

He forced himself to take a deep breath so he would cough.

"This chile's about to get pneumonia."

"These young uns now. Babies havin' babies.

Got no common sense about raisin' a chile."
This one rummaged through her purse, came
up with a little cloth wallet and opened the
clasp. "You just take this and get what your
momma told you and get on home before you
catch your death of cold."

Georgie pocketed the money and hurried
away. When he got to the corner he had to
cough some more but he didn't stay there long
enough to let the two old ladies catch up with
him. He might get them to help him out again.
But maybe he shouldn't come back here, with
the singing woman dead. Must be her they was
talking about. He'd sure better not let Padgett
know nothin' about it. Boy would never come
out at night no more.

That man what was chasin' them musta done
it. Police woulda caught him by now, else why'd
they still be there? He wished he knew how to
read. Bet it would be in the paper. No way he
could let LaShawna read the paper to him.
She'd really worry if she knew.

5

It was a little after twelve Monday afternoon when Marti went into the squad room. She and Vik had spent the morning in court and she was glad they wouldn't have to give any further testimony in that case.

She went home, changed out of her winter court outfit, a wool navy blue skirt and blazer, and into her work outfit—the slacks, jacket, and service shoes or flat, sturdy boots she always wore to work. She kept her gun in her purse, but on occasion used a shoulder or hip holster. She got teased a lot about always being ready for a pursuit, but when she worked in Chicago, that happened a lot. Here it was mostly comfort and habit.

She and Vik had three cases pending. This morning's she considered the worst. A fourteen-year-old who had shaken her two-month-old baby until the infant girl stopped crying. And breathing. Marti wasn't sure why she was depressed—if it was seeing the Christmas decorations attached to the street lights as she left the courthouse, or finding out that the teenager was pregnant again, or just the memory of the baby wearing a white nightgown with pink rosebuds and tossed on a chair like a discarded doll. Times like this she felt she'd had enough of the killing and crime and was ready to play the happy homemaker for a while.

Instead of handing her in her resignation she headed for the coffee pot. Cowboy, one of her vice-cop office mates, was prowling the space between his desk and the window; boots dragging, five-gallon hat pushed back on thick wavy blond hair. Mad about something, she guessed. He'd had a court date this morning too.

She circled around him, hoping that he had made the coffee before he went to see the judge. Smells strong like his, she thought as she filled her cup. She blew across the surface then tasted it. Not bitter. Good enough to drink without adding sugar or creamer. Cowboy made the best pot of coffee of anyone in the precinct.

Vik had come in by the time she sat down. Wiry hair pointing in half a dozen directions, nose skewed at an angle that seemed to be pointing at her, eyebrows locked together in a peppery scowl. "Need to lock her parents up," he muttered. "Things weren't like this ten years ago."

Marti didn't tell him that she had run across worse cases ten years ago. They had two more homicide trials pending, neither of which she felt like thinking or talking about, and a couple more that had been plea bargained down to manslaughter. She reached for the reports that had been left in her IN-basket and returned to what was nagging at her instead. Lauretta Dorsey.

The report on John, their mystery man, looked promising. When Vik stopped grumbling under his breath and began brooding in silence, she looked up. "I think we might have something here on our friend John. You know, 3B?"

"He exists?" Vik said.

"Checked into the Cramer the first of November. John Louis Clark, alias Jack Lewis, alias Clark Lewis, alias Louis St. John. Not much imagination. Picked that last name when he graduated from grabbing purses and snatching change out of cash registers to strong-armed robbery. Two years and parole on a manslaughter charge."

Vik's expression remained dour. "And Dorsey had money. And a bruise on her face. Looks like he might have graduated again, to homicide. What's the bad news?"

She began scanning the states he was known to have lived in. "Want these in alpha order?"

Vik glared at her.

"Alabama, Arizona, California, Florida, Georgia, Illinois, Indiana, Louisiana, Ohio, Minnesota, Nevada, Tennessee, and Wisconsin."

"At least we know where to look for him," Vik said with a scowl.

Slim, the other vice cop, came in preceded by the scent of Obsession for Men. "Think you got your man and don't know where to find him?" he said, giving Marti a wink that implied intimacy.

"Showered again with cologne," she said. "Gee, that makes twice this month and it's only the eleventh."

Slim lounged against her desk. He was six-two, slender, with coppery brown skin, a cupid's bow smile, dimples, and like a lot of vice cops she knew, an incurable flirt. "Bet this John, aka Louis, aka Clark, would have hung around a little longer this time if he knew someone like you would be looking for him."

She glanced at Cowboy, who was ignoring all of them as he paced. He had quit using chewing tobacco and was chomping on a thick wad of bubble gum. Watching him, her jaws almost ached. "Hey, Cowboy, slow down. We wanted to talk with both of you."

Cowboy walked reluctantly toward her desk, then doubled back to his own to spit out the gum and cram another pack into his mouth. "I suppose this is about the Cramer Hotel?" he said, leaning against a windowsill and chewing rapidly. "Your usual fleabag flophouse." He experimented with a small bubble. "Not as bad as the one three blocks over that they tore down a couple years back. Same clientele. You've met some of the residents."

"Know of anybody who might be useful?" Vik asked, irritably. "People we've talked with so far are all a bunch of losers. None of them know from nothing. And not lying either. Except for the night clerk, and he's still refusing to talk to us."

Cowboy spit into a wastebasket. "Wayne Baxter. Scrawny little weasel. Hope you threw the book at him. We might get a little more cooperation the next time we perambulate about the premises."

Slim smiled. "There is this little lady of the night there, Vik. Calls herself Clarissa. Great little woman. Forty-five maybe, hard to tell. Got a scar here"—he indicated a slit throat—"and lived to tell it. A couple of front teeth missing, but nobody's perfect."

"Want an introduction, Jessenovik?" Cowboy said. "She's not too far past her prime. Hear she's still real good at . . ."

"Lady present," Vik reminded them.

"Who?" Slim grinned. "Big Mac? This woman's all cop. Wouldn't want her to dropkick me."

Cowboy popped his gum. "Physically or verbally?"

"The holiday spirit's gotten to all of us," Cowboy said.

"Yeah," Vik scowled.

"Might have a lead for you, man," Slim said. "Little Christmas present a few weeks early to give you time to think up something nice to get me. Lenny Doobee. Nickname. Not your friendly type but a night owl. Too afraid to sleep at night."

"We met him," Vik muttered. "Sees little people. Hears enemy agents in the hallway. A real nut case."

"An observant nut case," Cowboy corrected. "Sees things nobody in their right mind would pay attention to."

"Yeah, right," Vik grouched. "Is any of it

real? Because if he saw anything real Friday night he's not telling."

Slim headed for the door. "Got to pick and choose, man. One man's reality, another man's dream. Or nightmare. What did you think, interviewing him?"

"You got any special code for distinguishing the dream from the nightmare from the reality?"

"Marti here is pretty good at that," Slim said, giving her another smile.

Marti said what she had been thinking. "I'm more concerned that he did see something, or someone, and can't or won't tell us. Shrink says he'll talk to him when he sees him this week. We'll see."

Slim stopped as he was about to go into the hall. "Doobee's real scared. He'd rather hide than fight. I don't even think the kid knows *how* to fight back."

"We've got our ears to the ground," Cowboy said. "We'll let you know if we hear anything. And we'll try to keep an eye on Doobee. He'll keep himself out of harm's way."

Marti thought about the mittens. "Heard anything about kids hanging around there?"

Slim shrugged. "Baxter leaves that door unlocked all night. Come payday or check day and there's pretty good pickin's. Probably got a few kids smart enough to take advantage of it."

"Heard anything special?"

"Can't say that I have. But for you, I will certainly check around."

"We need those two like we need more cold

weather," Vik complained. "And unless our friend John does something to call attention to himself, the odds on our finding him are the same as finding a robin on that windowsill this afternoon."

"There's also the small problem of why John Clark would hit her, kill her, and then leave without taking the money," she said.

"Unless someone in the hall interrupted him."

"Maybe," she conceded. "I'm not going to sit on my hands until we find him." She thought about the mittens. "I asked Denise Stevens to stop by when she got a chance. I hate all these loose ends." She picked up the reports on her desk. "Time to go through all this. What really worries me is that we're talking about people who aren't connected to anything or anyone. They wander through life with no attachments or commitments. When you try to find them or identify them or get to know who they are it's like trying to grasp fog."

The autopsy report indicated that Dorsey had died from pressure applied to the carotid artery. Someone had stood in front of her and squeezed her neck until she was dead. Whoever had done it had acted so quickly that she was unconscious almost before she knew what was happening. If Dorsey had scratched her killer, she had done it before he put his hands on her throat.

Marti looked at Vik. "The coroner's saying between eleven-thirty Friday night and one-thirty Saturday morning." A two-hour time span was a lot better than they usually got. "The bruise could have occurred one to two hours before death," she read aloud. "Perp was approximately five inches taller than Dorsey, which puts him at five-eleven. Degree of pressure indicates someone with good manual strength. Large thumbs. No prints. Knew what he was doing. The department's psychiatric consultant doesn't have enough data to commit to anything psychological but he thinks it's a person who would stay calm under pressure. Deliberate, not impulsive. He doesn't rule out a female perp."

"That sure narrows it down," Vik said. "From anybody to damned near anybody."

According to the report, Dorsey was in excellent health, had drunk white wine a short time before she died, and had never been pregnant. The date of birth on the VA ID indicated she was thirty-six.

"I'd like to know where that money came from," Marti said. "When I talked with her mother on the phone she was genuinely surprised that Dorsey was here, knew nothing about any money or anyone in the family who would give her that kind of cash."

Vik didn't answer.

"And those evening gowns and cotton underwear. What was that all about? Nothing else personal in that place but the way she kept everything in order. No personal effects except for that bottle of antihistamines prescribed by a doctor at the VA hospital. Strange."

"We don't know what the perp took with him."

"Well, I bet it's nothing that would give us a real handle on Dorsey," Marti said, frustrated by data that told her so little of what she needed to know. "She knew the perp. We have to get to know her. When we know her well enough she'll show us who did it."

Vik put down his pencil, put down the report he was reading, and leaned back in his chair, his eyebrows wedged into a frown. "I know we've only got six other cases pending and that must not seem like a lot when you come from a place like Chicago, but don't get your hopes up on this one. We've got a woman in the morgue with no roots, no ties, no friends. This looks like one of those cases that might stay in the open file forever. Don't let your curiosity get the best of you."

Curiosity, as far as Vik was concerned, ranked right up there with intuition.

"Look Marti, it bothers the hell out of me to know that this could be almost any other stiff and we'd be catching hell for not having it wrapped up already. But we're not going to take any heat on this one. We don't have to do a damned thing besides fill out the forms. Just one less crazy, and God knows we've got too many of those. A couple of years back we had five street people within the city limits and they lived in those shanties down near the lake because they wanted to. Now the *News-Times* is saying that our transient population has exploded. Well kid, it's been reduced by one. Dorsey won't even get an obituary."

He paused, rubbed his temples in a weary

gesture. "And that shouldn't happen. This is the United States of America. We're going to work our butts off on this one. Maybe it was Baxter. Maybe it was Clark. Eventually Clark will turn up. Maybe then we'll get lucky. One thing for sure, we can't give idiots like Burdett any reason to think that just because nobody's putting any pressure on us, that this, or any dead body is just another Jane Doe."

"Vik," Marti said, "I'm glad you don't let your emotions influence your work."

His scowl deepened. He stared at the reports for a minute. "What really concerns me is what if this perp didn't leave town and Doobee does know something he shouldn't. . . . And what if we do have kids mixed up in this?"

That worried her, too.

Denise Stevens, a juvenile probation officer, came in as they were getting ready to go home. She was the same height and size as Marti. Her skin was two shades darker. Unlike Marti, she wasn't comfortable with her size and wore plain, tailored suits and hats that drew everyone's attention to her face and away from her figure.

Tonight she looked dressed for church, probably a choir rehearsal. Her hat was black felt with a floppy brim and a huge red rose.

Marti looked from the rose to her face in spite of herself. Handsome woman, Momma would have said, describing classic black features, almond eyes, full lips, generous mouth, and a space between her two front teeth.

"Glad you stopped by," Marti said. When it came to juveniles, Denise had an informal network that was effective and far-reaching. Marti had seen Denise accomplish the near impossible just by getting on the phone.

"Cowboy make this coffee, MacAlister?" Denise asked. When Marti nodded, she poured herself a cup and pulled up a chair. "So you found a pair of kids' mittens near your scene of crime and think you've got kids hanging out at the Cramer."

"That possible?" Marti asked, hoping it wasn't.

"First," Denise said, looking at Vik, "despite what you would like to believe about this outpost of society, Jessenovik, we do have homeless kids right here in wonderful Lincoln Prairie. Homeless families come to our soup kitchens and shelters daily. Their numbers have doubled since this time last year and it's going to get worse."

She waited until Vik nodded, and went on. "Now, what I am also certain that we have, but are not acknowledging yet, is throwaway children. Kids nobody wants. Maybe they're abused at home, maybe they're just one mouth too many, maybe they cause trouble. When they leave, they're just gone. Nobody reports them, nobody looks for them. It's as if they never existed."

Vik's face was tense but he said nothing.

"Some of them come from someplace else and dead-end here trying to get to Milwaukee or Minneapolis or some other point further north.

71

But there are some that come from various parts of the county."

Vik clenched his fists.

"Now that we've covered the groundwork, Jessenovik, I have no idea whether or not any of what I've just told you impinges on your concerns about the Cramer. Anything is possible. I would much rather have you worry that there is a child out there than convince yourself that there is not. The only practical thing I can do right now is refer you to the second-shift beat cop who covers that area, Lupe Torres. She's young but she's a damned good cop. I've relayed this to her. She's in one of those walking patrols that have been set up in that area. She knows the people who are most likely to come into contact with the kids we might be talking about. She'll be in touch as soon as she has something."

As she got up to leave, Denise added, "And by the way. Whether they're street kids who are still with a family or throwaways, these kids adapt fast, learn how to take care of themselves and survive. Trouble is, most of what they learn is detrimental and illegal. They are not likely to thank you for finding them. If there are children involved and you can get them to me, I'll do whatever I can. But don't start looking for miracles."

For some reason, Marti felt better after Denise left. Maybe it was her grasp of the situation, or the feeling that they had at least one solid resource in an area where she would be in over her head. But most likely it was Denise herself.

"Good woman," Vik said. "I hope we won't need her help on this one."

"I'm glad she's around if we do," Marti told him.

6

Marti sat at her desk looking at the stack of forms the Dorsey case had generated. Instead of working on them she thought back to their visit to the Cramer the night before.

Vik had met her in front of the hotel just after midnight. She'd been waiting outside for ten minutes.

"Thought you stood me up, Jessenovik." The wind was beginning to penetrate the wool scarf she had pulled up to her nose, and her eyes were watering from the cold. At least her feet and hands were still warm.

"Bunch of fruitcakes in this place," Vik griped. "And we're as crazy as they are, coming here at this hour to check on Lenny Doobee."

"To question Lenny Doobee," Marti corrected.

"Sure, sure, MacAlister. Oddballs bring out your maternal instinct."

He spoke without rancor. Having a maternal instinct seemed to be a positive thing this time.

She pushed open the front door. Mud smeared the marble floor. Tracked-in snow had melted in small puddles. The day clerk had been pushed into night duty in Baxter's absence, and snored softly from behind the high oak desk. They had to look behind it to see him stretched out in the chair, covered with the flowered throw.

"So much for security," Vik said.

Upstairs they passed an open janitor's closet. The sink was clogged and the odor of sour water and disinfectant was strong enough to make Marti want to gag. Holes showed through the hardwood floor where the red carpeting had worn away. Lenny lived three doors down from Dorsey. Midway between the two rooms a saucer stacked with chocolate chip cookies had been left on the floor.

This time when they knocked, instead of a timid "Who's there?" a cheerful voice called, "Just a minute."

Lenny kept the chain on the door, took his time checking their shields as if he didn't remember them from his visit to the precinct. Finally he said, "I remember you. You're here about Dorsey."

Vik shrugged, indicating Marti should assume her usual role and ask questions.

"We thought you might have had time to remember something about the other night," she said.

"You'd better come in," he said. "You'll scare away the little people if you stay in the hall."

Lenny took the chain off the door, admitting them to a small room with a bed, a dresser, and a Formica-topped kitchen table with two chairs. A small cooking area with a bar-sized refrigerator and a hot plate was screened off by a curtain pulled across that portion of the room.

Lenny motioned Marti to a chair, took the other one, and paid scant attention to Vik. Vik took a long look at the sagging mattress covered with a grayish white sheet, then sat down.

Both of Doobee's chins seemed to rest on his chest as he leaned forward. His little eyes seemed to want to be friendly. He began to wring his pudgy hands. He didn't know how to trust her. Maybe he couldn't trust anyone.

"Lenny, you said someone came here last Friday night."

"You believe me?"

"Yes." She didn't think it was a paid assassin, but in her experience, a lot of fantasies began somewhere in reality and expanded. She wanted to find out what was real.

"He was there, he really was. He was looking for the little people. He wanted to kill them."

"There was one person?"

"There are more. There's a whole army but they only send a couple of spies here to catch the little people. They're small, they couldn't get away."

"And one person was after the little people last Friday?"

"There were three of them," Lenny stated with conviction.

"How many of them did you see?"

He looked at her, suspicious again. "I didn't see any of them and they didn't see me. But I heard them. I know there were three bad guys out there." His eyes became sad. "I just want to see the little people. But these men, they hide on the stairs and scare them away. I leave cookies out every night. They hardly ever make it through to eat them."

"Are the cookies ever gone?"

"Sometimes," he whispered.

"But you've never seen who takes them?"

"No. I can't. I would scare them too. But if you can just catch those men, make them go away so the little people don't have to hide and be afraid." His eyes widened with fear as he spoke.

He was the little people, Marti decided. He was talking about himself. But had some glimpse of reality contributed to his fantasy, like finding children at the Cramer or hearing or seeing a real killer last Friday night?

This morning, just thinking about last night made her feel frustrated. She pulled over to the typewriter, adjusted her desk chair to the height of the table, and fingered the keyboard while Vik started to fill out his stack of forms. Slim and Cowboy had a Tuesday afternoon court call. It was after six now and they hadn't returned to the office. She glanced out the window. It was dark. The quitting time sounds of doors slamming and cars starting had subsided.

After fifteen minutes of typing netted her only five completed forms, she got up, poured a cup of coffee, tasted it, and threw it into the wastebasket.

"Stale. Cowboy's going to have to remember

to make a fresh pot before he leaves for the day."

It hadn't been a productive day. There had been a call from the jail around four o'clock. Wayne Baxter had been released from the infirmary. He was still refusing to see her, claimed they had planted the wallet and the money. He'd be arraigned tomorrow. Maybe after he spoke with a public defender he'd be a little more cooperative. "That Wayne Baxter!"

"Any particular reason you dislike him?" Vik asked.

"Maybe it's the crack about us planting evidence. Whether he did it or not he knew she was dead and he left her there, went downstairs, and kept drinking. I haven't run across one person yet in this case who thought of anyone but himself. Total self-absorption. Even Lenny Doobee, for all his talk of little people and assassins. They all exist in relationship to themselves. What they see. What they hear. As if that gives them their existence. And maybe it does."

She looked down at the stack of forms waiting to be filled out. As she hesitated a woman came to the door.

"Officer Jessenovik? Officer MacAlister? They told me I could find the detectives assigned to Lauretta Dorsey's case here."

The first thing Marti noticed was the fur coat. The next thing was how much older the dyed black hair made the woman look. Worn loose in a windblown style, it aged her. Thick black mascara and arched eyebrows that accentuated the wrinkles aged the woman even more.

"I'm Lauretta's mother."

When Vik didn't speak Marti said, "I'm Detective MacAlister, ma'am. This is my partner." She scanned her notes, found place of birth, Shelburn Falls, and said, "You've come from New York?"

"Yes. It was difficult booking a flight but I came as soon as I could. My husband would have come, but he's in London this week." She swept into the room as if she were auditioning for the "Loretta Young Show."

Marti took a closer look and determined that the fur was sable, soft and luxurious and the best cut. She had worked a fur theft case once. She knew less about gems, but the rings on the woman's fingers, a ruby and several diamonds bigger than any she had ever seen before, looked real too. They would have to arrange for an escort to get the woman safely back to the hotel or airport.

Vik came to life and motioned the woman to a chair.

"Mrs. Dorsey?" Marti asked. She had the same deep brown eyes as Dorsey, and Marti bet without the dye she also had the same red hair, but graying.

Mrs. Dorsey looked uncomfortable, sitting on the edge of the chair as if she'd get something on her coat if she leaned back. She refused coffee and didn't remove her black kidskin gloves, acting as if she didn't want to touch anything.

Marti hoped something about the circumstances of her daughter's death would affect the woman—a little sadness, maybe, because Dorsey was dead at thirty-six. But the way she spoke, it was as if they weren't even related.

"She left home, officer. It was her decision." The East Coast accent along with the deep tan and dark hair made the woman seem like a foreigner. "We wanted her to go to Smith, just as her sisters had. She chose to join the navy right out of high school. Lauri always had to have a cause. If it had been the early sixties she might have joined the civil rights movement instead of choosing the conflict in Vietnam."

"But she didn't go to war, Mrs. Dorsey. Never left the states."

"Lauri didn't even become an officer, just a physical therapist." She said it the way another parent might have said thief or prostitute.

"Did everyone call her Lauri or was it just a family name?"

For some reason, Mrs. Dorsey seemed embarrassed by the question. "Everyone, as far as I know. We named her for my husband's grandmother. At the time Lauretta seemed like such a grown-up name for such a tiny baby."

There was a fleeting pensive expression in Mrs. Dorsey's eyes. "Of course she always was a tomboy. No frills and lace for that one. Nothing like her two sisters."

Marti's fledgling feelings of sympathy vanished. She wondered how Mrs. Dorsey would feel when she went through her daughter's effects and saw the shabby vintage evening wear. "Do you know why she kept returning here after she was discharged? Did she have friends here?"

"I assume it had something to do with that saxophone player she was involved with."

"Do you know his name, what happened to him?"

"No idea of who he was. I didn't want to know, and told her not to tell me. Thank God he died before they could get married. Car accident. She wasn't with him. The months we spent planning her sisters' weddings, impossible with Lauri's choice."

"Do you know of any friends, anyone else she associated with while she was in the service?"

Mrs. Dorsey turned up the collar of her sable as if she was cold. "I didn't want to know anything about those people. They had nothing in common with us. Lauretta didn't belong with them. I couldn't encourage her."

Marti persisted. "There were no letters, postcards, nothing?"

"We did not communicate while she was in the military or afterwards. I only know about this man, whoever he was, because she thought she was going to marry him. After she was discharged she never came home."

"Did you know that she was discharged with a psychiatric disability? That she was diagnosed schizophrenic?" Marti asked.

"What? Lauri? There must be some mistake. Not Lauri. She was always a stubborn child but certainly not . . . not . . . no one who knew her could ever believe that. And you are to suppress that from any public records that will come into existence because of this ... this ... unpleasantness."

"Not much I can do about that, ma'am."

"Well, I certainly can," Mrs. Dorsey told her and stood up.

"Just a few more questions, ma'am. Was Dorsey an especially neat person?"

"Neat? You've got to be kidding. I always had to remind her of the proper way to maintain personal hygiene, clean her room, sit at the table. Sometimes I thought she kept that room a mess just to spite me."

Well, Marti thought, if that was the case she's spent a lot of time making up for it.

"And you don't know of any money she might have received just before she died?"

"I checked with her brother. He's the only one in the family who might have sent her money. He said he hadn't heard from her since just before Thanksgiving. She did not ask for or indicate that she needed money."

Before Mrs. Dorsey left, Marti explained that so far it appeared that Lauretta was a loner, that they hadn't been able to locate one personal friend. She asked Mrs. Dorsey to speak with her brother and other members of the family to see if they could recall anything or find any correspondence that might help.

"Better to let Lauri rest in peace now, officer. I have no desire to see the person responsible apprehended. It will just create sensational headlines and fodder for gossip. Now, I have a cab waiting." With that she swept out of the room.

After the woman left, Marti finished typing her reports. Vik worked on his in silence. Neither of them had anything to say.

Just before she left the squad room Ben Walker called Marti with an invitation to dinner. They had been going out for dinner a couple of times a month since September. She wasn't sure if she wanted to see him or if she just wanted to avoid the health food cuisine her daughter Joanna had become dedicated to. Marti didn't turn him down.

"So, what'll it be?" he said. "This steak house in Racine that every paramedic in town's been to but me, or . . ."

"Or," she said. So far the only place they'd gone to was a restaurant with reasonably good steaks, an above-average house salad dressing, decent seafood, and a fantastic view of Lake Michigan.

"Pick you up at seven-thirty," Ben said. He didn't sound too disappointed.

"It's almost seven now. How about eight? I need a few minutes with the kids." Another nice thing about dinner with Ben. He was raising his son alone. Sometimes he was the one who needed the extra half hour.

By nine-fifty she had worked her way through a salad, two sides of fries with lots of ketchup, and a very rare steak. "Browned and raw," as Ben put it.

They practically had the room to themselves. Three couples sat at the other tables for two by the window overlooking the lake. Marti looked down at the candle burning in a round red globe, touched the glass with her fingernail.

"Why does someone join the fire department to ride the ambulance and not the fire truck?" she asked.

"Meaning?"

"If a sailor joins the navy to see the world, why does a woman become a Wave? They didn't see much of anything in 1970."

"The case you're working on. Got you stumped?"

"Why the navy?"

"Uniforms," Ben said.

"What?"

"Back then sailors could wear pants with thirteen buttons. Represented the thirteen colonies. Women loved them. I almost joined myself when the girl I was dating said they were romantic."

She thought about that. What would the uniform have signified to Dorsey? Discipline? Responsibility?

"Why didn't you join?"

"No control over your life. Somebody else telling you what to do and when to do it. Like having an omniscient parent."

That sounded right, now that she'd met Dorsey's mother. What about the man Dorsey was going to marry? Rebellion? Mother sure wasn't going to volunteer anything else. She could try the navy base, but there was nothing in their official records that had told her anything that she needed to know. It had been so long ago.

"All of that wandering and she never went

home," Marti said. "And her mother wasn't that bad. Not angry. Just a snob. She would have pretended the military service never happened. Everyone else would have taken their cue. Sort of like 'The Emperor's New Clothes,' everyone seeing what they wanted to see."

She looked out at the darkness. Water and sky seemed to meld. No clouds above, no breakers below. She couldn't tell where the lake ended and night began.

"I got a list of some military organizations, retirees, Vietnam vets," she said. "Nothing yet. She was scheduled to go to the VA hospital for a shot of Prolyxin on Friday. Maybe someone will turn up when I go there."

Dorsey didn't seem to have a recent past. Nobody who knew her at the time of her death had known her five years ago. Those who knew her now didn't know her well. That vintage dress world with everything tidy and in its place didn't seem to have a niche for friends or a past hidden in the dust-free nooks and crannies.

"Civilians," Ben said.

"What civilians?"

"Civil service. Always a lot of them working at the hospital. Some have been there twenty, thirty years."

"I already asked, Ben. Nobody on the wards now was there when Dorsey was."

"Then a lot of people around here know someone who works on the base. Start asking around. I will too. And tell Sharon. No telling who that girl knows." He chuckled.

Marti smiled too. Her friend Sharon wasn't a gossip, but she kept her finger on most of what was going on and could tap into a lot of informal resources. They had known each other since kindergarten. Now with Marti widowed and Sharon divorced, they were sharing a house. Sharon taught school and was home when her daughter and Marti's son and daughter were there, relieving an incalculable burden for Marti. And sharing the mortgage and other expenses took away Sharon's financial worries with a teacher's salary and an ex-husband who had stopped bothering to make child support payments.

"Good idea," Marti agreed.

They settled into a companionable silence, sipping wine. This wasn't a date, she reminded herself. She hadn't dated anyone since Johnny died. She and Johnny had grown up together. As long as she had known him he had been quiet, communicating as often as not in wordless signals that she had learned to interpret. After his death, it had come to her slowly that she needed to be quiet with someone who could feel comfortable with silence.

Ben, who was much more gregarious than Johnny and always seemed a chuckle away from laughter, understood and accepted that. And she could talk about the job with him because he did similar work. She wondered if that was why she was sitting here with him tonight. If so, she was sure that wasn't the only reason. Despite his silence, her relationship with Johnny had always been intense and physical and emotional. There was a inner calmness about Ben, an imperturbability that attracted her. But she wouldn't tell him that, not tonight.

7

When Marti got up the next morning, daylight was still approaching. Before going to work, she looked in on her kids. Joanna snored softly. Her pillow was on the floor, the blanket half off the bed. Blue sweats and a green basketball uniform were on the floor. Marti touched Joanna's hair, auburn like hers, and smiled at generous amber-toned features that mirrored her own. She adjusted the blanket.

When she went into Theo's room, Bigfoot was sprawled across the foot of the bed. He wagged his tail as she approached. Johnny had picked him out at the pound. As big as he was, part St. Bernard, Marti wasn't sure if he was much of a watchdog.

Theo's model airplane caught her attention. He and Johnny had been working on it when Johnny was killed. It was still unfinished, and Theo had kept it on his bureau. Now it was on the card table. She ran her finger along the balsa frame, wondered which pieces Johnny had glued together and if they had intended to paint it.

Theo was a light sleeper. He smiled as she sat

down beside him, but didn't open his eyes. In profile, his bronze face was all angles, like Johnny's.

"You awake?"

"Umm."

"What's with the model airplane?"

"Don't know. Cub Scout project. Be a Boy Scout soon."

His speech was often abbreviated. It was like listening to Johnny.

"Christmas break," he said. He sighed and went back to sleep.

Snow crunched as she backed out of the driveway. It had snowed enough during the night to cover the hedges and then gotten cold enough to glaze the barren oaks and birches with ice. Multicolored lights strung along the evergreen hedges had given off enough heat to peek through the snow-laden branches. Her kids called their street the gingerbread village. All the houses on the block were large brown or tan brick Tudors that sat back on lots sheltered by wide-branched evergreens. Manger scenes and Santa Clauses decorated the lawns. One neighbor had made a sleigh and three life-sized reindeer out of plywood and had filled the sleigh with brightly wrapped boxes. She drove slowly for two blocks, looking through the rearview mirror until she turned the corner.

After roll call, she spent the morning in court. Vik testified first. He was convinced they wouldn't get a conviction on the manslaughter charge. Marti thought they would. The man had a previous record of beating his wife. Too bad he was high when he stabbed her. He said the crack told him his wife was the devil and that she came at him with a meat cleaver. They couldn't disprove it, but Marti would have preferred murder one.

From court they went to the county jail. Wayne Baxter's public defender had called. Baxter was ready to talk to them. As they checked in their weapons and took the elevator to the third floor she wondered if it would be worth the trip.

They stepped out of the elevator into a small area located somewhere in the interior of the building. She never could get her bearings here. There were three rooms with glass partitions, each with a phone. Baxter hadn't been brought in yet.

Everyone else they'd been holding in connection with the case had been released, except those with warrants. There were no tissue matches and no fingerprint matches on any of them. Baxter's prints had been found in Dorsey's room.

"I wish I believed he killed her," Marti said.

"Me too. The only thing worse than having too many suspects is narrowing it down to one and not being able to put your hands on him or come up with any new prospects."

The lawyer arrived, a tall, thin man wearing a tan corduroy jacket with brown patches at the elbow. He extended his hand to Vik first. "Jack Boyd."

A metal door opened and Baxter came in. He was wearing jailhouse greens and slippers. His color had improved to brown without a grayish tinge; he'd had a shave and a haircut. A few fringe benefits that came with being incarcerated. He entered the small bare room, sat on the metal stool attached to the floor, and reached for the phone.

"Got something to say?" Marti asked.

"I been wantin' to talk with you."

"Then tell me what you know about what happened last Friday night," she told him. "And that's it. Anything else you discuss with Mr. Boyd."

"Yes ma'am. I understand."

She didn't like this subdued Baxter any better than she liked him when he was surly.

"I was asleep. Honest. Some kids coming in woke me. Woke me up again when they were running out. Time I got myself together and come around from behind the desk they was gone. Wasn't nobody there."

"How many kids?"

"Two."

"Boys or girls?"

"Boys."

"How old?"

He looked confused. "How would I know? Didn't get a chance to ask 'em."

"How old did they look?"

He shook his head. "Know less to nothin' 'bout kids. They was small though. Come to my shoulder maybe."

Marti made a quick estimate, came up with seven to nine years old. "What time was it?"

He scratched his head then rubbed his neck.

"If I went to sleep at eleven or twelve, it musta been between eleven-thirty and one."

That was within the time frame the coroner established as time of death.

"Do you know why they were running? Did they say anything?"

"Don't recall that they did. Happened real fast. Didn't actually see them when they was leavin'. Just heard them more or less."

"How did you know it was them if you didn't see them?" Marti asked.

"Sounded like kids. Wasn't no grown-up people running, least not till after they passed."

"What do you mean?"

"Well, somebody was chasing 'em. Time I came around the desk to run 'em all out, no one was there."

Behind her Marti heard Vik take a deep breath. "And you wouldn't tell us this last Saturday," he said, his voice menacing. "You wouldn't tell us that children were there."

Boyd looked at Vik, then Marti, and shrugged.

Marti spoke, forcing herself to stay calm and keep her voice quiet. "I think you had better tell us everything you know, right now."

"Y-y-yes," Baxter agreed. "Someone came in after the kids run out. A little old lady. I'd gone back behind the desk. I didn't want no trouble. I jus' didn't want no trouble, so I watch from behind the desk where no one can see me and the old woman carrying the shopping bag came in."

"And then?" Vik growled.

"I, um, my nerves was bad was what. All that

92

runnin' around and all. I jus' had to take something to settle my nerves. And I went to sleep. Everything was quiet next time I woke up. I thought I'd better check before the day clerk came in, see if the kids did any damage. Day man's been wanting my job. Pays a quarter an hour more than his."

"And?" Vik prompted, moving closer to the glass partition.

"And I found her. She was already dead. Wasn't nothin' I could do for her. Wouldn't get me nothin' but trouble if I said that I found her. Old man Arnie found her soon enough. I wouldn't have left her there long enough to go to stinkin'. I jus' didn't want no trouble."

He looked from Marti to Vik, back to her. "That's all. Swear to God. That's all I know. Can I get out of here now? Will you tell them to let me out?"

Marti stood up. "Talk with Mr. Boyd about that." She hung up the phone.

Mr. Boyd extended his hand to Vik as they left. Marti walked ahead to the elevator.

As soon as she got to their unmarked car she put in a call to have Lupe Torres report to her office. The young female officer came in about five minutes after they got back to the precinct.

"Coffee?" Marti offered.

"Might wake me up," Torres smiled. She slipped off her jacket. She was petite with broad hips and a narrow waist. Her straight brown hair was plaited in one thick cornrow that hung just below her shoulders. "This is about the kids you think might have been at the Cramer. What have you got?"

"Night clerk just confirmed that two little boys were in there, that someone chased them out," Marti told her. "Happened within the time frame the coroner set for the homicide."

"Only thing I've had in the past month that could be important is reports of petty theft in a neighborhood about three blocks from there," Lupe said. "But there were three boys, not two. Taking things like sterno and flashlights and batteries. I'll check back with the merchants."

"If we put our artist on it will they give us a description and help with a composite?"

"Don't see why there'd be any problem."

"And see if one or two won't look the other way until we catch them," Vik said. "I think we can get them some reimbursement. If these kids can't survive where they are, they might move someplace else. Then we'll never find them and find out if they're the right ones."

"They'll cooperate," Lupe promised. "And I think Joe the Arab might know something."

Joe the Arab owned a grocery store. He used the name of the former owner, Jose, and pretended to be Hispanic too because he feared retribution for the political situation in the Middle East.

Lupe smiled. "Joe always looks guilty if you ask him about anything, even when he isn't. Good-hearted though, feeds a lot of people in that neighborhood without getting paid. So I don't want to alienate him. One other thing. When I was trying to catch up with these kids a couple of times I thought I tracked them to that place east of Sherman, before you get to the lake. Those abandoned industrial buildings and houses. I lost 'em there."

Lupe stood up, reached for her jacket. "I can't promise you anything. We get too high a profile and these kids will disappear. But if your perp is after them we need to be more aggressive."

"We've got to find the kids," Marti agreed. "And you're the best person we've got to help us. We've got a meeting with the lieutenant in about an hour. Do you want us to get you put on special duty?"

"I'd rather work my regular shift and put in some overtime. It's not the money. I just need to keep up with things on my beat. Keep things in hand."

She worked a mixed area—low income housing, blue collar workers who lived in apartments or owned their own homes, small businesses that the community depended on.

"We'll clear it with the lieutenant," Marti told her. "We don't know for certain who the perp is, if he's still here or if he's left town. We have an APB on one suspect but nothing's turned up yet. I don't know how much danger these kids are in. I think it makes more sense to try to find them than to scare them away. We'll keep you informed too."

After Torres left, neither of them said anything for a while, then Vik muttered, "Damn."

"Got that right," Marti agreed. She put in a call to Denise Stevens, advising her of what Baxter had told them.

"These kids are smarter than you think," Denise told her. "But please find them as soon as you can. Kids become invisible. Nobody wants to see them. And these are probably too young to outsmart an adult for any length of time. Especially if he knows what they look like."

After she hung up, Marti remembered what Baxter had said about an old woman. She was reasonably certain that the old woman was a friend, not the killer. She wanted Lauretta Dorsey to have had at least one friend.

Lunch was a tuna fish sandwich out of the machine in the basement. It didn't taste like any tuna fish she had ever eaten before, but it was fresh. Vik had corned beef on rye brought from home. She tried not to watch as he ate.

"If we didn't have a rap sheet on John Clark," she said, "it would be hard to believe he existed."

"Gives new meaning to the word drifter," Vik agreed. "When we do catch up with him I think we ought to tell that ex-wife living in Santa Fe. She hasn't seen him in eleven years and she's still spitting mad because he walked out on her."

"He stayed there six months," Marti said. "That's about as long as he stayed anywhere else."

Vik munched on a pickle. "Man can't stay out of trouble more than six weeks unless he's in jail. Got into a few fights while he was there. He'll let that warrant catch up with him pretty soon."

A call came in about three-thirty. "Officer

MacAlister? I'm Edward Dorsey, Lauri's older brother." He spoke in a resonant baritone with a hint of an accent that didn't sound East Coast. "There will be no service, just cremation tomorrow. My father is in London this week."

"Yes," Marti said patiently, wondering what he wanted to tell her.

"I've heard from Lauri every couple of years. She'd call. I'd arrange to get her out of jail or into a hospital or whatever. She wouldn't have anything to do with anyone else."

He paused, took a deep breath. "Mother was talking. The gist of it seemed to be that you expected us to know who Lauri's friends were. She's upset because Lauri never called, never came home. It would have been worse for Mother if she had known the truth."

Marti wondered who had decided that but didn't ask.

"Anyway, she didn't have any friends that I know of, not for years, and I don't think this will help you. Lauri was going to marry this black guy named Weeks. Nelson Weeks. And she talked about this one nurse she called Jennings every time I got her checked into a hospital. Told me to call Jennings, that Jennings would help her but never told me how to contact Jennings or who she was. I think it must have been someone she knew in the service. She sort of fixated on that. I don't know why. I think there was a lot she didn't tell me."

Marti wrote down the names and thanked him. She asked him if he had sent Dorsey any money recently.

"She never asked me for money. Last time I talked to her, just before Thanksgiving, she sounded better than she had since she got sick. She really sounded good, like the old Lauri." His voice broke. "I thought things were finally going to be all right for her."

"I'm sure she was glad you were there for her," Marti told him, not knowing what else to say.

"Thank you for that. And officer, I do want you to catch whoever did this. Lauri was not a bad person. She wasn't a hooker or a junkie or anything like that. She just had a chemical imbalance in her brain and she didn't like to take the medication that could correct it. She was not a bad person," he insisted. "She was just sick."

Marti thanked him again. When she put the phone down she felt a little better about Lauretta Dorsey. At least there had been someone she could call on. She didn't suppose that many other residents at the Cramer had as much. She wondered about the yellow cat. Ginnie called the cat Samantha. Where had Samantha taken herself to? Did the cat know where to find Dorsey's friends?

She was learning more about Dorsey. Information received from military records indicated a discharge with full pension for a psychiatric disability. Medical records gave a diagnosis, schizophrenia, a moderate form with typical schizoid behavior: denial, wandering from place to place, refusal to take medication. Eventually Dorsey became delusional and thought everyone from the mafia to the FBI was after her. She had sought protection and sanctuary in more than a dozen VA hospitals across the country.

Dated entries provided a history of visits to the Lincoln Prairie VA hospital for a period of several months every three or four years. The file was updated with photocopied or faxed information detailing the hospitalizations in other states. As far as they could determine, Dorsey and John Clark had been in the same state, California, at the same time, once. But not in the same city.

Dorsey's pattern, established over fourteen years, had changed a year and a half ago. She had returned to Lincoln Prairie, checked into the mental health clinic, stayed on her medication, and remained stable with no hospital admissions. As far as they could determine, she hadn't established any social contacts and refused to participate in counseling programs or psychotherapy.

Vik said, "Hey, MacAlister, daydreaming?"

He had a street map and had made photocopies of one section. "Area around the Cramer," he said. He studied the enlarged copies, then began sketching a map of his own.

"Not in proportion," he told her, "but here's Sherman Avenue. Here's the Cramer, two blocks west of Sherman. Here's those industrial buildings about two blocks east of Sherman." He drew in some more squares and rectangles. "Now. Here on Sherman we got the old library right on the northeast corner, that long two-story apartment building to the north. Cross the street and those older one-family homes start on the northwest corner. Back here we've got those abandoned industrial buildings and maybe three, four houses that need to be torn down. If Lupe's been sighting the kids there, this is the area we need to look at."

"The local preservation society toured that old library last week," Marti said. "I read about it in the *News-Times*. They want the city to declare it historical so they can use it for a fine arts center. Good location. Right on a main thoroughfare."

"I used to go there," Vik said. "The place smelled like old books. Odd floor plan. One large room, four small ones. Shame to think of what it must be like there now. Been closed for twenty-seven years. I bet the basement is a mess. The city put in those clay pipes back then. No water, no heat, no electricity all these years." He shook his head. "The building's sound though. Be a shame to see it knocked down. They'd probably replace it with a parking lot."

He sounded sad at the prospect. Vik did a lot of reading when he was off duty and she'd bet he had checked out a lot of books as a kid.

"We'd better get this out to the beat cops," she said. She didn't know that area well so she kept a copy of the maps for herself. The day had been more productive than she'd expected.

They had a meeting with the lieutenant and then she could go home to her daughter Joanna's latest vegetable concoction and broiled fish.

Later, around midnight, she'd cruise by the Cramer, but she couldn't think of a good excuse to skip supper. Except for the food, she'd like having a few hours with her kids. When she was honest with herself she admitted that Joanna's cooking tasted pretty good.

Marti believed that Joanna's insistence on all of the dietary changes meant that Joanna hadn't accepted Johnny's death yet. Johnny was shot to death while on an undercover operation. The department psychologist told her it could take years for her children to get over the trauma. Joanna knew that cholesterol levels, blood pressure, and general health might have nothing to do with when or how Marti would die. But those were things Joanna could try to control, and she still needed to do that.

8

Before she went home Wednesday evening Marti had located a Marlena Jennings, who had served at the naval hospital when Dorsey was stationed there. She thought it would be a difficult, time-consuming task. Instead, when she had mentioned it during their meeting with the lieutenant, he picked up the phone and called an old college buddy who was career navy, now stationed at the finance center in Cleveland. Jennings was a retiree and was located through computerized payroll records.

Marti called her number all evening without getting an answer. When she tried again after the ten o'clock news a recorder clicked on and she left a message. Jennings returned her call at seven Thursday morning and they made an appointment to meet at 10:00 A.M..

Miss Jennings was a retired navy lieutenant, junior grade, who, according to their brief conversation, traveled a great deal and no longer worked. She lived twenty-five miles west of Lincoln Prairie.

Timberwood Trail was a subdivision that had been built eight or ten years ago. Some of the trees planted then had matured enough to provide shade during the summer months, and the light gray wood siding looked weathered. The condos were advertised for empty nesters, and Marti guessed that most of the people who lived there were retired or semiretired. Where garage doors were open she could see BMWs and Mercedes parked in the driveways. Wide expanses of lawn were evenly carpeted with a crusty layer of snow. The circular streets had been plowed but there were no dirty piles of snow along the curbs.

Miss Jennings' unit was midway along a cul-de-sac, and sat well back from the curving road. The path to the front door had been cleared. It was a bright, sunny day and Marti took deep breaths of the frigid air as she walked to the front door. Momma had always said cold winter air was pure and cleaned the lungs. Marti wasn't sure there was any such thing as clean air anymore but she still inhaled just as she had learned to do years ago.

Marti had assumed Marlena Jennings was an older woman, sixtyish maybe, even though she didn't sound that old over the phone. A much younger woman came to the door. Mid-forties, Marti guessed, hair still a natural strawberry blond, eyes a deep clear blue. Then Miss Jennings extended her hand. Marti adjusted her guess up to mid-fifties.

"Officer MacAlister. Won't you come in?"

Miss Jennings looked like someone in an ad for a health and fitness club, one of those women who smiled as they lifted two hundred pounds and spoke without sounding out of breath. She walked with the bouncy little spring of a cheerleader, and Marti would have disliked her at once if it wasn't for the openness in her face and the friendliness of her greeting. She took Marti's coat and hung it in the closet.

"Cold out, isn't it?" Miss Jennings said, leading the way into the living room. Bright splashes of color leaped out from the abstracts on the walls and the throw rugs and pillows tossed in deliberate disarray on the sofa and chairs. A fire crackled in the fireplace. "I just got back from Arizona. What a change," she said, waving toward the sofa. "Make yourself comfortable. So, you want to know about Dorsey. Can you tell me what happened to her? I don't have the paper delivered because I don't spend that much time here."

Marti wondered if navy pensions paid enough to live this well, but didn't ask. She explained the circumstances surrounding Dorsey's death. "We've had a lot of difficulty locating people who knew her, recently or years ago. She seems to have become quite a loner."

"That would be hard to believe if you knew Dorsey when she was first stationed here. She *had* to party and longer and later than anyone else. Came to work hung over. I always used to tell her it was a good thing she was a PT tech, because she had less chance of killing one of her patients. ' Miss Jennings hesitated for a moment. "That was just a joke. She was damned good. We had guys coming back from 'Nam with half their bodies either shot up, blown off, or no longer operational. Dorsey got as many of those who were severely depressed as I could push in her direction without dragging her down too. She was great with them, didn't feel sorry for them, didn't let them continue to feel sorry for themselves and made them bust their butts in PT."

Marti could almost see Dorsey, not as she was the night she died, but as she must have been sixteen or seventeen years ago. The change was so profound she wondered if she would ever get from there to the person Dorsey had become.

"Did she change at all, while you knew her?"

Miss Jennings had seated herself on the floor and was leaning against a chair. She looked at the fire for a few minutes. The flames had settled into a steady orange blaze as the thick logs burned. "Looking back, I think I should have wondered if she might have been manic-depressive, but that wasn't as common a diagnosis as it is now. Dorsey wasn't the kind of person you ever worried about. Totally self-sufficient. I would never have pegged her as mentally ill."

"Do you know what happened?"

"I know what triggered her problems. Dorsey got engaged to a black saxophonist in a band that played at the base. The members of the group had grown up together in Chicago. There was a war on, even though they still call it a conflict. Promoters would put together these shows and bring them to the base. This group must have been a cut above some of the others because they got to go on overseas tours as well."

Miss Jennings looked down at her hands for a minute. "God. This was so long ago." There was a tremor in her voice. She cleared her throat. "You get so much more involved than you're aware of." She shook her head.

"Anyway, there was a concert on base, Fourth of July. Dorsey had started hanging out with the members of the band. They were all going to go out for dinner and dancing and bar-hopping after the concert. And during the show Dorsey was going to be backstage. She was so excited. Dorsey was one of those people who made you feel more alive just being around them. The kind you can't keep up with, who make you wonder what they run on. She was really on a high that week. She had this laugh that made you laugh too." She was silent again, head down, rubbing the thumb of one hand. Marti didn't intrude.

"Sorry. I lost my family in an airplane crash around the same time. My sister, my father, my mother, my aunt. All the family I had. I had enough time in to retire in nine months. So, I took all of that insurance money, bought this place as home base, and haven't stayed in one place long enough to dredge up any memories since then."

"I can understand that," Marti told her. "I lost my husband a year and a half ago. Couldn't stay in the house, couldn't stay in Chicago. And I'm grateful for long hours and lots of other things to think about."

Marlena nodded. "Anyway, there was this freak accident while the band was warming up. Their singer, Julie King, was electrocuted. Dorsey saw it happen and got so upset that she had to be hospitalized and sedated."

Miss Jennings was silent again. Marti waited it out.

"A week to the day after the singer died," Marlena continued, "Dorsey's fiancé, Nelson Weeks, was killed. It was a terrible accident. They put the car on display at the entrance to the base as a warning not to drink or do drugs and drive."

"Weeks drank and used drugs?" Marti asked.

"Not according to Dorsey. A few beers maybe, but nothing else. It was just too much for her. She was admitted to the psych ward the following morning. She was hallucinating that government agents had killed him and there were armed men on the rooftops training weapons on her." She ran her fingers through her hair.

"I lost track of her. I had been scheduled to ship out the end of June but there was some problem with my replacement. I left that first week she was hospitalized. Then there was the plane crash in November. I cut all my ties after that. I'm a real rolling stone now. Smart enough to know why and content to stay this way."

"Miss Jennings, when Dorsey went to these concerts or to parties or dances, was there anything unusual about the way she dressed?"

"Sure, lots, at least I thought so, but there was a fifteen-year age gap, and everything those girls wore seemed unusual."

"She dressed like everyone else?"

"Basically, yes."

"Was she a neat person?"

Marlena Jennings laughed. "Dorsey? You've got to be kidding. I always told her she was going to have to hurry up and get enough rank to have someone else pick up behind her." She paused. "But Dorsey was very fastidious about her appearance and personal hygiene, things like that. Told me her mother's favorite word was proper. 'That is not the proper way to sit in that chair' or 'That is not the proper way to eat your soup.' Except for that, I don't recall her ever mentioning her family."

"Did she have any close friends, other corps Waves, someone she worked with?"

"Let's see . . . perhaps Adeline Greyson. She was a civilian nurse a few years younger than me, married to a captain. She didn't work directly with us in PT, but she was on the orthopedic ward. She would have known Dorsey. Adeline was a mother confessor to a lot of the girls. I'm afraid I didn't know her very well." She hesitated. "There is one friend from those days who I keep in touch with. I'm sure she didn't know Dorsey personally, but I'll mention this to her."

Marti put in a quick call to Vik, who spoke with the lieutenant. By the time she got back to the precinct Vik had gotten the name and address of a Captain Bernard Greyson and made arrangements for her to meet with his wife that afternoon.

"Don't know how much help the woman will be, but the husband is out of town. Colorado."

Marti filled him in on her conversation with Marlena Jennings. "I don't know how important something that happened that long ago could be, but it's a beginning. We've found one person who knew her and established a link to somebody else. And these people don't live that far away from Lincoln Prairie. This Greyson might know of somebody else. We might even get to someone who knew her when she died. Any word on John Clark?"

"Nothing," Vik said. "But Wayne Baxter told us about him, not Lenny Doobee. And we know he's not just another figment of someone's imagination. God knows we've got enough of that in this case. Baxter is so damned determined to be no help at all that when he throws you a bone you have to snap at it. Could be something else he knows that he's not telling."

"He's still in jail," Marti said. "At least until the charges are dropped or plea bargained down to a misdemeanor theft." She decided to skip lunch and go see Adeline Greyson.

The address was in a small community about twenty miles southwest of Chicago. Ten minutes in any direction and you were in the next town. It was an older wood-framed house with snow trampled and packed down along a long path to the front door; a rambling house with a porch that went across the front and along one side and upstairs rooms that had been added on. The steps creaked as she went to the front door.

An elderly woman answered the bell. If Marti didn't know that Adeline was a few years younger than Marlena she would have guessed she was at least ten years older. She looked like she was getting ready to go out, wearing a stylish paisley wool skirt and dark green blouse with a big scarf draped and tied across her shoulders. Lines as fine as a spider's web indicated years of sunbathing, or maybe tanning lamps. Foundation and blush couldn't disguise the wrinkles that added years to her appearance.

"Yes?" she said. A question in her voice. Her light brown hair was turning gray and was so thin Marti could see her scalp.

"I'm Detective MacAlister," Marti said, showing her identification.

The woman seemed reluctant to admit her. "Just what is this all about? The officer who called didn't say." A slight whistle on the silibants suggested she was wearing dentures that were either very new or old and loose.

"It's about Lauretta Dorsey."

"Dorsey?" The woman seemed astonished. She stepped back and Marti went in before she could recover and block the door again.

"What about Dorsey? I haven't heard from her in years. Not since her breakdown. What's happened?"

The living room was hot. Marti thought the thermostat must be set at ninety. Mrs. Greyson didn't ask her to take off her coat so she asked if she could. Sweat was forming on her forehead.

"Dorsey. She's schizophrenic you know, poor girl." She sat down stiffly, as if it was painful.

Marti sat too, before she passed out from the heat. "Dorsey is dead," Marti told her.

"Dead? But how? She was so . . . alive . . . until her breakdown. That was awful. Poor thing."

Marti waited.

"We worked together during the war. Dorsey wasn't . . ." She hesitated as if groping for the right word. "Well, she tried. No, she did her best. They weren't mature, none of them. Joined the navy to meet sailors and have fun."

This description didn't differ much from what Marlena Jennings had said. But Jennings had stressed Dorsey's competence, and Adeline Greyson seemed to be implying the opposite.

"How did she die?"

"It was a homicide."

Adeline gasped, looked sincerely aghast for the first time. "My God, you read about things like that. It's never anyone you know. Poor Dorsey. She would never have harmed a soul."

"Mrs. Greyson, have you had any recent contact with Dorsey?"

"Nothing. Not since my marriage fifteen years ago. She was still hospitalized when I married. And afterwards . . ." She put her hands palms up in her lap and was silent.

Marti took the opportunity to glance around the room. The chair she was sitting in was comfortable, looked to be a recent purchase. The room, all muted colors with a touch of mauve and several shades of teal blue, seemed recently wallpapered and painted. The room looked unused, no magazines or television or newspapers in sight.

A collection of medicine bottles and an inhaler, all with prescription labels, was arranged on the coffee table. An odd place to put them unless you wanted everyone to know you were sick.

The only other personal item was a large wedding photograph hanging above the mantel. A light affixed to the frame was turned on. Mrs. Greyson looked much younger and ecstatic. She was wearing an ecru dress and a small ruffle of veiling crowned with baby's breath. Bernard Greyson, staring straight ahead, was an ordinary-looking man, face getting a little fleshy, brown hair beginning to retreat at the hairline, light brown eyes, ears jutting out. He was wearing a suit and the tightness at the corners of his mouth suggested that the collar of his shirt might be too tight. His hands were at his sides. She had one arm around his waist.

"How well did you know Dorsey?"

Mrs. Greyson scratched at her wrists. "Know her? How well do you ever know someone you work with? How well do you ever know anyone?"

"Did you know the man she was going to marry?"

She laughed. A brittle sound, as if she didn't laugh often. "Dorsey and Weeks. He was col . . . black, you know. She always said how shocked her mother would be. I never knew why she wanted him. Stupid girl, thinking he loved her. He died anyway, didn't matter."

"Did she change after he died?"

"Change? She changed before he died." Her hand almost went to her mouth. It seemed she hadn't meant to say that. "We all change. War. It does that. You see them coming in with pieces missing, know they used to walk, feed themselves, wipe their own behinds. It's hell for them, being like that. Better that they die."

"And Dorsey helped with their physical therapy?"

"Dorsey was . . . competent."

"Did your husband work at the hospital too?"

"Bernard? Never came through the doors. Never saw what we had to look at every day. None of it. Never knew." Her eyes were bright now, as if she had a fever. "Bernard." When she repeated his name Marti realized that the woman lit up just mentioning him. She looked at the wedding photograph again. Nothing remarkable about him that she could see.

"Are you absolutely certain that you've not had any contact with Dorsey at all since your marriage?"

"Absolutely. I'm surprised she's still in this part of the country. She came from back east and schizophrenics do tend to wander."

"Do you know of anyone else in this area who knew her while she was in the service and might have maintained contact?"

"No. Dorsey . . . well, she was friendly with everybody . . . like a puppy lapping up attention. She was mentally ill, even then. Unfortunately none of us knew. People like that, they're so self-absorbed. I'd be surprised if she stayed in touch with anyone, even her family." She hesitated, then said, "I think they overmedicated her on Thorazine. She was like a zombie the last time I saw her." She looked down at her hands, then up at Marti. "It was . . . quick . . . wasn't it?"

Marti nodded. She had the feeling that Adeline Greyson was something less than Dorsey's friend.

9

On Thursday night, Marti went to the Cramer Hotel. She didn't know if the children or the killer would return, but if the children did come back they could be in danger. She was still without a motive for Dorsey's death. Did John Clark kill her because she rebuffed him? If the money was an additional motive, why had the night clerk ended up with it instead of the killer? Why had Dorsey's room been searched so carefully?

Scowling, Marti went into the hotel. The front door was still unlocked. She checked her watch. It was after midnight and the place was supposed to be secured. She had already advised the realtor, but apparently a homicide wasn't sufficient reason to provide adequate security. She would have to see if something else could be done.

She was wearing crepe-soled boots and walked across the marble floor without making any noise. As she approached the massive oak desk she heard snoring. Wayne Baxter had been released from jail. Leaning over, she could smell the alcohol before she saw him. He had slipped out of the chair, pulling the flowered throw with him. His head was resting against worn and cracked leather upholstery almost the same shade of brown as his skin. A thin stream of spittle was working its way from his mouth to the floor.

Marti headed for the rear Exit sign and went to the stairwell, feeling the reassuring heaviness of a gun in her purse. She would have preferred to have Vik along but didn't want to do anything to reinforce his budding impression that she had strong maternal instincts. For half a second she wondered if she'd ever just be a cop to him and gender wouldn't matter at all.

The cellar door was bolted shut but not locked. She had to push hard to open it. The nauseating odor reached up and enveloped her as she stood on the top step. Her flashlight revealed mounds of rotting trash. Scurrying sounds accompanied by warning squeaks and whistles indicated some good-sized rats. Satisfied that it was an unlikely place for anyone to hide, she backed out and pushed the door shut. The health hazard would be reported as soon as she got to her desk in the morning.

The stairwell to the upper floors was lit but the wattage couldn't have been greater than fifteen. She turned off her flashlight and went up all seven flights, checking each hallway and janitor's closet. On one floor someone was reciting a Shakespearean sonnet in a slurred theatrical voice. Otherwise the place was quiet except for the occasional sound of a television or radio, and on the fifth floor, an argument over a poker game.

The bathrooms on the top two floors had wooden water closets above the commodes with exposed pipes running down to the toilet. She couldn't remember the last time she had seen any like these. There was no sign of Samantha, Dorsey's cat. When she got back to the second floor she saw the plate with the cookies and went down the hall to Lenny Doobee's door.

When she questioned him before, she had tried not to do anything to make him feel apprehensive. Now she was hoping that if he had seen anything significant or dangerous to himself he would tell her about it. She knocked on his door. He opened it a crack, then let her in.

"Detective MacAlister." Pudgy hands gripped hers. He seemed glad to see her. He was wearing a Cubs baseball cap with the visor turned to the back. A lock of mud brown hair fell across his forehead. For a moment, as a smile creased his chubby face, she could see him as he must have looked as a five-year-old.

"Have they been eating the cookies, Lenny?"

He stopped smiling, shook his head. "And I've put everything out. Gingersnaps, hermits, double cream-filled chocolate. Everything. I put them out every night but nobody touches them." He looked at her, trusting her to believe him. "I think they're afraid now. I think they've left. And I don't think they're coming back anymore. Not ever. Not ever again."

He looked as if he was about to cry. "They

didn't want to be alone. I hope they aren't alone now. Or afraid.''

Marti debated telling him that before too much longer something would have to be done to see that the building was secured. Then she considered the sadness in his eyes and didn't want to be the one to take away all hope that these little people would return one day. That was cowardice at best, maternalism at worst.

"Lenny," she said, "I know you said you weren't here the night Dorsey died, but did anything different happen before she died, the night before or within the week before?"

"Somebody crushed all of my cookies," he said without hesitation.

She was hoping for more than that but persisted. "When?"

Lenny thought for a minute. "Wednesday. That's the day I always do my shopping. I bought some teddy bear graham cookies and somebody crushed them."

Two days before Dorsey died. "Did you see the person who did it?"

"No, but it was the man who lived upstairs. She was there. She just wouldn't let him in. She never wanted to let him in. But sometimes, if he knocked a long time, she did."

"How do you know it was him if you didn't see him?"

"I thought it was the little people. I peeked out to see them. He was knocking on Dorsey's door. Well, not exactly. He was turning the knob. He heard me and stopped. I came back in and put the lights out before he could turn around and see me."

"And he came back on Friday."

"Two times. The first time she let him in and they argued."

Then Al did hear an argument that night. Marti wondered if she should tell him he hadn't imagined it.

"Do you know what they argued about?"

He blushed. "Same thing they always argued about." He looked at the floor. "He wanted her to like him, to like him a lot, but she didn't."

"Did you see him the second time he came?"

"No. But he was there."

"Knocking."

"No."

"How did you know it was him the second time?"

"His coat."

He had to have seen him to recognize the coat again.

"What color was the coat?"

"Dark."

"Can you describe him?"

"Sure. It was the man upstairs."

She tried to get some kind of description; height, weight, hair color, something. Lenny countered with hat, gloves, scarf, coat with the collar turned up. Dark clothing, black or maybe navy blue. The light in the hall wasn't good. The second time at least, he didn't want anyone to recognize him.

"Do you know if Dorsey let him in?"

"No. I closed the door fast. He had already stepped on my cookies."

The plate was near his door. Whoever it was would have noticed them, would know where to find the person who could have seen him. She tried to explain that, but Lenny felt he had not been seen and was safe.

"Be sure it's someone you know before you open your door," she cautioned. "And don't let the man who lived upstairs come in. If he comes back, call me." Fear returned to Lenny's eyes, but it was reasonable and justified this time, not part of his delusions.

She didn't find out anything else that was useful. Tomorrow she would come back, talk with the other residents again, find out if anyone remembered seeing a man in the hall last Wednesday or Friday.

Outside, she circled the building, then got into her car. The squads that patroled this area were watching for children and loiterers. So far the only people questioned had turned out to be winos, prostitutes, and a dope pusher who was clean the night he was picked up.

At ten stories, the Cramer was one of the tallest buildings in town and large enough to hide or get lost in. It was warmer than being outside this time of year and had toilets and running water and places to bathe. At night the lighting was dim enough to make the place a little bit scary. Great playground for a street child. How long would it take for those cookies to lure them back again? And if they came back, would they be safe?

She drove past the Burger King on her way home. The place closed at midnight so it was too late to buy anything, but she had already checked on their nightly routine.

The food could only be kept for short periods after it was cooked. Then it was put into containers that were trashed at night. A computerized system determined how much of each item to have on hand, based on daily traffic patterns such as the average number of people who would order an egg-and-sausage croissant from ten to ten-fifteen on Tuesday morning. There was very little waste, but some food was thrown away.

That information did nothing to narrow down the time when the person who dropped the hamburger could have been in the hall. Either they bought it by midnight or came to the dumpster anytime before five in the morning. She didn't see anyone near the place and after circling in a three-block radius, didn't see any children out after curfew. Giving up for the night, she went home.

Friday morning she yawned through roll call. A third cup of coffee seemed to be enough encouragement for her eyes to stay open at least until midmorning. Just as she was sitting down for a briefing with Vik, the door opened and Lupe Torres came in.

"Morning, ma'am. It's about those kids."

Marti sat up, suddenly wide awake. She had found out that Torres did a lot of Officer Friendly work in the Hispanic community.

Short, with a quick smile, she could pass for a teenager out of uniform.

"There are three boys, preteens, one black, one Hispanic, one with black hair and blue eyes, stealing from my merchants. These are mom and pop operations with limited inventories. I haven't had any complaints lately because all but two of the proprietors have banned the kids from the premises."

Lupe helped herself to a doughnut. "The artist is working on a composite but I can't find kids who fit this description anywhere, not in the low-income housing units, not at either of the nearest schools. I've asked the two merchants who still let them in to look the other way if they take anything. Said we'd reimburse them."

"And you haven't got any idea of where they might be staying?"

"They're the kids I tracked as far as those abandoned buildings. Couldn't find a trace of them once I got there."

"We talked with the lieutenant. Work as many hours as you need to and keep us informed. Anything else, anything, and you let one of us know immediately."

As soon as Torres left, Vik yelled, "We do not have throwaway children in Lincoln Prairie." He didn't sound convinced or convincing. That said, he sat slumped in his chair until the door burst open and Slim and Cowboy came in.

"Might have a little something for you, ma'am," Slim grinned. "One of our little ladies of the night recalls a blue-eyed, black-haired darling who stole fifty bucks from her purse and took off."

"That the last she saw of him?"

"Yup."

"When?" Vik asked.

"End of October."

"Did she say where he lived?"

"No, but she got the impression he lived with a family somewhere on Sherman."

Marti stared at Vik's map. They were still at square one.

By 8:30 A.M. Marti was stationed at the clinic where Dorsey received her antipsychotic medication every other Friday. The clinic opened at 9:05 A.M.. As the doctors interviewed each of the patients, they let them know why she was there. Talking with her was optional. Twenty-three patients came in. Five came over to her. Three asked her to find whoever did it but had no idea of who that could be.

The other two were different. One was an introspective young man who walked with his shoulders hunched and kept his eyes averted. Thick, light brown hair curled at his neck and fell over his eyes. As she watched his progress through the clinic, he never made eye contact with anyone. He didn't look at her either. His earnestness got her attention, that and a shy smile that seemed to indicate that he had liked Dorsey.

"What's your name?" she asked.

"Dave."

"Did she talk to you, Dave?"

He nodded.

"What did you talk about?"

"She used to work in a hospital."

"Did she tell you about that?"

"No. Just said that's what she used to do."

The answers to the rest of her questions were the same. Dorsey had given this young man some information about herself without sharing anything important.

"Dave, what did she talk about the last time she saw you?"

"How her family used to have a big party on New Year's Eve and she'd get all dressed up."

"Did she seem any different that day?"

He shook his head.

A woman with a shopping bag got her attention next. Marti watched her go from the nurse to the doctor's office and back to the nurse to get her injection. At a glance, she seemed like an elderly woman who paid little attention to her surroundings. Watching her, Marti realized that was a deliberate deception.

When the woman came over to her, Marti took in her plain but neat clothes; the thick wool scarf, the cloth coat, well-made and heavy, the sturdy leather boots. Her face was the color of polished pecans and there were lines at the corners of her eyes and mouth. Marti guessed her age at near forty.

"You gonna find whoever done it?" the woman asked without preface. Her voice was a rich contralto. Marti wondered if she'd ever sung in a choir.

"I need a little help," Marti said. "Want to tell me your name?"

"Folks call me Nessa." The woman scrutinized her face for a minute. "This just another killin' to you?" she asked. "Dorsey just another one of us crazy folks?"

"Maybe," Marti said. "But Dorsey's being dead is reason enough for me to find out who did it. Doesn't matter who she was. Got the same right to live that you and I do."

The woman studied her face again. "Well, I can't help you none, but I'll tell you this, Dorsey, she don't hurt no one. She don't drink, lessen it's somethin' special. She sleeps a lot and gets a little absentminded on accounta the medication. Sometimes she gets a little down, but them moods don't last long. She be singing again in a couple of hours. Sometimes she don't dress like other folks and she talks to herself but that don't make her no crazier than the rest of us. She wasn't thinkin' nothin' 'bout dyin' and it ain't right that she did."

Marti looked at the woman's hands, clenched. She was certain that Nessa was the 'old' woman who went to the Cramer the night Dorsey died.

"Nessa, you know why she got depressed?"

"Same reasons most folks do. Mad about something she can't do nothin' about or rememberin' things that used to be or just wishin' life could be like she wanted it to be."

"Had anything special happened to her recently? Anything, good or bad?"

Nessa looked her right in the eye. "No. Nothin' special."

Marti wondered what Nessa wasn't telling her.

"Did she have a boyfriend?"

"No. Couldn't stand that John what kept comin' around. You talk to him yet?"

"Should I?"

"I would sure enough if I was you. He just made up his mind that Dorsey an' him was goin' to get somethin' goin' but Dorsey, her man is dead. Some women are like that."

"We can't find John."

"Well," Nessa said. "Can't fault you none for that. Not that hard not to be seen if'n you don't wanna be."

No, Marti agreed. Especially not if you've had years of practice. "You liked Dorsey, didn't you?"

The woman's eyes filled and she rummaged around in her purse and took out a crumpled Kleenex. "Good people, Dorsey was. Real good people."

Marti believed her, wanted to ask her more questions, but thought she might alienate her if she did. Already the woman was looking at the door and shifting from one foot to the other.

"Nessa, there's just one more thing. The night clerk says there were children in the hotel the night Dorsey died. We're afraid they might have seen her killer. And we can't find them."

"Children." There was no mistaking her concern but she seemed more thoughtful than surprised. "I see any children what could've been there, I sure will let you know. And I sure enough would keep lookin' for them if I was you."

"Thank you, Nessa. I think you must have been a good friend to Dorsey."

Marti watched Nessa assume her old woman's shuffle as she walked away.

"Wait," Marti called.

She caught up with Nessa at the door. "You be careful. Dorsey's already dead. We don't want no more killings. You think of something, you call me." She gave Nessa her card. "You show this to any police officer and they'll call me right away."

"Nessa be real careful ma'am. And thank you."

As Marti was getting ready to leave, the nurse looked up. "I'm surprised you got old Nessa to talk. That's the first time I've ever seen her talking to anyone."

"She never spoke to Dorsey?"

"Not a word, to anyone. Nods that she's okay. Polite, thanks me for giving her the medication. That's it. Otherwise I've never heard her say a word and I've seen her six years."

Then she must have spoken with Dorsey someplace else. Marti thought about the food in Dorsey's apartment. She went to see the director of the facility, explaining only as much as necessary to get Nessa's full name and address. She couldn't begin to imagine what it had taken for Nessa to speak to her. She just hoped Nessa had told her everything that was important.

Back at the precinct she talked with Vik. "She lives in a two-bedroom bungalow in one of those subdivisions on the north side. I'm not sure she told me everything."

"I'm surprised you couldn't get more out of her, MacAlister. These odd types can't wait to talk to you."

"The nurse said I'm the first person she's ever seen Nessa talk to."

Vik groaned. "You're getting a hell of a reputation, Marti. Next thing you know they'll be making you the nut case detective, assign all of the cases and interviews with the oddballs to you. And me too."

"Different, Vik," she said. "Not odd." And there wasn't even that much that was different about Doobee and Nessa. She didn't think they were that different at all.

10

Friday afternoon right after lunch, Marti walked the three blocks to the *News-Times* building. The temperature was hovering a few degrees above zero but the sky was clear and there wasn't much wind coming in off the lake. Snow crunched under her feet. She loved days like this.

A brief discussion with Vik and they both agreed that until John Clark turned up they'd reached a dead end. Checking what they knew of Dorsey's past could provide some thread that would lead them to the present. The odds might be slim, but two people Dorsey knew and presumably cared about had died violent deaths fifteen years ago. They could either check it out now or second-guess it forever.

Vik had known the detective on the case involving the singer who was electrocuted, but he'd died of a heart attack a few years ago.

The reporter currently covering the crime beat was out with the flu, but he had pulled everything they had on the case and had it ready for her perusal. When he asked why she was interested in something that happened so long ago she admitted that she wasn't sure. She could tell from the sound of his voice he didn't believe her.

The *News-Times* building was four stories high and took up an entire block. There were two afternoon printings each day. When she got there the early edition was stacked on the loading dock and two hefty young men were tossing the bundled copies into vans. Inside, a young woman showed her into a small room where one manila folder and two brown envelopes were stacked on a desk. Yes, there was coffee, but they would prefer that she not drink any while going through the files.

"Matter of fact, ma'am, food, beverages, and smoking are not allowed in this room."

Marti suggested that someone post a sign.

The young woman looked startled. "What an awesome idea."

Marti opened one of the envelopes. The glossy eight-by-ten photographs were all of the victim, taken from various angles. Juliette Kingsland, professionally known as Julie King, lead vocalist for EarthStar, now defunct. In the photos taken at the scene of the electrocution, Julie had long black hair cut in bangs across her forehead. Her head was turned to the side, round features narrowed by the camera angle.

The photographs taken at the morgue captured the flaws. An overbite that made her upper teeth jut out. One side of her broad nose made flatter by a piece that was sheared. A thin scar above her upper lip. Her own hair cut in a short kinky afro. The long hair was a wig. A minor outbreak of acne on mahogany skin.

The second envelope was filled with publicity photos touched up until they looked like pictures taken of somebody else. In them, Juliette Kingsland's skin was much lighter; the protruding top front teeth had been airbrushed out of her smile. One of her trademarks seemed to be wearing enough jewelry to create an occupational safety hazard. Huge dangling earrings pulled at her earlobes; at least six chunky necklaces with elaborate metal settings and multicolored glass stones in all shapes and sizes hung from her neck. Enough rings on each finger to make it impossible to bend them at the second joint.

Marti made a list of all of the band members' names in case she wanted to question them later.

She had gone through all the police reports of the accident without finding Dorsey's name. Special services was responsible for providing and setting up the electrical equipment and microphones. The entertainers provided their own speakers, synthesizers, and other acoustical equipment as well as their own instruments.

Juliette Kingsland had died almost an hour before the show was scheduled to begin. Marti knew little about the preparations for a performance. Once, years ago, she had gone to a concert early enough to wait while various people walked across the stage, picked up a cord, touched a keyboard, strummed a few chords on a guitar, then walked over to the microphones and said, "Testing, testing." She seemed to recall at least ten people doing that before the band ambled onstage in twos and threes. Then there was another series of the "testing" routines before anyone got around to starting the show.

How could anyone plan to electrocute a specific person under those circumstances? Police reports indicated seventeen people had access to the microphone that Juliette had picked up, and of those each said that the microphone hadn't been working properly. Then Juliette Kingsland had come out to check it herself. If she had been killed deliberately, timing would have been critical. The killer would have to be knowledgeable about electrical wiring and systems. It would have taken a lot of planning and more than a little luck to zap the right person. Homicide seemed as unlikely to her as it had to the detective who had investigated the case and concurred that it was accidental. She couldn't come up with any reason to dig any further than he had.

If the electrocution had been deliberate, crimes with complex methodologies were often easier to figure out than those with simple, straightforward plans, but that was mostly because the perps got tangled up in their own cleverness. Catching them still required a lot more legwork. At the moment she couldn't even get a handle on Dorsey's recent past.

The newspaper articles had been microfilmed. The copies provided were on slick glossy paper that curled at the edges. Whoever made the copies hadn't gotten the film in focus on the reader and the print was a little blurred. There were only three articles, but Marti's eyes hurt by the time she finished reading. She kept the copies. Something was missing. There was some background information, but the writing was dry, disinterested. She checked the byline, went back to the receptionist, and asked for the person who had written them.

"Herb Mansfield?" Squinting, the young woman checked several lists, then with a heavy sigh, went to a closet and pulled out a large designer purse. Searching through that she came up with an eyeglass case with the same designer logo. "Lost one of my contacts," she explained, sounding annoyed because she had to put on her glasses.

She went through the lists again, using her finger as a guide. "Not here," she said, putting the lists away.

"I want to talk with him," Marti said.

"Well, I'm sorry, but he's not on any of my lists."

Realizing the young woman had come to the end of her resources, Marti showed her the byline and suggested she speak with personnel. It took less than five minutes to find out that the man had retired, and more than thirty minutes to get clearance to find out his address. No telephone. He lived in Wisconsin, but not too far from the state line. She decided to drive up there and talk with him.

She took Route 173 west, passed Antioch, turned north on a road that twisted around a number of small lakes. Tall, bare trees with snow-dusted branches overhung the road in thick clusters. The road was slick in places. She drove slowly, found out she'd missed her turn when she stopped to ask directions, made a U-turn and drove south for half a mile.

A dirt road curled around part of a large pond called Lake Vista, went past five cabins, none with names or numbers visible, then ended. Cars of various vintages from a '73 Nova to an '82 Eagle wagon were parked alongside each cabin. Smoke curled from each chimney. She called to a man carrying a stack of firewood and he pointed to the third cabin.

A path had been shovelled and the steps were clear. An elderly man opened the door before she'd reached the top step. He gave her a big smile.

"Well now, don't see many strangers hereabouts. And you got cop written all over you. Been a long time since anyone's wanted to question me."

She followed him into the cabin, certain that an old crony at the *News-Times* had mentioned the new black, female homicide detective in town. A cast iron, wood-burning stove heated the place. One big room with lofts for sleeping. There was a sink, a footed range with bottled gas, and an old refrigerator with the motor on top that hummed noisily in one corner. No couch, but two overstuffed chairs near the stove with a table between them. Each chair had its own brass floor lamp, the kind with three bulbs.

Both were lit. The shades were getting brown with age.

A chess set was on the table, a game in progress. She guessed that the wooden pieces had been hand-carved. She sat in the chair that didn't have a hassock.

Her hair and clothing would be saturated with the smell of burning wood by the time she left. Washing her hair would be a nuisance tonight. Blow drying didn't get it straight enough despite the chemical relaxers she used. She'd have to set it with rollers and sit under the dryer. She had just washed it Monday night, was hoping to get by until next week.

Herb Mansfield went over to the kitchen area and fussed with a pan and some crockery. He had been a big man. Now his back was bowed with age and his step was infirm. He was in his seventies at least, Marti thought. The lower half of his face was covered with a gray beard, his eyes were getting filmy with age, his fingernails were yellowing. It was hard to believe he was the *News-Times* crime reporter fifteen years ago.

He served her hot cider with a cinnamon stick in a fat ceramic mug and sat down, putting his feet up. He reached for a pipe, stroking the bowl. "What brings you out here? Ain't been near that old rag in twelve years and this has got to have something to do with that."

"Juliette Kingsland. Singer. Electrocuted. . . ."

"Fourth of July, about fifteen years ago. Naval base," he finished. "Not much of a case. Why's it interest you now?"

"Not sure it should. Just a tangent maybe. We've got a homicide on our hands. A woman who was backstage that night and knew Kingsland."

He chuckled. "You're right. Real tangent. You're not from Lincoln Prairie."

"I was on the force in Chicago for ten years. Moved to Lincoln Prairie a year and a half ago." She was certain he already knew that.

He began to stuff his pipe, taking tobacco from an old leather pouch he had tucked behind the chair cushion. "Too many local boys on the force there. Sometimes you need a different perspective."

It was the first positive thing anyone had said about her being a "big city cop" since she'd left Chicago.

"You remember the case?"

"Sure. Only one like it the forty years I was at the *News-Times*."

"You didn't have too much to say about it."

He laughed, a deep belly laugh that made him seem robust and younger. "You noticed. Word was to soft pedal it. Routine, no big exposé. Military, you know. Not because of the possibility of a suit. They could settle those kinds of things without the publicity back then. Morale, they said. Bad for morale to make too much of it. Wartime. Even though they weren't calling Vietnam a war. The patriotic thing to do, playing it down."

"Doesn't sound like you bought into it."

Another deep laugh. "Nah. But I was ready to retire, what the hell."

"Was it a gag order?"

"Oh sure. Somebody somewhere didn't want too much said."

"Would it have taken someone like the base commander to keep it quiet?"

He finished stuffing his pipe, struck a long wooden match. "Could have been anyone, a second lieutenant in charge of the garbage detail. All it took was a phone call."

"Nothing in writing?"

"What?" Mansfield said. "So some cop could come nosing around fifteen years later and find out who it was?"

"Anything not in those articles that you would have liked to have written about?"

Puffs of smoke wafted from the pipe. She could catch just a hint of the tobacco aroma, hickory she thought, not sure because of the cedar logs burning in the stove. She enjoyed the smell of a pipe.

"That band made a lot of visits to the base, made a lot of trips overseas—the Philippines, Japan, Hong Kong, places like that. I would have liked to have checked for a connection."

"Drugs?"

"Nah. They were smuggling that back in cadavers. All kinds of ways to bring drugs back without using a live mule."

"Intelligence?" she persisted.

"Nah. Nobody in that band was smart enough for that. Don't know what it could have been, maybe nothing. You know how it is. You want

137

to dig, can't poke your nose into anything. Just makes you strain at the leash. Didn't have any definite ideas. Nothing I could put my finger on." He pondered the bowl of his pipe for a few minutes. "Not sure I was that interested at first. Not even an odd way to die. It's happened before, happened since. No reason to play it up or play it down. Routine until I got orders. Made me wonder why. Still makes me wonder why."

He puffed on his pipe. "Hope it wasn't the one that got away." He chuckled, then said, "So, you work with Matthew?"

She had to think for a minute. She had never heard anyone call Vik that.

"My partner."

"So I heard. Thought they must be joking. His dad and uncle and I were best friends. Poor Matthew, daddy a cop, one uncle a priest, the other a fireman, two younger brothers. And not a woman among 'em. Eugenie, Matthew's mother, died in childbirth. Hard to imagine him being partnered with a woman."

It gave her something to think about too.

They talked for a while. He asked her a lot of questions about Lincoln Prairie, not too surprised by the changes. He didn't remember anything else about the case, but she enjoyed the small talk. It was getting dark by the time she drove home.

11

Georgie kept to the side of the building, walking fast to the alley behind the hotel. The snow was shiny like ice and his Converse didn't make any footprints. He ran to the dumpster and hid in back of it, peeking to see if anyone was following him. When it seemed like a long time had gone by, he stood up. He was getting cramps in his legs and his fingers had got cold right through his mittens. His feet had been cold before he got here. At least his ears were still warm. Funny how he'd be cold in places but was sweating all the time and feeling hot.

When nobody came into the alley, Georgie went to the first floor window he had left unlocked. He opened it and looked inside, seeing the dark shapes of the bed and bureau and table. Nobody living here yet so he climbed into the room. The floor made noise as he tiptoed to the door, and the lock made a real loud snap as he turned it.

He looked into the hall, heard the man who sat behind the desk snoring. Didn't see nobody at all. He waited again, just to make sure, till it seemed like a long time had gone by. Crouching, he went to the hallway and up to the second floor.

The plate with the cookies was here. Too bad he couldn't come here no more. Man was nice, leaving stuff out for them. But the singing woman had got herself killed and the man who chased them must have done it and he didn't know who the man was, or where he was staying at. Maybe he was still here and would come chasing him again if he saw him.

A door opened and Georgie ran back to the stairwell, his heart jumping in his chest. He wanted to run, but couldn't make his legs move. Then a door closed and the toilet flushed. He wiped the sweat from his forehead, tried to stop breathing so hard. Whoever it was went back to their room.

He leaned against the wall, wanting to sit down. Then he checked out the stairs and the landing. His mittens weren't here. There wasn't another pair and he didn't even have any extra socks he could use when he and Padgett went out together. He'd have to find a way to get some.

He eased into the hall and grabbed the cookies, stuffing them into his pocket as he ran down the stairs. He checked the lobby again but didn't wait. His legs were beginning to feel funny, like he wouldn't be able to walk in a few minutes. He ran into the room, climbed out the window and ran down the alley. A man was standing in the doorway. No telling if it was the man he was hiding from. No way he was gonna stop to find out.

He slipped as he ran, fell and hit the back of his head. His hat fell off. He grabbed it, rubbing his head. Then, pulling his hat down over his ears, he kept running. He didn't stop until he was in back of the police station. He ducked in back of the box where they kept the sand and sat, squeezed against the brick wall behind it. He cupped his hands over his mouth, breathing into Padgett's mittens so no one could hear him. He was crying but he didn't care. The pain in his chest was bad, like someone was slicing at him with a knife. At first the tears had felt warm on his face but now they were cold, like ice.

Somebody was walking close by. He tried to hold his breath and couldn't. He breathed slowly instead, holding the mittens to his face. The footsteps went by, then came back, crunching on the ice. He heard the man say "damn!" and knew it was him. He squeezed his legs together to keep from peeing and didn't move.

The man went past the box, feet stomping. Maybe the man couldn't see him. Georgie didn't look up, didn't move.

A car drove past. The man said "damn" again, then his footsteps went away.

Georgie knew it was the man he had heard in the singing woman's room that night. He liked her. She always gave him all of her silver money. And now she wasn't gonna sing no more. And there wouldn't be no more silver money so he could get some mittens. Good thing they'd be going to Minneapolis soon, then he wouldn't miss going to the Cramer late at night, eating the cookies and listening to the scratchy records on that funny old stereo and the woman who sang.

Georgie waited. He tried to wait for a long time but it started to snow. His chest hurt, and his head. He was cold. When the footsteps didn't come back he got up, almost too stiff to move. He peed, then kept to the wall and went around the corner, moving closer to the police station. Not that he wanted to mess with any cops, but it was better than being dead.

When he reached the place where an alley was right across from him, he ran across the street. Then he ducked behind a pile of cardboard boxes and began to feel safe again. He wanted to go back to the empty building where everyone else was in the basement. But it was Sissie's birthday tomorrow. She'd be ten, a year older than he was. He was supposed to be getting her a birthday present. The wind blew the snow in his face. It was starting to snow harder.

He went to the Salvation Army, cutting through alleys and keeping away from the streets. There was a big box there with clothes and things inside. He climbed in, feeling safe in the dark. It was warmer out of the wind. He jumped up and down, letting himself fall because it was soft in the box, like a pillow. Then he began holding the clothes up to the light where the opening was, looking for something for Sissy. He found a sweater that was too big but it was yellow, her favorite color. He wished people would give away socks and mittens and boots and more Converse. He had to steal those.

When he got close to where they were staying

he got scared again. If the man followed him home he might kill all of them. He looked behind him. The snow was already filling in his footprints. He went to the street where the houses were all close together, went into the first open door just like he lived there, ran to the back door and went out. He kept to the backs of the buildings till he came to the field. When they first came here the leaves were still on the bushes and trees, but everything was dead now and there was just snow, deep snow that got in his Converse.

He walked in a wide circle, crossing the street and going behind the old building where they were staying, to the window that could only be seen from the back. He had seen someone walk around like that in a movie on TV and the man who was chasing him never found him.

The old building was all boarded up. They got one of the boards off the door in the back and kept it there like no one had touched it. No one had come there since they moved in when it started getting cold.

Georgie scooted through the opening and put the piece of wood back in place. He braced wooden boards against it to keep people out now that all of them were inside. He went upstairs first, through the funny-shaped room, then one long room with bookcases mostly empty except for smelly old magazines.

The little room in the back with Mickey Mouse and Donald Duck painted on the walls still had a few books on the shelves. He'd taken some downstairs to look at the pictures. La-

Shawna could read a little. He'd like to know what the words under the pictures said without having to ask, but didn't think he ever would.

Opening a door, he went into the bathroom. There were no lights so he lit the candle. La-Shawna said they couldn't use candles nowhere but in here and down in the basement. She was worried that the light would show at the tops of the windows where the plywood didn't cover the glass.

Georgie held up the sweater to the mirror, saw his chipped front teeth when he grinned. James Arthur had hit him too, just like he hit Momma. There was a bad-looking scratch on his face. He must have hit some ice when he fell. "You black, boy. Black and ugly. Stupid too, like you momma," James Arthur would say. But James Arthur wasn't his daddy. No reason to believe him. He touched the back of his head. It was just a little bump.

Too bad there was just the toilet in here. A bathtub or a shower would've been nice. At least there was running water. Just cold water, and at first it tasted like something that had sat in a tin can for a long time, but after a few days it was okay. It was a lot warmer here than outside, even thought they had to keep sweaters on.

When he got downstairs, Sissie was sleeping on the bed in the corner. Padgett was mumbling something in his sleep and Jose was all curled up in the other corner. They each had a bed here, just coats and old clothes piled on the floor, but more than what they had in St. Louis.

Georgie, Padgett, and Sissy got to have the three blankets they found in the Salvation Army box because they were the youngest.

Georgie tiptoed over to LaShawna. She was the oldest, thirteen. They had left home in the summer when James Arthur killed Momma. LaShawna had lived with them for as long as he could remember. She was awake, waiting for him.

"I found her a sweater," he told her.

"You see that man?"

"No," he lied.

"You be careful. Take Jose with you or Padgett next time you go out."

They'd come across Padgett in Peoria, found Jose in Chicago. Said they didn't have a momma or poppa, but probably did, somewhere. LaShawna didn't think they should be by themselves, said if they wanted to go to Minneapolis they could come along. Jose was eleven. They could both steal out of stores better than him, but they didn't like going out at night like he did. He knew they were scared of the dark but they wouldn't say so.

LaShawna pulled him against her, rubbed his hair.

"Need a haircut," she whispered. "All three of you do."

Georgie leaned against her belly. She was getting fat now with the baby. That's why they were staying here. She couldn't travel no more until after it came unless they could figure a way to get them all bus tickets. While he was leaning against her the baby moved.

"We gonna be all right," she told him. He knew she was worried about what they'd do when it was time for the baby, but it would be a couple of months yet. They'd have something figured out by then.

"You sure this man ain't James Arthur?" she said. Worrying again.

"No, a white man. I saw him real good. Sure ain't no James Arthur. He in jail anyway for killin' Momma. No way he got away. Too drunk that night to catch us when we run, sure couldn't run from no cops."

He shivered and LaShawna held him tighter, rocking him, knowing he was remembering Momma on the floor and all of the blood. When he was asleep he'd dream of Momma singing at the stove, cooking supper. Then, when he woke up it was like his head was awake but the rest of him wasn't. He would blink his eyes for a while until the rest of him woke up and he could move. When he was awake he knew Momma had never been like he dreamed her, spent most of her time drinking and hardly ever cooked.

"You wanna sleep here with me?" LaShawna said.

He wanted to, but she'd sleep better by herself.

"Need to sleep in my own bed."

She held her hand on his forehead. "You real hot, Georgie."

"Been runnin'."

"You take more of that medicine, right now. How come you ain't coughin' no more? Still got that cold. I can hear it in your chest. I think we gonna have to figure out how to get you some penicillin or something. We got us some SpaghettiOs for breakfast. You eat some, you hear. You ain't eating enough no more."

He didn't feel much like eating. And the food was better here than what they'd had most days when they was home.

He took the medicine Padgett had stolen for him without making a face. He took off his Converse, pulled his pile of coats closer to La-Shawna and closed his eyes, intending to sleep. Then he remembered the cookies he'd got from the hallway. He gave one to LaShawna, kept three for the others and bit into one. LaShawna loved chocolate chips. Georgie huddled further under the covers, glad the man hadn't caught him.

12

Marti sat up in bed and looked at the luminous dial of the clock, wondering what had awakened her at four-thirty on a Saturday morning. A winter storm had begun moving in when she got home a little before midnight. She had fallen asleep to the sound of the wind making little whooping sounds as it whipped around this side of the house. It was quiet now. No storm sounds at all. Maybe that was what had awakened her.

She sat up, groping for her robe and slippers without turning on a light, then did what she always did on those infrequent occasions when she woke during the night. She went to check on the children.

She peeked in on Sharon's daughter first, then pulled up the covers Joanna had kicked off, then continued down the hall to her son Theo's room. Bigfoot, their sleeping sentinel, wagged his tail twice without opening his eyes and gave one deep sigh. Theo didn't stir.

The model airplane was still on the card table. Newspaper, glue, and more wood had been assembled. She didn't see any diagrams, but it looked like Theo was going to finish it. She wasn't sure what that meant, but Sharon knew a lot about kids and she thought it might be Theo's way of coming to terms with Johnny's death. Marti picked up the balsa frame. It felt light, but wasn't as fragile as it looked.

She thought of three other children, little boys close to Theo's age, wondered where they were sleeping tonight and if they were warm. Did the little one who had lost his mittens have another pair? Did he have boots and a heavy winter coat, things her children took for granted?

She shivered, hugged herself, wondered what more she could do. They had the artist's drawings now and had distributed them to every cop on the force. They were all doing everything they could think of. Time. They needed time to find those few people who had seen the children and might know where they were. Would Dorsey's killer stalk these little children if they could identify him? She didn't find that impossible to imagine, not even difficult to believe.

She could remember growing up on the west side of Chicago, watching her mother go to clean houses in Lake Forest and her father go to clean trains at Union Station. There were nights when they ate pinto beans and rice and corn bread for supper, poor fare compared to what her children ate now. They had a cramped apartment filled with odds and ends, not a nice, roomy home like this. But in that city, on those streets, she had been safe. Neighbors watched out for her. The beat cop wasn't always friendly but he was there, on foot, and whether they liked him or not everyone knew him. They all knew his top priority was a crime-free shift. And, because those police officers knew their beat and the people who lived there so well, for a long time she thought they were omniscient.

For all that she could buy her children that her parents had not been able to provide for her, she couldn't promise them safety. Even though they felt secure, this was not a safe or caring world if you were a child. It was a place where three little boys became invisible because so few chose to see that they were there.

She made a cup of herb tea and went up the two steps into the living room. It was seldom used, always tidy but frequently in need of dusting, like now. She had come to love this old Tudor house with its pointy eaves and leaded glass windows and beamed ceilings. When she had moved in they put her furniture in here, brown and gold and rust with brass lamps and wall decorations, and moved Sharon's furniture downstairs to the den.

The children had begun to decorate for Christmas. White and red poinsettias on the coffee table. A ceramic Mary and Joseph waited on the mantle on either side of an empty crib. One angel and a donkey observed them. On Christmas Eve Baby Jesus and the shepherds and a few sheep would join them, followed by the three wise men on January 6th. She wasn't sure why they did this. Theo and Joanna had sort of taken over and that's the way it had evolved.

At work there was an artificial tree. A local charity had brought in a basket filled with cards and a sign asking everyone to pick one. Hers had said "Queenie, age 56." Queenie had requested a blouse and her favorite color was pink. Marti had bought two, one for church and one for everyday, and added a sweater. She knew the others had done much the same. Wrapped, beribboned boxes were piled beneath the tree. They all took part in Toys for Tots, but it wasn't just kids anymore, it was everyone. And more and more, Christmas was ceasing to be merry until she came into her own house and closed the door and locked out the rest of the world.

She moved the table away from a floor-length window where they were going to put the tree. She hoped she would be able to take everyone out this evening to pick out a fat spruce, tall enough for the angel's halo to almost touch the ceiling. The kids had stacked boxes of ornaments in a corner. They would make popcorn and cocoa and sing carols while they decorated the tree.

Had Ben and his son Mike been invited? Should they be? Did she want this to be a family occasion? Funny, she didn't think of Ben or Mike as outsiders. They weren't family, but Ben was comfortable to be with. And there were all of those dinner invitations. It would be a great excuse to order pizza—they could get a vegetarian pizza for Joanna. She waited until six to call Ben. He sounded sleepy but seemed pleased to hear from her and said yes, they would come. When she asked, he agreed that if she got tied up at work, he would take care of getting the tree.

Joanna came down while she was untangling the lights. Without speaking, Joanna sat on the carpet beside her, flipped her single long braid over her shoulder and began to help her. Marti didn't speak. It took Joanna half an hour to wake up after she got out of bed.

Eventually Joanna said, "Have you had time to do any Christmas shopping?"

"Sort of," Marti hedged. She had picked up a few things right after Thanksgiving.

"I'll wrap, but you'll have to pick out your gifts yourself."

"Deal," Marti agreed. "Ben and Mike are coming over tonight to help decorate the tree."

"That's great. Ben brought the boys to my game night before last," Joanna said. "And Theo will like that. Are we inviting them for Christmas dinner?"

"Too far ahead to think about."

"Only a couple of weeks. Ben doesn't have family here. We should at least ask."

"We'll see."

Marti thought back to last Christmas, their first without Johnny. They had opened their gifts with feigned enthusiasm, then sat down to dinner. Sharon had prepared turkey with all the fixings, but Theo wasn't hungry and Joanna refused to eat the collard greens and candied sweet potatoes and black-eyed peas. For Marti it was more depressing than not celebrating Christmas at all.

"When I was kid," Marti said, "Momma would start baking a week after Thanksgiving. Cookies and fruit cake, then pound cake and pecan tarts, and finally fried apple pies. I'd come home from school and I could tell by the aroma how long I had to wait to open my presents. Whole house would smell like Christmas. No matter how poor we were, we always had a good Christmas. Caroling at the nursing home and the Christmas play at church and everybody in the neighborhood stopping by to sample Momma's cooking. Our family was small but there was always somebody who didn't have anyone else at all sharing the table with us. Not a lot of presents, but memories to keep you going all the next year."

Joanna smiled, said nothing. Marti smiled too, remembering.

The call from the precinct came ten minutes later.

"Got another stiff for you over at the Cramer, Mac."

"Who?"

"Guy named Leonard Horvaster, better known as Lenny Doobee. Found him out back in the dumpster. We called Jessenovik. He screamed obscenities. Something to the effect that he was going to kill the beat cop if his scene of the crime was messed up. Hard to mess up a dumpster in a blizzard, know what I mean?"

"Who found him?"

"Desk clerk. Day man. Board of Health had been there and they'd started cleaning garbage out of the cellar. Dumpster was full of stuff they'd cleaned out yesterday. Horvaster was thrown on top of it. If it had happened before they started cleaning up and they'd dumped the stuff on top of him, might have taken a while to find him. If we had found him at all."

Marti hung up, looked around the living room at the lights strung up at the windows and around the mantel; at the candles on the window sills and the small ceramic manger with Joseph and Mary waiting for Baby Jesus. "Merry Christmas," she said, feeling depressed.

The only people at the scene were with the department. The coroner, Janet Petrosky, was stamping her feet as she paced, waiting for the doctor to certify death.

"Doctor Cyprian," Vik complained. "Must like playing around with stiffs. Can't even hurry in the cold." He blew on his hands.

"Put your gloves on," Marti said. "Must be ten below out here." She hadn't noticed the cold until she saw how red his hands were.

"Left in a hurry. Didn't bring them."

"Hold on a minute. With kids I've always got some in the car."

She found one of Joanna's green mittens and a black glove belonging to Theo.

Vik stared at them for a few seconds but it was too cold to argue. "Guess our perp hasn't left town yet," he said, then coughed.

"Now look, Jessenovik," Marti told him, handing him a cough drop. "Just don't bother getting sick on me. No time for that. Case load's getting worse by the day."

"Yeah. So much for Christmas. Got any Kleenex?"

"In the car. Get them yourself." Maternal instinct. Now she was in trouble for sure.

Dr. Cyprian, a tall, austere East Indian, was standing on a stepladder and leaning over the dumpster. He seemed impervious to the cold. He was thorough and concise and Marti liked him.

Janet Petrosky came over to her. "No visible marks. I wouldn't be surprised if this corpse had some pressure applied to his carotid artery, too."

"That would make it too easy," Marti told her.

"Look what we've got." Vik pointed to one clear set of tracks partially obliterated by the snow.

"He's got big feet."

"Size twelves," Vik told her. "Must have been snowing and blowing out here pretty good when it happened. He must not have thought there was any need to get rid of 'em."

Three and a half prints near the dumpster, walking away, must have been sheltered from the wind. A break maybe. Or at least they could eliminate anyone with small feet. Or else the person was wearing boots that were too big, or else . . .

"Wanna bet it was the guy he saw in the hall?" Vik said.

"I don't bet on sure things," she told him. Neither of them said what if there were kids around and they saw him, or he saw them. But she thought it, and she was certain that Vik did too.

While they were waiting for Dr. Cyprian to finish they went up to the second floor. The plate for the cookies was still on the floor. The cookies were gone. Marti's stomach lurched. The day clerk, a short, thin Hispanic man with a smattering of freckles, let them into Lenny's room.

"Where's Wayne?" she asked.

"It's day time," the man told her. "Won't see old Wayne till tonight."

Marti stood in the doorway with Vik just behind her and surveyed the place. It seemed different without Doobee there. Shabbier. Dirtier. The clean but grayish sheets, a muddle of olive army blankets, dust curls under the bed, dishes unwashed for several days. Spills on the linoleum had dried in uneven splashes and globs.

She went in, already disliking the task of going through the bureau and closet. Clothes crammed into drawers, dark socks, drab underwear, laundered shirts that still had rings around the collar. A drawerful of papers. The envelopes his social security checks came in, advertisements, flyers, notices from the last three political campaigns, local and national. One black-and-white photograph of a pudgy little boy, much as she had pictured he would be, standing between two adults the right age to be his parents. The man was tall and thin, the woman short and fat.

There was no correspondence, no personal letters or cards. One invoice from the Christian Children's Fund. Based on the year to date contributions, Doobee hadn't missed any this year.

The journal was under the mattress.

"First place someone would look," Vik grumbled.

"But nobody did. And I bet his room keys are on him. Nobody's searched here. He must have left his room, got killed somewhere near where we found him." She flipped open the book, a black ledger with cracks in the maroon binding along the spine. Pale green paper frayed at the edges. Handwriting neat. She opened to a random page near the front. "The little people didn't come again last night." The page was dated.

She flipped to the back. "Two pigeons came to the windowsill and ate the cracker crumbs. The same two birds who came yesterday. Maybe they'll come back again tomorrow." That entry was dated almost two years ago. She suspected that she would find the same simplistic entries throughout the book, but she would read it tonight, page by page.

"Look at this," Vik called.

She went over to the closet. There was a jumble of boxes on the floor. All kinds of Keebler cookies. Girl Scout cookies. Boxes of chocolates. Boxes filled with candy bars that had labels identifying schools and other organizations.

As they left Marti wondered if Lenny had any living family. She was getting an impression of a person in search of connections. She tucked the ledger in her purse almost reluctant to read it, already saddened by the two entries she'd read so far.

They went back to the alley. The wind had picked up, penetrating the scarf she wrapped around most of her face. They were ready to move Lenny Doobee. She shot a roll of black-and-white film, then a roll of color film. His face was so white. He didn't look like the little boy in the snapshot anymore. The desk sergeant had gotten it right when he called her: Lenny was a stiff now.

She put the camera in the trunk. They would have to canvass the building, ask if anyone had seen or heard anything. Eventually she'd go back to the precinct and write up her reports. By midafternoon she'd be in a hurry to get home and hoping nothing came up to delay her. She had to get home as soon as possible—they had a Christmas tree to pick out.

13

When the telephone rang Sunday morning Marti felt too groggy to open her eyes. She groped for the receiver, dropped it before she got it to her ear and tried again. "MacAlister." She closed one eye to get the numbers on the digital clock into focus. 4:55.

"Morning, Mac." It was the coroner, Janet Petrosky. How could anyone sound that wide awake before daybreak?

"The Horvaster autopsy is scheduled for six with Doctor Cyprian attending." Janet sneezed.

"I thought allergy season was over."

"It is. I'm coming down with a cold. What's going on at the Cramer? We got a serial killer running amok over there?"

"No, just a couple of isolated incidents."

"You believe that, MacAlister?"

"No. I know there's not much of an M.O., but see what kind of a psych profile you can get for me, okay?"

"We'll see what we can put together." Janet blew her nose, then sniffled. "You're that sure it's the same perp?"

"That sure," Marti answered.

"I haven't called your partner yet."

"Don't. Tell him I said so." Vik's cold hadn't sounded any better when they left work last night and she knew he planned to check out the Cramer around midnight. They had reached an unspoken agreement to go by there every night and it was his turn.

"Are you going to violate Jessenovik ordinance 6892 again? View another deceased male and watch us undress him?"

"If I can keep my eyes open long enough to get out of bed."

Vik didn't approve of female officers attending autopsies if the victim was male or badly disfigured. As with most of his idiosyncrasies involving women, Marti ignored his protests. Now he said nothing at all.

"I've got to admit it, MacAlister. I didn't think you two would remain a team this long."

Marti smiled. "He's adjusting."

Janet chuckled. "Out of necessity, I'm sure. I think he's met his match."

By seven-thirty Marti was standing outside of the coroner's facility, glad that the autopsy was over. She shivered even though it didn't seem much colder outside than in. More than just the temperature made the morgue seem cold. Cinder-block walls painted white. Stainless steel tables and instruments. Bright lights. The odor of chemicals and antiseptics always made her stomach churn, that and the anticipation of viewing someone who had died by violence before the undertaker made the body look more presentable.

She stood in the sunlight, squinting in the glare of the recent, still mostly white snow. She took a few deep breaths of the cold, crisp air and let the wind buffet her face for a moment before she headed for her car.

Lenny Doobee had died the same way as Dorsey. Someone stood in front of him and applied pressure to the carotid artery in his neck. He died quickly and did not resist his killer. Did that mean that he knew him or that he was too frightened to defend himself? Was John Clark their perp? This method of strangulation was something that Clark could have picked up while in jail. Would Doobee have tried to defend himself if it was Clark? It looked like the psychiatrist was right. Doobee did let someone kill him.

The only reason he had seen anyone in the hallway was because someone had crushed the cookies. He didn't identify Dorsey's killer. He hadn't and he wouldn't, even if he could have, because Marti had not penetrated that barrier of self-absorption that everyone at the Cramer seemed to have. She had not made him see the reality of his own danger. She had told him to be careful but that hadn't been enough. Maybe she hadn't been certain enough that the danger was real.

Slim and Cowboy were in the squad room when she got there. She waved at the air with the Sunday edition of the *Chicago Tribune* as she walked to her desk. "Do you have to take a shower in that stuff?" she complained. Slim's Obsession for Men seemed stronger than ever this morning, but that wasn't why she felt cranky.

Slim mouthed "p-m-s" to Cowboy, who looked at one of the calendars and shook his head. Their pantomime made her feel like throwing something. When she reached for the phone they both ducked. Turning away from them, she called the Respite.

Doobee had phoned them about one o'clock Saturday morning. He was frightened. The killer was after him. He said he was going to call a cab but he never showed up.

"He couldn't," Marti told the cheerful, impersonal voice. "He was murdered."

There was a gasp at the other end of the line. "My God. He wasn't imagining it. So many things happened inside his head, we thought that's all that it was."

"How long had he been imagining that someone was after him?" Marti asked, touching the cactus in the terrarium on her desk with the tip of her finger.

"This time? Just a few weeks."

"He had imagined this before?"

"Sure. He got real paranoid when we set the clocks back in the fall and stayed that way until we put them an hour forward in the spring. Then he just imagined things all summer, and nobody was trying to hurt him."

Marti felt the stiff bristle of the cactus against her skin and moved her finger away. She thanked the woman for her time. After she hung up she wondered if anyone from the Respite would go to the funeral. She couldn't be annoyed with them for not recognizing danger when Doobee's fear had settled into that kind of a pattern. Maybe that was why she hadn't been more concerned about his safety. Even Doobee had seemed used to being afraid.

Marti thought of his parents, wondered if they would understand the significance of 122 boxes of cookies, including six cases of Girl Scout cookies. There were 215 candy bars, all purchased from groups representing local schools. Doobee had sought out a family the best way he could. She felt sorry for the man and woman in that photograph. Maybe they would just think Lenny was eccentric.

She looked away from the window as Slim came over to her desk. "You and Jessenovik are going to have to spend a little time away from the job."

Cowboy pushed his five-gallon hat back far enough to show off his wavy white-blond hair to best advantage. "Not that we can ever expect Jessenovik to be in a decent mood," he drawled. "We ought to get some kind of combat pay for being in here with you two."

Slim saluted her with his cup of coffee. "Get you some, Mac?" he offered.

"I'll get it myself," she snapped. "Got anything else on those kids?"

Slim and Cowboy got serious all at once.

"Hadn't thought of them," Cowboy said.

"Me neither," Slim agreed. "Fool out there killin' folks could be after these children. Damn."

"What's Torres got for you?" Cowboy asked.

"Nothing since we got that description of the three boys. We haven't distributed the artist's drawing outside of the force. Don't want to scare them away." She showed them Vik's map.

Slim stroked his chin. "You can get more volunteers for an increased patrol in that area, no sweat. Not much more we can do."

Cowboy finished cramming a pack of chewing gum into his mouth. When he'd chewed it to a manageable consistency he said, "They ain't hanging out with our crowd. I got three pimps out there real scared so if any of our little ladies do see any of them again we'll know about it real fast."

Vik came in while they were talking and dropped a metal canister on his desk.

"Cookies!" Slim said, homing in on the container and opening it while Vik hung up his coat. "Mrs. Vik must have made these."

While Vik scowled, Slim passed them around. Marti took a couple of the chocolate chips. Then she thought about the plate of cookies Doobee wouldn't be putting in the hall anymore and couldn't eat them.

"M.O.'s the same as Dorsey's," she told Vik.

"Figured it would be," he muttered, picking up the phone. In five minutes he managed to yell at the desk sergeant, the coordinating officer in charge of locating John Clark, Lupe Torres, and Slim when he reached for the tin of cookies again.

"Lordy, Lordy," Cowboy drawled. "Sure hope you all nail somebody for this soon. We'll have to work out of the hallway if things keep up like this."

"Too bad it's happening at the Cramer," Slim said, favoring Marti with one of his cupid's bow smiles. "Place is a hell of a lot better than that flophouse that burned down a couple of years ago. Soon as this hits the *News-Times* we'll have folks wanting to close it down."

"Be a lot more work for us having all them folks scattered around town than keeping 'em together in one place," Cowboy said. "Got us maybe a hundred oddballs in there. Probably talk to themselves more than they talk to each other, but I think it must be kinda reassuring to be around people who are a little off like you are, a little touched in the head. Be a shame to close that place down."

Slim went over to the spider plant and dumped in the dregs from his cup. "We're lookin', Mac. We've got all of our snitches with their ears to the ground. Let you know if we come up with somethin'. Course now we been looking a while. Kids must be real good at hiding."

After Slim and Cowboy left, Marti took out Doobee's diary. She had stayed up half the night reading it and opened to the first page she had marked. "I thought Daddy was in the hall tonight but it was just that one who tried to go in Dorsey's room." Looking at Vik she said, "That's dated two nights before she died."

"Any entries about John Clark so we can get some idea of whether this was him or some other man?"

"No. He mentions 'that man' going to Dorsey's door seven times."

"Anything about what he looks like?" Vik asked, sounding weary.

"Not unless you call 'I thought it was Daddy' a description."

"John Clark is forty. That's not old. Unless he meant 'daddy' as in when he was a kid or 'daddy' as in when he was a teenager, or 'daddy' is generic for anyone over twenty-five. Damn thing's no use to us."

"No," she agreed, thinking of the shiny black-and-white snapshot of Lenny when he was a little boy. There were other entries in the diary where Doobee thought he saw his father in a barber shop or passing by on a bus. No telling what triggered the association that made him think complete strangers could be his father. "Not unless someone else can corroborate what he says. There's also the small matter of apprehending a suspect and having enough evidence to charge him with being the man who was there."

"Evidence," Vik grouched. "A couple of size-twelve footprints and someone who knows about or has been trained to apply pressure to that particular artery. I think our primary witness just got killed. And don't forget the small matter of motive."

Feeling discouraged, Marti agreed. "If we could get any handle on Dorsey's recent past, she'd tell us the motive herself. Trouble is that she kept to herself." Except for Nessa, the lady at the clinic. Marti was certain Nessa had left the food and if she did, she and Dorsey must have been friends. She made up her mind to go see her as soon as possible.

About half an hour later a uniform came to the door. "Mrs. Horvaster to see you," he said. He turned to the short, bespectacled woman standing not quite behind him, said "Ma'am," and hurried away.

The woman just stood there, swathed in homemade hat, mittens, and a scarf wrapped around her neck several times, all knitted in variegated green yarn.

"Are you the officers who found my Leonard?" the woman asked in a weak, quavering voice.

Vik started to push back his chair, eager to avoid all contact with the next of kin. Marti gave him a look that dared him to try and escape. He began shuffling the papers on his desk instead. The woman took one hesitant step into the room.

Marti stood up. "Come right in, Mrs. Horvaster, I'm Detective MacAlister. This is my partner, Detective Jessenovik."

The woman waddled into the room. Marti wasn't sure if it was body weight or layers of clothing.

"Have a seat," Marti offered.

The woman put a satchel-sized purse on the floor and pulled off her mittens. Her hands were as pudgy as her son's. "Did you find my Leonard? I had to go in this morning and tell them it was him."

She sniffled, stifled a sob, then stared at her

hands. "Funny he was, you know, in the head. Never was right. Not even when he was a little boy. But harmless. He wouldn't ever do anything to hurt anyone." There was a catch in her voice. "Harmless. And frightened. All of the time so afraid. That this should happen to him."

Vik looked like he was praying, hands together, the tips of his fingers under his chin as he stared at the ceiling. Woman's work, comforting the bereaved, notifying the next of kin, asking questions that might help solve a homicide. Calling it woman's work was just an excuse to avoid unpleasantness.

"Mrs. Horvaster, we didn't find Lenny, but we had spoken with him a few times."

"I know, about the other killing, right there at that hotel, just like Lenny. Seems to me they should have done something. Negligent, letting it happen again. I'm seeing a lawyer first thing tomorrow morning."

The first question Marti asked was the one that had been bothering her the most. "Can you tell me about Lenny's father?"

"He talked to you about his father, too?"

"Not exactly. But he did mention him."

The woman pulled a wad of soggy Kleenex out of her pocket, dabbed at her eyes, and began to twist it in her hands. Little bits of wet tissue fell to the floor.

"My husband is not a well man. He's always had a weak heart. Raising Leonard, well, it was just too much of a strain, put him in the hospital with chest pains and palpitations. We had to put Leonard in a place with other children who were like he was."

"When's the last time he lived at home?"

"Not since he was four years old. I couldn't send him to school, you see, like a normal child. But I always went to see him. Every other Sunday and it was way to Elgin and I had to ride the Greyhound, but I went. The trip, it was too much for my husband with his heart and all."

Another Vik, Marti thought, avoiding anything he might get emotional about by letting the little woman take care of it. No, maybe she was wrong and Mr. Horvaster really was in poor health.

"How long had Lenny been living at the Cramer?"

"Seven years now. I went to see him once a month. Took the city bus. Not that far from home."

Marti was afraid that if she asked why Lenny didn't visit his parents at home she'd get another explanation of the father's health. "When's the last time you saw him?"

"Monday, December fourth. He always took me to lunch when his social security check came."

That would explain the monthly visits.

"Did he ever talk about anything that happened at the Cramer Hotel?"

"We went to a restaurant nearby, ate. I'd tell him about the family. He never said much of anything at all."

"Did anyone else in the family come to see him?"

She looked down, shaking her head. The Kleenex looked like snow on the brown tweed carpet. "No. When we put him away, it was like he didn't exist anymore. To everyone but me. Now he doesn't." She began to sob. Marti put her arm around the broad heaving shoulders, patting until the crying subsided.

"It's hard," Mrs. Horvaster said. "Hard to know what to do. You just do the best that you can. Leonard was my boy and I loved him. He didn't deserve to die like this. Did he know? When it was happening?"

"No." Marti hoped that was true. She would have said it regardless. "He never knew."

Mrs. Horvaster nodded and didn't ask for any details.

"How are you getting home?" Marti asked.

"The bus. Another one will be leaving in fifty minutes. I'll get some coffee while I'm waiting."

"We'll see that you get home," Vik said, voice gruff.

After the woman was gone, Vik snapped, "We're becoming a damned escort service around here."

Marti looked at the stack of forms still to be filled out. "Secretarial service," she corrected.

14

When Marti arrived at the precinct Monday morning they had something on John Clark.

"He's wanted for questioning," Vik said. "Man delivering Domino's Pizza Saturday night was robbed. His assailant wore a ski mask and an olive parka. The guy makes regular deliveries to the building, recognized the parka. Described the guy he saw wearing it. Cops took a look around, and somebody's been sleeping in the furnace room. They lifted Clark's prints."

"Where?" Marti asked.

"Kankakee. Hour and a half drive from here. Clark must be getting a little desperate for cash. Held a knife on the guy and escaped with $13.75."

Marti reached for the report, stared at it without reading. "He hasn't left the state, and he didn't do anything big enough to buy a ticket out of here. Kankakee. Sounds like he's lying low, trying to survive without calling attention to himself or getting caught."

"He might be smart enough to keep moving, try something different, someplace else," Vik said. "But maybe we'll get lucky."

"Maybe," Marti agreed. "But why hasn't he gone farther away?"

The call came in from the Cramer Hotel at 9:17 A.M. They were due in court at 9:30. Vik called the state's attorney's office to say they would be detained, while Marti headed for the parking lot.

By 9:30 they were looking at what was left of Wayne Baxter. Marti passed around her jar of Vicks VapoRub and Vik, the two uniforms, and the doctor put more on their upper lips. There wasn't much more they could do about the stench. The garbage that she had smelled more than seen Thursday night was knee deep in places. A path had been cleared by the crew cleaning it out. She followed the path to where the mounds of garbage began again and looked at Baxter. She'd seen worse, but not in the past couple of years. She looked away.

"Rats got him," Dr. Cyprian explained. "I haven't seen anything like it since I interned in New York."

He put on a pair of surgical gloves, made a few exploratory efforts at examining the body. "He's probably been down here a couple of days now. I'm not certain that we will be able to pinpoint a cause of death for you."

Cyprian turned to the evidence techs, spoke to the one who hadn't vomited. "We will need samples of the garbage. Make a diagram so I can see where you take each sample from. Get some of what is under the body when we remove it." Looking at Vik and Marti he said, "I'm not sure we can pinpoint time of death either.

If we do, it will probably take longer than normal." He dismissed everyone with a brisk "we will do what we can," and continued his examination of the corpse.

Marti looked around. With all of the bright lights that had been set up it was possible to see the extent of the refuse that had been piled here.

"Bet they got stuff here going back ten, fifteen years," Vik said.

Old mattresses spilling stuffing, broken chairs, couches that were little more than frames and exposed coils, rotting clothing and bedding. And the garbage. Marti passed the Vicks again.

"Let's go," she said.

When they got upstairs she asked if the owner had been located yet.

"Manager, ma'am?" the day clerk said. His English wasn't very good.

"The *owner*," Vik said, menace in his tone of voice. "The owner, not the manager, and now."

In Spanish the man asked, "How do I call someone I do not even know? This man, the owner, I do not even know his name. How do I call him?"

Marti identified a Mexican dialect and answered in rapid, fluent Spanish. "Call the number that you have been given. We will speak with whoever answers the phone."

The man did as he was told. Marti handed the phone to Vik. He was angrier than she was and needed someone other than her to vent it on.

"The owner!" Vik yelled. "Now. Understand?"

Half a minute later he said, "Ownership is not privileged information. We've had three homicides here in a week and you will contact the owner now and have him call this number within the next five minutes."

"Or?" Marti asked when Vik hung up.

"I'll call the mayor. I went to school with him."

She smiled. Sometimes Lincoln Prairie did seem like a small town.

She surveyed the residents who had gathered in the lobby. They looked like the two groups of old men and women who had been here when Dorsey's body was found.

She remembered the black woman with five or six slips hanging below the hem of her knee-length blue bathrobe. As she looked at her the woman moved away from five other old ladies and came over.

"Who's down there, chile?" she asked.

Marti liked being called the familiar 'chile' and smiled.

"Won't none of them tell us who 'tis," the woman complained. "Sadie says it's Little John what lives on the fifth floor, but her sister Sarah says she heard it's old Arnie, our janitor. Sure wouldn't want it to be either of them."

Marti looked at the four women again. Now that this lady had said sister, she could see a resemblance between two of them.

"It's Wayne Baxter," she told the woman.

"You don't say! Serves that fool right. Sure glad it weren't old Arnie."

"What's your name, ma'am?" Marti asked.

"Cynthia Wright. Most folks call me Cindy."

"Well, Miss Cindy, your friends got any more questions?"

The woman shrugged. "Nah. We old. Ain't much none of us can do about any of this no way. Can't afford to be movin'. Sure would be nice to have a safe place to live though."

"We're contacting the owner," Marti told her. "Why don't all of you just stay here and you can tell him that yourself."

She turned to Vik. "He'll be here in another ten, fifteen minutes," he said. "Lives in Wilmette."

"This is Miss Cindy, Vik. This is my partner, Detective Jessenovik."

Vik said, "Stick around, ma'am, and you can tell the owner, Mr. Dunlap, anything you'd like."

The woman gave them a big smile, showing about seven teeth, all crooked, and spoke to Marti. "We sure 'nuff will, chile. We sure 'nuff will."

Vik motioned a uniform over. "Tell them not to cover or remove the body until the owner gets here."

Marti walked with Miss Cindy and spoke to her and her friends. "Did any of you see or hear anything last night?"

The four old men came over. "Wayne wasn't here last night," one of them said. "Wasn't nobody on that desk at five to twelve. Cops came out because there was a fight on the third floor. Wayne wasn't nowhere around. Not in his room either. Door was open, though. You should see that place. Hard to believe anyone could live in it."

Marti had seen Wayne's room when they arrested him. She sent a uniform in to have another look.

"Anyone see or hear anything Saturday night?" she asked.

The same man answered. "We was all playing gin rummy in Ed's room up front on five. Nothing happened up there. Don't think none of us had any occasion to come down here." He looked at the others. They all agreed.

The uniform came over and suggested that they might want to take a look at Baxter's room. It was much worse than it had been a week ago.

"Whoever did this was in a hurry," Vik said.

Even the pot of sour food, what looked like neck bones and cabbage, had been thrown on the floor.

"We keep asking if anyone heard anything last night or the night before," Marti said. "But I don't expect to get much. Drunks were midway through their weekend binges. Old folks were playing cards."

Vik groaned. "That leaves the crazies, and two of them are already dead."

When the owner arrived, the two groups of elderly people converged on him. Marti and Vik got out of their way.

"We need this door locked at night."

"People at the welfare office said this place was secured."

"We don't wanna go to no nursing home. We can take care of ourselves well enough."

Dunlap, a tall man with wavy white hair and a generous smile, didn't try to back away from them or shut them up.

"How long have you been living here?" he asked one man.

"Six years, ever since my Lucy died. Had a waiting list for senior citizen housing."

Miss Cindy said, "Be a good enough place if'n you'd just keep the door locked at night. All of us here, we look after each other. Share what we have so's none of us need nothin'. We just want a safe place to live. Three people killed here in the last week."

Dunlap turned to Marti and Vik. "Three? I thought there was just some woman."

Marti brought him up to date.

Vik volunteered to escort him down to the basement. Behind Dunlap's back, Marti held out the jar of Vicks VapoRub. Vik shook his head and grinned.

Mr. Dunlap lost his breakfast before he got to the deceased. One look at Wayne's remains and he dry heaved. They escorted him back to the lobby. Vik scowled at the rookie who offered Dunlap a Pepsi.

Dunlap used it to rinse out his mouth, then took a couple of long swallows. "They are cleaning up that cellar?"

Vik nodded. "Have everything out of there today. The clean-up crew has been told to watch for dead children."

Dunlap blanched, swallowed, and didn't ask any questions. He turned to Miss Cindy. "I don't know how long it will take to get a security system installed, but the door will be kept locked from dusk to dawn and there will be a guard. Any other problems?"

She shook her head. "They keeps the place heated well enough and we ain't in any of the top floor rooms that got leaks. And don't worry yourself none about fixing the elevator. We wouldn't get no exercise if it worked. About the only time we miss it's when someone goes out in an ambulance."

Dunlap made a cursory inspection of the lobby and hall. "Think we might have a liability problem if we don't get the elevator fixed," he commented to nobody in particular. Turning to Marti and Vik he said, "Bought the place maybe three years ago. First time I've seen it. Could use some fixing up."

After he left, Vik said, "He'll take the depreciation on the place for another three, four years. Then he'll sell it to someone else and the depreciation will start all over again. Bad cycle. Property just keeps deteriorating. I think he'll do what he says, but the only investment he has in this place is as a tax write-off. He won't spend a dime more than he has to. Cuts into his profit."

On their way out, Miss Cindy and her friends stopped them. "That was a good thing you did, getting him to come here."

"Yes," one of the two sisters spoke up. "Don't know what will happen to that little boy, though."

"What little boy?" Marti and Vik asked, almost in unison.

"That fat kid on the second floor what they found Saturday mornin' kept putting out cookies for him, didn't he Sarah?"

"Don't know what this world is comin' to, Sadie. Women lettin' their children go 'round begging like that."

"Gave him five dollars last week, didn't we?" Sadie said.

"Sure 'nuff did. Not that we believed he'd lost a five-dollar bill outta that hole in the thumb of his mitten."

"Woulda given him more, wouldn't we sister, if'n we had it. We done decided that if'n he comes around again after we get our social security that we gonna take him and get him a coat and some boots. Catch his death of cold with what he's got on."

Marti showed the women the composites they had of the three boys. Sarah identified the little boy who was black.

"How old do you think he is, ma'am?" Marti asked.

" 'Bout the size of a seven-year-old, but I'd say nine or ten, way he talks," Sarah said.

"And can lie just as fast as he can breathe," Sadie told her.

"What day did you see him?"

"Saturday, wasn't it sister? Week ago Saturday."

179

The day after Dorsey was killed. Marti bet he was looking for his mittens. "How often does he come around here?"

"Couldn't say," the sisters agreed. "We up on the fifth floor. Drunk lives down the hall. Gets up a few Saturday mornings wondering where all his money went. That's when we started watchin'. Only strange person we noticed was this little boy. Figure it must be him."

"Mother needs a good whippin'," Sarah concluded. "The way that child was coughin'. Ain't gettin' no kind of upbringing at home."

Vik looked at her. Marti shook her head. Once the building was secured, would this little boy still be able to get in? And if he did come back, would the killer be waiting for him? Marti tried not to think about how he was dressed or if he was sick. Bad enough wondering where he was.

They considered stopping for lunch, decided not to. Filling out a couple dozen forms back at the precinct would change their memories of Wayne Baxter's remains from vivid to blurred with aggravation at the work his dying had caused. By the time Marti finished writing up her notes she was angry with him again.

"Took him four days to tell us about those kids," she grumbled.

"Got what he deserved," Vik agreed.

They were both silent, thinking about the children. Marti got a call through to Lupe Torres. When she hung up she got out Vik's map and said, "Torres suggests a sweep of these abandoned industrial buildings and a ten-block door-to-door canvass. Can we organize that for this afternoon?"

"Watch sergeant can talk to the first shift when they report in. They'll go back out and look for the kids."

They had just decided to break for lunch when Mr. Horvaster, Lenny Doobee's father, came in. He wasn't thin anymore but at least as large as his wife. His hat, mittens, and scarf in variegated browns were also handmade. Thick brown hair streaked with gray escaped from the sides of the hat.

Mr. Horvaster walked with the aid of a wooden cane and a tripod-based metal cane. A young woman hovered behind him as if ready to catch him should he fall. She was thin. Store-bought hat, too. Maybe she was the family rebel.

"My wife came here," the man said without preamble once he'd sat down by Vik's desk.

Vik gave Marti a look that said *help me*. Marti smiled *your turn*, and sat back to watch.

"Actually," Vik said. "Mrs. Horvaster spoke with my partner here, Detective MacAlister."

Mr. Horvaster tried to twist around far enough to see her, couldn't see her more than peripherally, and turned back to Vik.

"I'm on my way home from the doctor's. This here's my daughter. Mother's home prostrate. Saw all them cookies and candy bars, got a little upset. Most things upset Mother, really upset her if they got anything to do with our Lenny."

He was wheezing a bit from exertion. Marti decided to be a good female cop and brought

181

everyone coffee to order. Vik glowered at her but couldn't say anything.

"Our Lenny was a good boy. Not quite right in the head, but a good boy. Gentle. Never did nothin' to harm anyone. I know Mother told you the family just couldn't handle it, but you see, her sister's got six kids, five of 'em boys, four in the building trades and doing quite well, youngest is just a real screwup. But Mother, well, she just had the two, Rachel here, and our Lenny."

He rested again, told Marti she made a great pot of coffee, then went on.

"Anyway, our Lenny was easier for Mother to deal with from a distance, and to be honest, he was strange about things and it was easier for all of us. I'm not trying to say it was right, but you make it right in your own mind till something like this happens and then you just wish he'd been safe with you at home."

He spoke without emotion, dry-eyed and calm. Marti felt more sympathy for him than she'd felt for any parent she'd seen in awhile.

"Now what I really came here to tell you is that Lenny was just a little bit off in the head. But just because a person's called crazy and might be a little slow doesn't mean they're stupid or don't have good sense. Our boy did real good at takin' care of himself and a lot of what he said did make some sense sometimes."

Vik began to lean forward. He started to drum his fingers on the morning *Tribune* while the man took a few deep breaths, caught himself and tried to pretend he had a little patience.

"Right after a holiday, any holiday, Lenny would go off to that Respite cause he'd have to be by himself, instead of with us. I'm pretty confined, except for these doctor and hospital visits. Mother gets around a bit more but it was too much for her, taking care of us at home on a holiday and getting down here too, what with the bus schedules and all and not wanting anyone to drive her so's they would see Lenny too. Lenny, he would always call when he got to the Respite, just to be in touch. The night that woman got killed, when he called he was too upset to make much sense and real scared."

This time when Mr. Horvaster stopped to catch his breath, Marti wanted to urge him on.

"Lenny had seen a man in the hall the night before she died. He thought the woman was pretty. He wanted to tell her, but Lenny, he was too scared to talk to most people. Then when he saw she was dead he was really afraid."

"He told you he saw her?" Vik said.

"Said she got into an argument with the man 'cause she didn't want him coming to her room no more. Said he saw her on the floor dead."

John Clark.

"Did he describe the man?" Vik asked.

"No, just said that at first he thought it was me. That's all."

"Do you have any idea of what it would be about another person that would make him think it was you?"

"Never could figure that out," Mr. Horvaster admitted.

He had no further information. Marti explained to him about the diary, that they would keep it for now but would be turning it over to the family. She tried to give him some idea of what was in it. The man was sensitive enough to recognize that his son had been reaching out for some kind of family ties.

"Call the house," Mr. Horvaster told her. "Rachel can run down here and get it. I'll see that Mother doesn't even know."

After he left Marti felt overwhelmed. Her primary responsibilities involved victims who were far beyond helping themselves and she could distance herself from them when she needed to. Many times she felt inadequate when she dealt with their survivors because there was nothing she could do to help them. Then there were times like these, when she just felt a dull ache inside.

15

By two o'clock the search was organized. The first shift volunteers would be off duty by three-thirty. As they walked to the car Vik said, "See today's *News-Times*?"

"No."

"Headline reads FRIDAY KILLER AT CRAMER STRIKES AGAIN. Second page has an alderman saying they should close it down. I'm going to call Brian tonight. No way we should turn those people out of there."

Brian was the mayor. It wasn't the same as picking up the phone and calling the mayor of Chicago, but Marti was reasonably impressed.

Lupe was already out looking for the children. They got her location and drove over to the area not far from Lake Michigan where the abandoned industrial buildings were located. Marti had never been there. It was one long block with two buildings still standing on one side of the street and three on the other. The street was narrow and neglected. She had to drive carefully to avoid the potholes. The tires bumped over lumpy ice.

She could see where two buildings had been

torn down, with foundations jutting up just above ground level. Several lots were cluttered with rusting odds and ends of equipment and abandoned cars and garbage.

Four of the buildings that remained were concrete or cinder-block structures discolored to dingy grays and tans. What was left of their chain-link fences was rusty and sagging. In some places just the posts remained, held in place by concrete. One building was made out of tin. The walls were collapsing inward, dragging the roof down until the corrugated metal almost touched the dirt yard in places.

"What did they do here?" Marti asked.

"Freight handling and warehousing, mostly," Vik said. "Some small boat repair. Used to be a place where the crews from the fishing boats sold their catches. I'd come down here every Friday with my cousin and pick out a fresh salmon for supper."

They spotted Lupe's squad car and parked behind it. Lupe was making her way through some brittle weeds and bushes behind the tin building. Vik grabbed a handful of Kleenex before he got out of the car. He still hadn't shaken his cold.

Marti followed the path in the snow, Vik behind her. "What have you got?" she asked.

Lupe was squatting in the snow. "Footprints," she said. "Lots of 'em. Not like someone was walking, though. Looks like they were playing or dancing or just making sure nobody could make any sense of them. I'm not sure they're new."

She stood up and pushed back her visored cap. "It's always like this. Plenty of prints. They come down here from those apartments," she pointed to the row of brick apartment buildings about two blocks west. "And they hit that embankment over there." It was about halfway between the apartments and where they were now. "I've come here during the day, at night, nothing. I don't think anybody's living in any of these places. It isn't just that they're not habitable. The rats are huge. We're always calling the dog warden to pick up strays. And inside, God. These places have standing water, some stink like hell, there are bugs big as your fist, cats mean as junkyard dogs."

"So you're sure these kids are not here," Marti said.

"I think they want me to think they are, or that they just want to lose me. Part of my beat is combined foot and scout patrol in an eight-block area adjoining this," Lupe explained. She pointed toward Sherman Avenue and indicated the row of brick apartment buildings on one side and single-family homes on the other. They were older structures, reasonably well maintained. The streets and sidewalks were clean. The farther end of her walking beat included public housing, the projects. The old library squatted on the corner, a gray brick building with plywood covering the windows.

"There's always something about that place in the newspaper," Marti said. "They decide what to do with it yet?"

"Restoration proponents were supposed to

look at it about a week ago," Vik said. "They've been trying to save the place for over a year now. I think they should save it, turn it into a restaurant or something. They don't have too much more time to make up their minds. I'll bet the water pipes have burst, and the roof probably leaks. It's a good, solid building though. At least it's secured from vandalism. Location helps. Real visible."

"This is a pretty stable area," Lupe said. "Owners live in all of the homes. Not too much turnover in the apartments. Not too many young kids either. Older people. A few middle-aged parents with teenagers, a few singles. Biggest problem we have here is break-ins, homes and cars. Over in the projects the foot patrols have really cut down on drug dealing, break-ins, theft. We know just about all of the kids who live there. I've talked with some of them. Nothing."

"Well, we can confirm whether or not anyone is living in these places and have a look at those three houses over there too," Marti said. "From the looks of it a thorough search is long overdue."

The search took several hours. They called in some off-duty firemen because they were more familiar with structures that looked ready to collapse. When Marti saw Ben, she and Vik went over to him.

"Didn't know they let paramedics volunteer for these complicated operations," she said.

"Some dumb cop might fall through the floor and lose his shoe," Ben said, close to laughing at a previous experience he had been involved in with Vik.

"Nice to see you, too," Vik said.

They followed Ben into the tin building.

"Nice thing about this one," Ben said, "is plenty of ventilation."

There were large rusted-out holes in the walls and places where the roof and wall had separated.

Ben motioned to an area that looked like the foundation for a vat. "Gets rid of the odors, too."

Debris and what looked like animal carcasses were frozen in about eight inches of ice.

"We could have bodies in these places," Vik said.

The rest of the interior consisted of stall-like structures, some empty, some with odd bits of metal lying on wooden trestle tables as if someone had put them down at the end of a workday and never came back. A desk had been left in one stall, a metal file cabinet in another. Marti opened the drawers of both and found a couple of manila file folders filled with invoices.

A fireman came over from the three abandoned houses. "Someone was living in one of them," he reported. "Not for a while though." He opened a plastic bag. "Found these sterno cans and Burger King wrappers. Place is wide open. Walls down, no windows. Miracle they didn't get hurt. No protection there at all from this weather."

Marti stared at the Burger King wrappers for a long time. Too late, she thought. We found out about them too late. Would have found them if all of this had happened a month or so ago.

Everyone gathered outside at five o'clock. It was dark and there were no street lights. They used flashlights. One dead body had been found. A male, mummified and preserved by the cold. Probably a vagrant. Nobody had found any place in any other building that looked like someone was attempting to live there. They hadn't even found liquor bottles or beer cans or fast food packaging. Nothing. In all probability the buildings were not being used.

Just before they disbanded to write their individual reports the mayor drove up, got out of his Buick and thanked them. Every so often the small-town touches surprised her. When a photographer from the *News-Times* showed up she thought about the stalemate in the city council over how to revitalize this area. Maybe they needed a walking tour.

Then the mayor came over to them and extended his hand. "Hi Matt, how you doing? Good to see you're keeping Lincoln Prairie safe for mankind."

Then he looked at Marti. He was her height with a long nose and a prominent forehead that made his look seem penetrating. "And you're our highly recommended cop from the force in Chicago. Nice to meet you. I'm Brian Esiason."

As they shook hands Marti decided she liked him.

"Has this got anything to do with what's happened at the Cramer or are you at liberty to say?"

"You see today's paper?" Vik asked. "If that bandwagon gets rolling we'll have one hell of a time on our hands once those people are scattered all over the county."

"You think so," Brian said, noncommittal.

"Yes. We ran a make on everyone in there and came up with seven out of a hundred and twenty with felony convictions. Sure as hell beats what we could find in the general populace."

The mayor smiled. "Still quoting statistics. You used to do that when we were in school. How's Mildred? She driving a car yet?"

"Fine and no," Vik snapped, but he wasn't annoyed.

"Nice gesture," she said as Vik got in on the passenger side.

"Conned his way through high school," Vik said. "Had a smile and line for everyone. Decent people, though. Funny how surprised we were when he went into politics."

"I bet you went to school with a relative of every politician in town."

"Probably," Vik agreed. "Only had one high school until ten years ago, hard not to know most of 'em."

She felt tired. Her legs ached and her head hurt. Vik was sniffling again.

"Think I'll swing by the Cramer tonight. You get some rest and take something for that cold."

"I drove past there last night," Vik said. "Cowboy, Slim, and Lupe Torres drove by too. Didn't see any kids. They're outsmarting half the police force."

"Hope they outsmart the killer, too."

Beside her Vik swore, something he almost never did in her presence.

"This is really getting to you."

"We're looking for kids," he said angrily. "We've got a crew digging garbage out of a cellar and looking for dead kids. We're here in this rat-infested, godforsaken part of town looking for children." He spat out another profanity. "We are looking for little children because we think someone is out there who wants to kill them. And you know what the worst part of it is? I don't think we're looking for some kind of madman. I sat in that court and watched that little girl, six months pregnant, who shook her baby until it stopped breathing. She was sorry, she didn't mean to hurt her. She just wanted her to stop crying. And we sat in the courtroom and listened to that dopehead say he was sorry. He didn't mean to kill his wife, the crack told him she was the devil. And she wouldn't shut up. He just wanted her to shut up."

He sneezed, blew his nose. "And you know what? Six months or a year from now we'll sit in a courtroom and listen to this idiot say he's sorry. He didn't mean to do it. He just didn't want three little boys to tell the cops they saw him off poor schizo Dorsey. What in the hell is this? You don't even have to be nuts anymore. Just hang your head and say sorry. And then get angry when that isn't enough and you can't just get on with your life as if you hadn't taken someone else's."

They sat there in silence. She had felt that

way once. Said much the same thing to Johnny. She told Vik what Johnny had told her. "You do your job. You do it right. You don't take shortcuts, you don't go home early, you don't leave anything undone. You build a solid case against them. You bring them in. You don't let them get away with it. And that's all you can do."

"Cop tell you that?"

"My husband."

Vik didn't speak for a minute. Then he said, "Been, what, year and a half now?"

"Seventeen months, four days, and about sixteen and a half hours."

"Yeah," Vik said. "I hear you, kid. I hear you."

"I know. And I hear you, too."

16

It was dark when Georgie woke up. He had fallen asleep with his head in LaShawna's lap. Now he was on his own pile of coats. Through the cracks where the boards didn't come real close together on the windows he could see the light the moon made on the snow. It must be late. He could hear Sissy talking in her sleep, heard LaShawna telling her to be quiet when her dreams got bad and she talked louder. Sometimes LaShawna had to wake her up, but not tonight. Not yet.

It had scared all of them, having all those people searching the old buildings where they pretended to go. It was almost as scary as when the man was after him, even though the old buildings were farther away. He didn't want anyone to find them. They'd never get to Minneapolis if they got caught.

He must have slept through supper. He wondered if Padgett or Jose had gone to Burger King or if they'd opened more of the cans. There had been Spam behind the store the last time and a big can of chicken and a whole bag of apples. LaShawna was worried 'cause he didn't feel like eating. Not even thinking about food made him hungry. He didn't feel sick, just tired. And he wasn't hardly coughing no more.

Padgett had gone to the Osco and took some cold medicine and Tylenol and cough drops without getting caught. LaShawna thought it was making him better but he just couldn't stop being tired. Didn't want to do nothing but sleep. He'd have to go out tomorrow. Jose didn't know enough yet to go out by himself and Padgett had gone for two days now. And it was his turn. He wanted to go find his mittens. And besides, Padgett was scared of the dark. When they was talking about him going to the Burger King tonight he was scared, but he still said he'd go.

The people who was looking for them hadn't come close to finding them, but what if they came back, started looking someplace else, started coming closer? He didn't know what they would do. No sense in trying to run, they'd just get caught. He'd been trying to think of something while he was laying there but just ended up going to sleep.

If they could just stay here till after New Year's he'd go back to the Cramer and this time he would find enough money to buy them all bus tickets to Minneapolis. He felt better deciding that. He wondered how much he would need. LaShawna would know.

It wasn't hard pretending to be asleep when LaShawna came over and put her hand on his forehead. That was all he felt like doing, being asleep.

17

Marti went to the Baxter autopsy Tuesday morning. Vik showed up, too. They both watched without gagging or even flinching. She knew she was just proving that she was a tough cop and could handle anything, but Vik was there for the same reason. A couple of rookies had even asked to attend, as if looking at Wayne's ravaged body was some kind of a test they should pass and then brag about over beer. Vik glowered at them until they went away.

Outside of the coroner's facility they both took deep gulps of fresh air and turned their faces toward the wind blowing in off the lake.

"Glad that's over," Vik said.

"Me too," Marti agreed.

"You must have seen worse in Chicago."

"It's not exactly something you get used to, just goes with the job. You had breakfast?" she asked.

"Nope."

"Want to?"

"Nope."

"Me neither."

Marti's beeper went off and they rushed to

the car to call in. There had been a purse snatching at an Osco drug store.

"We're not investigating petty theft today," Vik snapped.

"Uniform suggests you see the man," the dispatcher said. "Two children involved."

Vik blew his nose. "Don't get your hopes up," he warned as Marti turned the key in the ignition. "Didn't say they were caught."

The woman working the customer service desk directed them to the manager's office. It was a small room, too cramped for the desk, chair, and file cabinet that took up most of the space. Papers were stacked everywhere: invoices, orders, newspaper ads, pads of coupons. The manager, a short, thin man with a pot belly, paced in the narrow space between desk and door.

"You're the detectives." Lacking space to move around, he rubbed his hands on his pant legs and rearranged some of the piles of paper on his desk.

"Sit down," Vik directed.

The man seemed relieved at being given an order. "Yes, yes. Holiday season, crazy. This morning someone walks in, grabs a handful of checks and money from the register, runs out. Last night two men got in a fight and went through the window. Now this."

"What can you tell us?" Marti asked.

"Two kids, boys, maybe seven, eight years old. They'd been hanging around where the windows are at the prescription counter. We've got a toy display there. I thought that's what they were after. We got a complaint on them yesterday, put them out twice. They came back today. This time they followed a customer outside and took her purse. The officer found the purse near the loading dock out back.

Vik blew his nose. "Where is the officer?"

"She's out looking for the kids. She had a drawing of two of them."

"Which two?" Marti asked.

"The Hispanic kid and the one with the black hair and blue eyes. Even the woman who had her purse stolen thought he was cute."

They found Lupe Torres out back. "Those were our kids," she said. "I drove around the block, went over to those apartment buildings where I lost them. I don't know how they got away. And I don't know why that stupid manager didn't call us yesterday." She sounded upset.

"Hey look," Marti told her. "We know that they're okay. They're smart enough to get away from us and evade the killer, too. If he's even looking for them."

"Oh, I'm sure he is," Torres said. "I'm watching for this John Clark, too. No sign of him either. It's as if they vanish into thin air."

"What was taken from the purse?" Marti asked.

"Forty-seven dollars and nineteen cents and a bottle of erythromycin."

"Oh," Vik said. "You think one of the kids might be sick?"

"I thought of that," Lupe agreed.

Vik looked worried. "Antibiotics."

"If one of them is sick," Marti said, "that might flush them out. Maybe they'll go to a hospital."

That did nothing to relieve their concern.

Marti dropped Vik off at the precinct. He wanted to continue going through the reports and his notes. She wanted to see if Nessa was home. The woman couldn't stay out all of the time. Marti drove over to the small bungalow without feeling like she would accomplish anything. This was one case she might never solve, but if she just got to the kids before they were harmed . . .

When she pulled up across the street from the bungalow with beige siding, Nessa was at the side of the house putting a large black Labrador pup on the lead attached to the dog house.

The dog barked as Marti approached. Nessa just stood there, waiting. She was wearing a shapeless brown coat, a gray watch cap pulled over her ears. Marti wasn't sure if she was coming in or going out.

"You remember me?" Marti asked.

"Sure. You're Officer MacAlister." Even her voice sounded old.

Marti had to look closely at her oval face, at the unblemished brown skin to remind herself that Nessa was close to her own age.

"I've got a lot of problems," Marti told her. "You read the paper?"

"Not unless I run across one from Seattle, which ain't often." Nessa squinted as she spoke and there was a vagueness in her speech and attitude, as if she was old and absentminded.

Marti didn't ask why Seattle. Maybe that was part of her old lady routine, nonsense answers.

"Two more people were found dead at the Cramer," Marti said.

Nessa looked interested. "Who was they?"

"Wayne Baxter, the night clerk, and Lenny Doobee, kid who lived down the hall from Dorsey."

"Fat guy who put out them cookies?"

"Him."

Nessa forgot to act old long enough to stand straight up. She was an inch taller than Marti, not two inches shorter. Then she remembered and hunched into herself. "Strange goings on in that place."

"Real strange," Marti agreed. "Bags with chicken and dumplings left there and no telling who cooked it. Cats that disappear. Lots of strange things seem to be going on."

"You run across anyone yet named Henderson?" Nessa asked.

"No."

"Can't say for certain but it might be somebody you'd like to know."

"I'll keep an eye out for them. Man or woman?"

"Can't say. Someone Dorsey knew."

Nessa began her old-woman walk to the doorstep where she'd left a canvas bag. Marti thanked her and headed for her car. By the time she got the car started Nessa was standing in the doorway holding a fat yellow-and-white tabby.

Marti rolled down the window. "You take

good care of Samantha," she called as she drove away.

She called her lieutenant as soon as she got back to her desk. This time he was not able to help her. If a Henderson was attached to the navy base while Dorsey was there, whoever it was must have been a civilian. The name might not have anything to do with the service. She knew it was important, though, because Nessa had told her.

On impulse she called Marlena Jennings the navy nurse. She got the answering machine.

Marlena Jennings returned her call Wednesday morning.

"I've been meaning to call you," Jennings told her. "I talked to that friend I mentioned and she sent me a snapshot of Dorsey. I wanted to pass it along to you before I left for Jamaica. My plane leaves at three. You're more than welcome to pick it up if you can manage it this morning. Or do you want me to try to remember to put it in the mail?"

Marti said she'd be there in about twenty minutes.

Marlena Jennings came jogging up the walk just as Marti rang the bell. "I wanted to get a little exercise. I've been keeping an eye out for you," she said, not a bit out of breath. Her face was flushed and wisps of blond hair escaped from a bright blue cap almost the color of her eyes.

Inside, she removed a glass screen placed in front of the fireplace, poked at the logs until they flamed orange and sent sparks up the chimney. She added more wood, adjusted the damper. "I like a little bit of winter," she said. "Not three or four months of it, but a few weeks around the holidays. This is the last I'll see of it this year."

Marti settled into the thick sofa cushions. She got the impression that Marlena Jennings was lonely even though she said she was content with her life-style. While she waited for Marlena to get the photograph, she studied the abstract on the wall directly across from her.

"Here we are," Miss Jennings said. "Like that?" she asked, nodding toward the canvas.

"Is it supposed to mean anything?" Marti asked.

"Couldn't say. An elephant at the Racine Zoo painted it."

They both laughed.

Miss Jennings gave Marti an envelope with two pictures inside.

"Dorsey's hair isn't red?" Marti said.

"She didn't want to be a redhead then, dyed it black. Brown would have looked better with her coloring."

Dark hair, like her mother's. Red hair when she died, but wearing vintage dresses her mother would have dressed up in. Contradictory. She looked at the next picture. Dorsey with a group of women in white, some in navy uniforms, others in nurse's uniforms. And one of them was Adeline Greyson. She was the only one who wasn't smiling.

"My friend, Quinella, wasn't taking pictures of Dorsey," Miss Jennings said. "Dorsey happened to be part of the group. These were taken before Dorsey became engaged to her saxophone player."

"And before the entertainer got electrocuted," Marti said.

"Yes. Perhaps her family would like to have these."

Maybe the brother would. "How well did you know Adeline Greyson?"

"I take it you've met her."

Marti nodded.

"Unpleasant woman, isn't she?"

"But everyone confided in her?"

"I didn't want to say anything until you'd had a chance to meet her. She was very protective of 'her girls,' anyone who worked for her. Wouldn't let the doctors give them a hard time. Very good about lending an ear, or lending money. Young sailors, even women, are notorious for getting their paychecks and blowing them by the weekend. There's always someone out there smart enough to hold on to his money so he can loan it, with interest, of course. Adeline didn't charge any interest."

When she spoke with her, Marti had gotten the impression that Adeline Greyson either didn't like or didn't approve of Dorsey. She didn't think their relationship could have been as close or as friendly as Marlena Jennings thought it was. "How did you feel about her?"

"I didn't know her personally. She never worked with me. We worked different wards on different floors. She had a reputation for running a tight ship. No carelessness or negligence tolerated on her ward."

Miss Jennings sat cross-legged on the floor by the table, poured herself some coffee. "People are very seldom called by their first names in the military. She was. That's unusual. Sometimes I wished the girls would confide in me the way they did her. Sometimes I wondered why they'd talk to her at all. She wasn't a warm person, not maternal. Must have just had a way of getting people to open up to her. And she wasn't much older than they were. But she acted older, much more mature."

Marti looked at the snapshot again. Adeline's face was pinched, almost disapproving. Of what? She looked older than the others, but mostly because she seemed so aloof from their carefree camaraderie. Her uniform emphasized large breasts, a small waist, and full hips. She sure looked a lot different now.

"She must have been popular with the sailors," Marti said.

"The only one I know of is the one she married."

"Who sent you these pictures?"

"Quinella Jones."

"Could I talk with her?"

"Probably not. Quinella just checked into the VA hospital in Milwaukee. She's going to have thoracic surgery. Got lung cancer."

"You've kept in touch, though?"

"We have one of those odd friendships where you just hit it off and it's like you've known each other all your lives. She was my ward secretary most of my tour. She got transferred to Adeline's ward temporarily not long before I transferred out. Quinella and I were friends my entire four-year tour and still keep in touch."

"Do you remember anyone by the name of Henderson?"

"Sure, that was Adeline's maiden name. Is that important?"

"I'm not sure yet," Marti told her.

18

Marti met Vik in front of the county building the next morning. They were due in court at 9:30 A.M. Last Friday's snow was still white where it had been blown into mounds near the building. It had turned to gray-black slush along the curbs. Vik kicked at an icy mound and said, "More due tonight."

"We've already got plenty for Christmas." It was December twentieth already. She hadn't done much shopping but had ordered a computer and software for the kids. "This storm might miss us and keep to the south."

"Right. Tulips might start coming up this afternoon, too." He coughed, a dry cough that sounded more like a bark. His cold wasn't helping his disposition.

"Why don't you break down and take something for that, Jessenovik?"

"It's getting better."

"Well it sounds worse."

Vik stomped up the steps to the courthouse. By the time they reached the third floor the defense attorney had already got a continuance.

"Damned nuisance," Vik complained.

Marti was glad her whole morning wasn't tied up. "Want to drive up to Wisconsin?"

"I want to go over to The Barrister and have breakfast for the first time this week."

He fumbled around in his pocket until Marti gave him a Kleenex. If he still had an appetite his cold must not bad as it sounded.

After they ate what her daughter Joanna referred to as the "cholesterol special," Marti took Interstate 94 to Milwaukee. The hospital wasn't hard to find. It was near the stadium where the Brewers played, and she took the kids to a couple of games there every year.

The VA hospital had an old-fashioned switchboard, with cords and a board to plug them in and two operators wearing headsets. Marti stopped and watched them. She'd never seen anything like it before except in old movies.

In contrast, the elevator was so modern that a computerized voice announced the floor every time they stopped. She got lost looking for the right ward. The hallways were twisting and mazelike, stopping at a ward, or sometimes a dayroom, and once ending at a patient's room.

Quinella Jones didn't look sick at all. She was a big woman like Marti. A multicolored granny-square afghan was draped around her shoulders like a shawl. The table beside her bed was crowded with snapshots of dark-eyed, brown-skinned smiling children. Crayon and magic marker get-well greetings were taped to the wall.

"All yours?" Marti asked.

"Had two girls. Between them they've given

me thirteen grands. We have to rent a pavilion in the park to have a picnic."

Quinella Jones's laughter turned into an extended period of coughing and spitting.

"Bad lung," she explained. "I smoked two packs a day till three months ago. Always said I'd rather smoke than quit, even if it meant getting sick. I hate to admit it, but now that I am sick, that sure ain't the case."

Marti waited while Mrs. Jones put on a mask and breathed oxygen.

"So you want to know about Dorsey. Last time I saw her she was on the psych ward. They zombied them out with Thorazine in those days. And that's what she looked like, a zombie. Then they wondered why patients didn't stay on their medication. We weren't friends. I don't think Dorsey had any close friends. She knew just about everybody, and loved to party, but in spite of that, Dorsey really was a loner. I'm not sure how I can help you."

"Neither am I," Marti admitted. "But somebody killed her and it's not likely that I'll find out who it is unless I find out more about her. I'm having a hard time finding people who knew her."

"Probably because nobody did. Her people come for the body or just have her shipped home?"

"Her mother came."

"That's surprisin'. Can you tell me how she died?"

Marti shook her head.

"Was it quick?"

208

She nodded.

"Did she know?"

"I don't think so. Not for more than a few seconds."

Quinella let out her breath slowly, as if she'd been expecting to hear something worse. She lay back on the pillow, eyes squeezed shut, hands open, palms up. Marti knew she was praying. After a few minutes she opened her eyes, adjusted the bed to raise her head, and looked at Marti, trying to smile.

"Lord, the way Dorsey went on about her momma," Quinella said. "She'd prance around the dayroom and talk in a real thick New York accent. 'This is the propah way to do that. You must do this propahly, Lauri.'" There was a rattling in her chest as she coughed. "Always said how she didn't belong nowhere or just didn't fit in. Never could figure out why she felt that way. Everyone liked her."

"Was she good friends with Adeline Greyson?"

"Oh, Adeline." Quinella Jones paused, gave her a shrewd look. "That's really what you want to know, ain't it? All the gossip?"

Marti nodded.

"Well, you come to the right place. I don't know why those silly-acting young girls liked Adeline. Saw her use three of them to get to their men, then once she got 'em she didn't want 'em and threw them right back in their faces. Thing was, with so many transferring in and out folks sorta forgot, and there she'd be all folksy with 'her girls' again."

She paused, inhaled some oxygen. "She stayed friends with Dorsey longer than most. It took me awhile to figure out what she was after but it must have been that man she ended up marrying. I'm not sure how Dorsey helped, but it had to have been something to do with that band."

She put her head on the pillow and reached for the oxygen mask again, breathing hard. A woman accustomed to talking.

She took the mask off. "Guy she married was in charge of special services, booked that band in, even sent them on trips overseas. He was already married with five or six kids, but crazy about Adeline. And jealous. Course now, she was a looker." She lay back, laughed, then coughed. "I always did wonder what happened when Adeline got to keep him and couldn't give him back. Course this was a little different. An officer, not an enlisted man, and one with plenty of money. Never could figure out how that man could support a family that size and drive a Mercedes and just seem to have money to burn."

"He was in charge of the show where that singer got electrocuted?" Marti said.

"Right there when it happened, too. Dorsey wasn't never right after that. Got real withdrawn. Never knowed her to laugh again. She might have snapped out of it if Weeks hadn't gone and got himself killed. Rough on both of them, that Julie King dying. Real bad break, happening when it did. They had just arranged to go audition for some music company right after that concert. Dorsey said Weeks just knew they were going to make it real big. Weeks wasn't much of a drinker. Didn't even smoke pot with Dorsey. He must have really been torn up by what happened to go out and do both the same night. And that car. Wrong of them to put it right at the gate where Dorsey had to see it. One look and she just went off."

"Was Adeline married by then?" Marti asked, mostly out of curiosity. It was still difficult to reconcile the wrinkled, arthritic woman with the picture of the busty, leggy nurse that Marlena Jennings had shown her. It was hard to believe that the picture had been taken only fifteen years ago.

Quinella stayed on the oxygen for a few minutes. "No. Greyson got a Mexican divorce about a month later. They got married right away. Course Dorsey knew Adeline was pumping her for information, but she said most of the questions Adeline asked were about that band. Said it wasn't nothin' important, just silly stuff like where they had been or what hotel they stayed in and she was always asking for pictures of that Julie King. Seemed odd though, her being interested. Adeline didn't like blacks."

Quinella sighed, plucking at the afghan. "I told Dorsey about the other guys Adeline had messed around with. We had this runnin' bet on Greyson. Whenever Dorsey thought it sounded like Adeline would get him she'd change the odds. Right before all of this happened, well she was setting them at something like twenty-five to one against. Adeline was thirty-five. Greyson was a good ten years older, all the other guys she had dated were real young. I got the impression Adeline might've been kinda wild in bed."

She rested again, not using the oxygen. "Could you pour me some a that juice over there? I'd offer you some but they don't allow it. Like cancer is some kinda germ."

Marti poured juice from a blue plastic pitcher into a glass with a straw.

"Ah, thank you. Coupla days now and I won't be knowing nothin' or drinkin' nothin', maybe not till the weekend, assuming that I wake up. We used to have this joke about them always gettin' you offa the operatin' table alive and not losing you till you got to intensive care. I'm sure hoping I can make it back to this room."

Listening to the cough and seeing how often she needed the oxygen, Marti hoped that surgery would be enough. "Was Dorsey gullible? Did she trust Adeline?"

"Dorsey was fun. She thought life was some kind of game. She always made remarks about being a loser, but I think that was all tied up with her leaving home and saying she didn't fit in nowhere. Dorsey's biggest fault was probably what got her killed. She didn't take things seriously when she needed to. Trusted people too much. If there was any kind of misunderstanding it had to be her fault. Took the blame for everything. Always saying 'I'm sorry.'"

The rumbling cough stopped her again. Almost breathless, she said, "Like with Adeline, so what if Adeline was using her, big deal, who could that hurt, who cared? Adeline was fun. And she went after a man like it was a game she had to win and then gave back the prize. That's what was in it for Dorsey, finding out what Adeline would do if she won and kept the prize. Too bad she never got to know. I wouldn't mind knowin' myself."

Quinella began gasping. "Any of this helping you? I sure want you to find out who killed Dorsey. When you find whoever did it, you be sure to let me know."

Quinella looked cheerful but exhausted. Marti thanked her for her help, leaving just as she was reaching again for the oxygen.

Light snow was falling as she drove back to Lincoln Prairie. It tapered off just over the state line. By the time she got back to the precinct the sun was shining.

Vik was working on some kind of tick sheet. Sometimes he played games with whatever statistics they had.

"Don't tell me," she said. "The odds on us finding three different sets of prints in Dorsey's room are seventy-six and a half to one."

"No," Vik said. "Nothing that good. We might have something else on John Clark. Pizza Hut this time."

"Another delivery man robbed? Where?"

"Champaign."

"Then he's still in Illinois, but heading south," Marti said. "I take it he didn't get caught."

"Not yet, MacAlister. Be patient," Vik chided. "Clark's not going to stay lucky much longer.

He got fifty-three dollars this time. Might think he's on a roll."

She sat down and pulled off her boots, changed to her service oxfords. "And he might think this has played out and try something different the next time."

"No way," Vik scoffed. "Guy's not that smart. I called down to Champaign. Looks like the same M.O. as Kankakee. Apartment complex that rents mostly to college kids. The guy was wearing a ski mask and an olive parka. Sound familiar? And a storage room had been broken into. Looks like he was staying there."

"So what's with the statistics?" Marti asked. At this rate it could take all winter to catch Clark. The only reason anyone was taking the pizza delivery robberies seriously was because of the possible link to a homicide.

"Just trying to figure out where he might strike next."

Marti noticed a cake tin on Slim's desk. She got a whiff of mint when she opened it. His mother had made candy cane cookies. She helped herself. "What's your best guess, Jessenovik?"

"Carbondale's next."

"Bet it's Normal," she countered, only because that was a college town, like Champaign.

"Nah. He'd have to head south," Vik countered.

"You could be right," she admitted.

She relayed what Quinella had told her. "We need to get our hands on Clark, get the tissue matches, decide if he's the one. Meanwhile I think we're going to have to take another look at this Julie King accident. Maybe the Weeks accident, too. If either one was a homicide, then Dorsey's death could be connected with it."

"Wonderful. Check out the past," Vik groaned. "We can't even find out what Dorsey did last month. The real key could be finding out how she got that money. I've come up empty. No government windfall from the VA or social security or any state agency. Nothing."

Marti got on the phone, called the lieutenant again. A half hour later she had the Colorado address for Greyson's ex-wife. "Adeline said he was in Colorado. Didn't say that's where the ex was. Maybe that's why she was in such an unfriendly mood. No harm in confirming that he's there and asking him if his wife's been in touch with her old friend Dorsey."

One of Greyson's sons answered the phone. He sounded like he was in his late teens. Marti identified herself but didn't say why she was calling. When she hung up she said, "He's there, but not home right now. He'll call as soon as he comes in. Meanwhile, I think I'll pay Adeline another visit."

Before she left, the phone rang. Vik answered. "Man says he's Greyson," he said, handing her the phone.

"Mr. Greyson. Hope I'm not interrupting your vacation but I need to ask you a couple of questions about Lauretta Dorsey."

"Dorsey?" He didn't sound old or young either. Moderate voice with East Coast inflections. "Can't say the name rings a bell."

"She was a friend of Juliette Kingsland. Julie King. The singer who died."

"Oh. Yes." He still sounded vague. "Look. I just can't place this Dorsey at all. Let me think about it, give you a call back." After he took down her name and number he said, "Why are you calling?"

"Because Lauretta Dorsey is dead."

"Dead? What happened? What has this got to do with me?" He sounded genuinely puzzled.

"I think it could have something to do with your wife."

"My . . . um, Frannie?"

That must be the first wife.

"No. Adeline. They knew each other."

"Oh. Well. If I think of anything I'll be in touch."

She hung up and stared at the receiver.

19

Marti took the scenic route when she went to see Adeline Greyson. She needed a little time to relax and ruminate.

It was a pleasant drive, past farmland first, wide expanses of snow drifting against fences and fields with snowmobile tracks. Fallow land gave way to broad lawns with shoveled walkways. As she got closer to the town where Adeline Greyson lived, the roads were more heavily traveled, the snow banked against the curbs became splattered with mud and gravel thrown up by the plows.

The house with the wide porch where the Greysons lived seemed isolated today. It sat back from the street, separated from neighbors by a lot on either side. Although there was no fence, Marti had a feeling that nobody trespassed. The Greysons must own all of the property. All three lots were a good size; someone would have developed the adjoining two by now if the Greysons didn't own them. Nobody had been out since last night's snow and Marti made fresh tracks as she went to the front door.

There was no answer when she rang the bell.

She persisted because she had seen an upstairs curtain twitch. After almost ten minutes an angry voice called from inside.

"What do you want? Go away."

"It's Detective MacAlister. I need to talk with you again."

"Well, I don't want to talk to you. I don't want to talk to anyone." Adeline hadn't been friendly the last time Marti was here. Now she was downright hostile.

"This is a murder investigation, Mrs. Greyson," Marti reminded her, although legally Adeline did not have to let her in.

After a few moments the door opened and Marti followed Adeline inside. Adeline walked stiffly, as if her back was bothering her.

The living room was unchanged since her last visit, but dulled by a layer of dust that muted the walnut tables. Teal blue curtains were drawn. The air seemed even hotter than before and again Marti asked to slip off her coat as Adeline Greyson waved her toward a chair.

Mrs. Greyson was wearing another paisley skirt and scarf outfit, this time in fawns and tans with a brown blouse. Her makeup had been applied with care. Every curl was in place and stiff with hair spray. Marti got the impression she might be expecting someone. Or maybe she was just waiting for her husband to return from his trip.

The wedding picture caught her eye again. A joyous, smiling Adeline, ecru veil and baby's breath. Bernard, somber, looking younger than the bride even though she didn't look wrinkled or old then. Her arm was around his waist. His arms were at his sides. That and the pinched expression on his face made him seem less than an eager bridegroom. Marti thought of what Quinella had said. If there was any prize in Adeline's game she couldn't see what it was.

Adeline saw that Marti was looking at her wedding picture. "I waited so long," she said, sounding like her throat was dry.

"Your first marriage?" Marti asked.

"Not something to be lightly entered."

"Religious ceremony?"

"Civil. Because of her."

The first wife. "Oh. Then your husband was married before. Any stepchildren?"

"Five. She bred like a cow."

Marti was curious why Adeline still felt so much animosity toward the first wife. She wondered why Bernard was in Colorado instead of here, especially at this time of year, but that wasn't why she had come. "I need to ask you a few more questions about Lauretta Dorsey."

"That one," her voice rasped.

"How long did you know her?"

Adeline shrugged. "A few years."

"You worked on the orthopedic ward."

"One of them. Head nurse, second shift," she corrected.

"Dorsey worked with your patients?"

"She was a PT tech."

"So far all I know is that Dorsey was competent, friendly, outgoing, energetic, dedicated, and well-liked."

"A wonderful human being." Spoken with bitterness.

Why did Adeline dislike Dorsey? She apparently had used her in some way to get Bernard. Maybe what she got wasn't quite what she wanted. But she couldn't blame Dorsey for that. "Why don't you agree with that, Mrs. Greyson?"

"She was a tramp. Slept with every man who could move, legs or not."

But Adeline slept around too, according to Quinella Jones.

"I liked her at first. Until I found out."

"Found out what?"

"She stole. Little thief."

"Stole from you?"

Laughter, dry, harsh. "Oh yes, from me."

"What did she steal?"

Mrs. Greyson looked at her, eyes narrowing. "Nothing of importance," she said. "Nothing valuable."

She was lying, Marti knew, but from the tight-lipped expression on her face, she was not to be challenged. At least not today.

"Did she ever confide in you, Mrs. Greyson?"

"Sure. They all did. When you're over thirty and still not married they all think you want to be somebody's mother. Or need to be, since nobody wants you as a wife."

Resentment. Had she ever done anything with those confidences? Told others? There was something about her attitude now that suggested that she could have spread rumors, told secrets, without anyone realizing it was her.

"What did Dorsey tell you?"

Hazel eyes appraised her for a minute. As she waited, Marti noted how quiet it was, how muted the sound of a car horn was, how distant the sound of a woman calling "Jason" again and again.

"She talked about her mother, mostly. They all talked about family. Or home. Or men. Dorsey's mother was a mental case, but you know how those wealthy families are. Send them to a private sanitarium for a few months every year or so and say it's a trip to Europe or the Caribbean. Keep them on tranqs. That kind of thing. Her mother had bad mood swings. Docile one minute, violent and throwing things the next."

"Did she abuse her children?"

"If living with that is abusive. Nothing physical." She sounded disappointed.

"Is that all she talked about? What about the man she was going to marry?"

Mrs. Greyson looked away, knuckles getting white as she clasped her hands. "Nothing personal, officer, but I didn't approve. Dorsey resented me for that. Said her mother didn't like the idea of a mixed marriage either. As if that meant I was supposed to."

"Did knowing that her mother had a history of mental illness ever make you think that Dorsey might have a similar problem?"

"Didn't act crazy. Crafty maybe. Like a fox."

She was sitting straight up now, back rigid and away from the chair, shoulders stiff, hands in her lap with the fingers pressed to her palms.

"Why do you say that?"

Again the look, tight-lipped and silent.

"What kind of work did your husband do, Mrs. Greyson?"

"What?"

She repeated the question.

"He worked for special services." She began a visual inspection of the room, looking everywhere but at Marti. She didn't want to talk about this.

"Recreation, not spying. In charge of everything from day care to bowling facilities. Important reponsibilities. A critical position, essential for morale, especially with so many passing through who were coming back from Vietnam."

Marti translated that to mean that his rank and position had been much more important to his wife than to the navy. If the build-up meant the same thing in the military as it did on the force, Bernard Greyson was an obscure pencil pusher who signed his name with a flourish on documents that nobody took time to read.

"Did he have anything to do with entertainment?"

Another hesitation. Her eyes restlessly looked about the room. "That was just one area of his responsibilities."

"When they had that accident, the woman who got electrocuted—"

"We were dating then. Bernard never spoke of it."

One hand gripped the other, knees together. There was something she didn't want to say.

"Was your husband divorced then?"

"Not yet."

Okay for Mrs. Greyson to date him though, but Dorsey was immoral.

"Were you there the night it happened? Was Bernard?"

"I never went to things like that. Wouldn't know about my husband." Tight-lipped again. She was lying.

"So you didn't go?" Quinella said she was there.

"No." Jaws clenched.

"Did Bernard go?"

"I said no!"

Angry now. Marti backed off. "Did Dorsey go?"

She looked away, inspecting the closed curtains. "Kind of thing she'd do."

"Did she say anything about it afterwards?"

Mrs. Greyson shook her head.

"Did she seem affected by it at all?"

"Dorsey? Of course not. Fun-loving girl, that one."

Nothing like what Marlena Jennings and Quinella Jones had said. "This entertainer's death had no effect on Dorsey at all that you were aware of?"

"No."

"Were Dorsey and Julie King friends?"

"I wouldn't know." She stood up. Interview at an end. Getting too close? To what? Her smile was triumphant. Mrs. Greyson was a woman with secrets. It could be something important. It could be material to Dorsey's death. As Adeline escorted her to the door, Marti had the feeling that there had been times during their conversation when she had been talking about one thing and Adeline another. If that were true, she didn't know how she would ever find out what the unspoken things were all about.

Marti retraced her steps in the snow and got into her car. She took the interstate back. The sky was clouding up. They might get more snow.

By the time Marti got back to her desk, the area just above her eyebrows felt like someone was using his thumbs to try to push his way in. She rarely got headaches and wasn't sure if this was from inadequate sleep or her repeated attempts to sort through what she'd been told the last couple of days to determine what, if anything, was significant to the Dorsey case. Maybe it was just late hours and too little sleep. They had to catch up with those children soon.

Vik was sniffling when she walked into the squad room. "If you don't do something about that cold—"

"I'm taking Contac," he snapped. "And Tylenol."

"Oh, that's just great. Ignore it until it's completely out of hand and then O.D. on every over-the-counter product you can get your hands on."

She kicked at her wastebasket, heard a satisfying metallic ring and kicked it again.

"Interview went that good?" Vik said, leaning back in his chair.

She went over to the coffee pot, got the last half cup. It tasted like melted rubber. "Who made this?"

Vik didn't answer.

"Haven't we told you to stay away from this coffee pot?" she demanded.

Vik shrugged. "Everybody else drank it and nobody said anything."

"Because it took their breath away," she said, dumping it into the spider plant. The liquid seeped out of the bottom of the flower pot and dripped on the carpet. "This is where it went. Look at that. Must be another dozen of those baby plants sprouting. Damned thing's going to take over the office. Bet it can't get enough of your coffee."

Kicking the wastebasket again she sat down. At least her headache was abating. "Nothing on those kids?"

Vik shook his head.

Marti began rotating her neck slowly to ease the tension. "I think we have to pursue this Julie King electrocution. I don't know if it has anything to do with Dorsey, but something isn't right. Adeline Greyson really bothers me. She did not like Dorsey. And Adeline lied to me about not being there the night it happened."

She pulled out her copy of the investigating officer's reports. "Too bad Greyson's in Colorado. I'd like to ask him a few questions."

"It'll have to wait until he gets back. Let me see that report," Vik said. "Frank was a good cop." As he read it he said, "Doesn't sound like he was thrilled about dropping the investigation. Ordinarily the military is cooperative. Maybe it was because of the war, maybe it was just whoever they spoke with. Hmmmm. Charles Smith. Says we couldn't justify the questioning of military personnel."

Marti realized she was drumming her fingers on the desk because she couldn't curl them around a coffee cup. Must be caffeine withdrawal. Joanna would have a fit if she knew.

"Let's see if we can track down the person who was contacted," Vik said. "See why they wouldn't give us access."

The lieutenant came up with another blank. According to his contact in Cleveland, the person who refused to authorize the questioning of military personnel didn't exist at this installation as far as the U.S. Navy was concerned.

"Okay, MacAlister. I can see your nose twitching. This one is fifteen years old. We got three bodies within the past two weeks and someone out there who may do it again. This will keep."

"The *News-Times* reporter who covered the case," Marti said. "Herb Mansfield. I wonder if he had a contact on base."

Lupe Torres came in just as they were getting ready to go home. She was in uniform. Moisture glistened on her jacket. Short, dark bangs hung below the visored cap.

Marti looked out of the window. A scattering of tiny snowflakes drifted past the window. "Got any good news?" she asked.

"No." Lupe straddled a chair. "I thought about that hamburger again and went back to the Burger King. Teenager behind the counter asked me if we'd found the kids yet. When I said no she got a little upset. Seems the black kid used to come in and give her some change, she'd give him five of whatever she had that'd been sitting out the longest."

"Five?" Vik slammed the palm of his hand on his desk. "Why five?"

"First time he went in there he said that's what he needed and he showed her how much money he had, about a dollar in change. Pretty good little con artist."

"Why was she upset?" Marti asked.

"Hasn't seen him in two days now. Brought his blue-eyed partner in with him a couple of times. Now old blue eyes is coming in by himself, says the other kid's got a cold."

Vik got up and went to the coffee pot.

"Empty," Marti reminded him. She winked at Lupe. "You got lucky tonight. Missed out on heartburn."

Vik scowled at her.

"I don't do coffee," she said.

Lupe laughed. Marti joined in. Vik almost smiled, even though nothing was funny.

20

Marti woke up with a headache Friday morning. By the time she arrived at the precinct she was convinced that the throbbing at her temples was caused by an allergy to the low-fat cheese sauce in the turkey-and-vegetable casserole Joanna cooked for supper the night before. It tasted good, but if she didn't continue to put up some resistance everything they ate would be good for them.

They had gotten another case during the night. A sixty-seven-year-old woman had stabbed her son-in-law because he was beating her daughter. The woman had only lived with them for three months. Now she was in the hospital, heart attack, and he was in the morgue. "At least the wife didn't do it," Vik had commented. "She'll be home with the kids for Christmas."

Now Vik looked as lousy as she felt. His eyes were red and the dark pouches underneath were puffier than usual. It had been his turn to check out the Cramer last night. He had gotten even less sleep than she had. "Herb Mansfield?" he asked. "Today?"

She pulled out the folder with the forms she hadn't felt like filling out at three this morning. "I guess."

"The old lady could have picked a better time to knife him," Vik complained. "Middle of the night. Why are people compelled to do their killing in the middle of the night? When is the last time we got a homicide call at two in the afternoon?"

"August. That pool room stabbing."

"See what I mean? Four months ago. Total lack of consideration."

She sniffed, didn't catch even a whiff of Obsession for Men. "Slim and Cowboy been in here this morning?"

"Cowboy stopped by and made coffee. Told me to tell you Merry Christmas. They've got a heavy court schedule. Remember the porn shop they closed down last summer? Finally coming to trial."

Marti had filled her mug while he was talking. She inhaled the aroma. "Thank God." There were doughnuts, too. Calorie, cholesterol, and caffeine heaven.

Vik threw his folder of blank forms into his IN-basket. "Let's hit the road if we're going up to Wisconsin. I haven't seen old Herb in three, four years now."

She was looking forward to the visit if not the drive. Good reporters were a lot like cops. Squirreled away all kinds of irrelevant information on the off chance that something might lead them to paydirt.

It was a little after ten when they approached

Manfield's cottage. Smoke was wafting from the chimney in a lazy stream. There was something inviting about the warm fire Marti knew would be waiting inside.

"Matthew," Mansfield said, throwing his arm around Vik.

Vik was taller than Herb by a few inches but seemed surprised at having to look down at him.

"My God, it's good to see you." Herb gripped Vik's hand, pumping his arm up and down. He put his arm about Vik's shoulders as they went inside. "How's Mildred?"

Vik held out the bag he had brought. "Stopped by the house on my way out. She thought you'd like this. Made some dumplings and some of those beef-and-potato pastries and froze them last week. Got some other stuff in there, too."

"Always said you got the best cook of the bunch when you married the youngest Kowalski. How's the kids?"

Vik filled him in.

"Two grandkids!" Mansfield led them to the two easy chairs near the fireplace and brought in another chair from the kitchen area, straddling it over Vik's protest.

Herb stroked his beard. "So, you didn't come here for small talk. It's the Kingsland case, ain't it? I was going to call you next time I went to town. Got my files out on that one a couple days ago." He reached for his pipe.

"Actually," he said, waving his arms toward a stack of boxes, "I had 'em in there. Took a while to find 'em. Thought there was something interesting about that case." He tapped his forehead. "Memory just ain't what it used to be. Needs a few nudges every now and then."

"Find anything?" Vik asked.

"More like what I didn't find. I thought I'd check on who gave that gag order. I knew we didn't get a name but somethin' kept nudging at me. Seems we *did* get a name, Charles Smith."

Vik looked at her. That was the same name the lieutenant couldn't trace yesterday.

"Just couldn't track him down," Herb said. He pulled his leather pouch from his pocket and began filling his pipe with tobacco. "Couldn't find any Charles Smith on base who mighta had something to do with issuing that kind of order. Nor a Chuck or a Carl or even a Charlie."

Herb lit his pipe. "Got this note that when my editor tried to get them to change their minds they wouldn't."

He chuckled. "The military way, ain't it. Can't find hide nor hair of someone who was supposed to have given the order but no way in hell would anyone countermand it. You two thinking about looking into the Kingsland and Weeks cases?"

"Maybe," Vik conceded.

"Let me fix you some coffee. Made some banana bread too, just getting cool."

Crockery rattled for a few minutes and Herb came over to them with two fat, steaming mugs, then a plate of sliced bread loaded with walnuts and a saucer with a soft stick of butter.

"Gag order put a stop to everything. Be almost impossible to find out anything now. I think they would have taken a different look at the Weeks accident if the body hadn't already been shipped back to Jamaica. Even your man wasn't satisfied with the verdict."

"Why not?" Vik asked, leaning forward. He seemed as eager to dig into those old accidents as she was. If she wasn't so tired today she'd probably feel more enthusiastic. As it was, it just seemed like something unfinished that had to be resolved.

"Well, Weeks's blood alcohol level was so high that there was no question of what caused the accident. He was drunk, alone in the car, and smashed it up so bad that both he and the car were mangled. So they let them ship the body out of the country, released the car so the base could put it on display and then a couple weeks later got a toxicology report saying there was something different about the alcohol."

Vik was at the edge of his chair. "And?"

"High methylate content or something. Stuff he drank was bottled liquor with an alcohol content that was more like bad moonshine. Case was really hushed up then. I only know about it 'cause Frank and me were buddies."

They stayed long enough to eat smoked salmon for lunch. Marti listened while Vik and Herb talked about Vik's dad. Vik didn't often speak of his father. When he did it was usually to contrast police work in his father's day with the way it was now. Marti had assumed they hadn't been close.

As she listened to him now, recalling the time his dad caught the kids who were stealing cigarettes from a gas station, and the night he helped the feds track down an escaped felon, and then the time he had to go to a neighbor and speak with him about not hitting his wife again, she realized that Vik must have been very close to his father.

When Mansfield began talking about different cases Vik had solved and said how proud his dad would have been, Vik smiled for the first time in days.

"My old man knew the people, knew the streets, the neighborhoods. He said he did a lot of guesswork solving cases, but I don't think that's what it was," Vik said. "Times were just different then. There wasn't any big crime in Lincoln Prairie. We went three years once without a homicide. Can't go much more than a couple of weeks anymore."

And Vik missed those times. Missed his father. And he thought her hunches and intuition were better suited to then than now.

Marti didn't say anything as they drove back to Lincoln Prairie. She was becoming convinced that if they solved the old case they'd get closer to the current one, but she didn't have enough pieces yet to put the puzzle together.

When they got back to the precinct, Vik sent a uniform to the archives for the Weeks file before she got a chance.

He flipped through the pages, grunted a few

times and closed the folder, pushing it toward her.

The same cop had investigated Weeks's and Julie King's deaths. A methyl or wood alcohol had been identified in Weeks's toxicology reports. Weeks had gone to the Kit Kat Klub, Marti noticed. "That club still open?"

Vik shook his head.

Weeks had ordered three mixed drinks, gotten into an agitated conversation with one of the other men he was with, tossed off the third drink, and left. When questioned, the waitress felt that Weeks could have consumed more alcohol than she served him. At least six pitchers of beer had been brought to the table while he was there, and lots of times the sailors drank from each other's glasses.

"Weeks was at that club with five sailors. One of them was Bernard Greyson."

"Makes sense," Vik said. "Greyson booked the band on base. They must have had a lot to talk about. Replacing Julie King. When he could set up another tour."

"I suppose," Marti agreed. "But I sure wish Greyson was in town." His statement didn't differ from those of the other four sailors, which concurred with what the waitress said.

"Doesn't say who he was talking with just before he left." She went through the statements again. "Nobody's sure what was said or why he got angry. They all agree that the last thing he said was 'We'll see about that,' and he walked out."

Frustrated, she put the photocopy of the file

back into the folder. "Our first priority is finding these kids. I think I'll call Colorado, though, find out when Bernard Greyson will be coming back."

A woman answered the telephone. "Bernard?"

"Your ex-husband, ma'am."

"Yes, I know, but why are you calling him here?"

"I'd like to know when he'll be returning to Illinois."

"Returning to Illinois?"

"Yes, ma'am," she said.

"Well, um. I don't know. Let me have him get back to you."

When Marti left her name and number the woman said, "Why on earth would the police want to talk with Bernard?"

"A woman was killed here, ma'am. Name of Dorsey. Lauretta Dorsey. We think Bernard might have known her about fifteen years ago."

"While he was stationed at the base?"

"Yes, ma'am."

"I see."

Marti waited.

After a pause the woman said, "Well, his second wife might be a better person to talk to."

"I have, ma'am."

"Did she tell you Bernard was here?"

"Yes, ma'am."

"I see," the woman said again.

Marti was getting annoyed. She knew it was because she was tired. She tried to be patient while she waited for wife number one to say something else.

"Well. Umm. I'll have to tell Bernard to get back to you on this."

"Sometime today, ma'am. When I talked to him before—"

"You talked to him?"

"Yes, ma'am." She picked up a pencil, tried to snap it in half with one hand the way Vik did. She couldn't.

"Here?"

She had known that would be the next question.

"Yes, ma'am. Called, talked with one of your sons. He had his father call me back."

"I see."

Marti propped the phone under her chin and used both hands to break the pencil.

She was reaching for another one when wife number one said, "I will have Bernard call you. Today if I can."

Marti put the unbroken pencil on her desk. "Weird group out there. First Bernard sounds like he doesn't know much more than his name. Now the first wife does the same."

"Must be the air." Vik said. "Thinner up there."

"Whatever it is, Adeline is much more talkative. If only she didn't lie."

The first wife was certainly friendlier. Puzzled, as Bernard had been, but friendly.

Snow flurries were visible in the darkness outside the squad room windows when Denise Stevens came in.

"Work late?" Marti asked.

"No regular hours on this job," Denise said. She removed her gloves but left her hat on and unbuttoned her coat. When she sat down she rubbed her eyes.

"Any good news?" Marti said.

Denise shook her head. "Not enough good news in juvenile. By the time we see them the bad news is already well entrenched." She sounded weary. "Got something for you on your kids, though."

Vik put his hands over his ears, then straightened up in his chair and sat back, waiting.

"I'm sure we've got a positive I.D. on this one." She showed Marti the artist's sketch of the little black boy. "George Sanders. I've been calling around, sending the pictures out. Social worker in St. Louis thought this looked like a kid who belonged to a family she had worked with." Denise looked at the coffee pot but didn't seem to have the energy to get up.

Marti fixed her a cup.

"Thanks, MacAlister. Long week."

"You're telling me."

Denise put her hands around the cup to warm them. "The reason this social worker remembered the kid is because the mother got killed by the boyfriend last August. As far as she knew, all three kids had been placed with an aunt. I asked her to check on it. Kids took off right after it happened. Nobody knows where they are."

"Their family doesn't know where they are?"

Vik said. "Three kids and everyone just doesn't know where they are? And it didn't occur to anyone to report them missing?"

"Vik," Marti snapped. "You know the odds on getting a handle on kids from out of state? These are juveniles. We don't have any system in place to correlate information among states. All juvenile records are sealed." To Denise she said, "Thanks. You must have put in a lot of hours."

"These are kids," Vik yelled. "Little kids who go to school and come home and play in the snow. Why wasn't anyone told they were missing? Didn't anyone notice?"

Marti thought a better question might be why did they leave.

Denise turned to Vik. "Look, Jessenovik. These are throwaways. I don't like that any more than you do and yes, I can think of a lot of people who are responsible. That isn't going to do these kids any good. Fact is, there might not be any way to help them. After their families get through with them the system gets them. What one starts the other finishes. The end of the line is prison or the morgue. Damn few of them escape both."

Denise stared at the dark liquid in the styrofoam cup. Marti tapped her finger against her terrarium cactus and Vik broke a couple of pencils with one hand.

"Now," Denise said, sipping the coffee, "you've got a couple of problems on your hands. Five kids, not three."

Vik exploded. "Where could five kids be?

We've looked everywhere. No way we've got five kids out there."

"What else?" Marti said. From the queasiness developing in her stomach she knew she didn't want to hear any more.

Denise drained the cup.

"More?" Marti asked.

"No. That'll keep me alert enough to drive home."

"What else?" Marti asked again.

"The fight, when the mother was killed. They were arguing because the boyfriend had gotten a niece she was raising pregnant."

Marti went over to Cowboy's desk, got a bottle of Tums that he kept in the drawer. "And?"

"So there's George, aged nine, his sister Cecile who's ten, and this cousin LaShawna, thirteen."

"Who is pregnant," Marti said.

Vik's eyebrows had come together in a scowl but he said nothing.

"And the other two little boys?" Marti said.

"Yes," Denise said. "I have no idea of who they are yet. No kids fitting their description have been reported missing and nothing has turned up from distributing the flyers."

"Did Lupe Torres tell you one of them is probably sick?" Marti asked.

"I know. When you find them"—Denise said when, not if, but Marti wasn't sure any of them believed it—"Lincoln Prairie General will put them in a room together. Best place for them to be over the holidays. The nurses will make a big fuss over them. Don't send any of them to the juvenile facility, don't let any caseworker from DCFS take any of them. The hospital. Together. Until we can sort things out."

After Denise left, Marti sat and watched the snow blow. She had heard of worse, seen worse, she reminded herself.

"Nobody kills five children," Vik said.

"A man in Chicago set fire to all five of his," she reminded him. "Nothing new about children dying."

"That's not all that worries me," Vik admitted. "This man kills methodically, without passion. That's the kind that can kill again and again. I think they might be as sane as I am. I'm just not sure they have a conscience."

Without speaking they pulled out the files again.

It was almost eleven when she got home. The house was quiet but there was a light on in the kitchen. Joanna was at the table rolling out pastry.

"What's that going to be?" Marti asked. At fourteen, Joanna was already as tall as she was.

"Pecan tarts," Joanna said.

Marti sat down, yawning. She rubbed at her eyes.

"I'll fix you some sassafras tea," Joanna said, wiping flour on her jeans as she went to the stove. "Sleep deprivation," she added as Marti yawned again. "With these hours you've been working, Sharon and I have been trying to decide the best time for Christmas dinner."

"Middle of the afternoon," Marti said. Vik was right. Everything important happened at night. "Didn't you have a basketball game this evening? Aren't you tired?"

"No, winning's a real hype." Joanna brought two mugs and a teapot to the table. "The roots need to steep for a few minutes."

By the time the tea was ready she'd be asleep.

"I'm using grandma's recipe for the tarts," Joanna told her. "The one with the cream cheese crust. I found the one for fried pies, too."

"Fried apple pies," Marti said. "And you're making them? Healthful fried pies, right?"

"Probably not. But I'm substituting canola oil for lard. My God, lard. It's a wonder you're still alive."

Marti gave Joanna's braid a tug. "It's going to be nice to come home to some fried pies and pecan tarts. No way I'll miss this Christmas dinner. Does this mean you'll have just one tart and one fried pie, too?"

Joanna added honey to the tea and poured. "I suppose that just one day a year we can all sit around and clog up our arteries. Maybe the memories are more important."

"They are," Marti told her, glad Joanna had figured that out for herself.

21

Nessa waited until after midnight before getting ready to go out, same as always. She switched on the light in the empty bedroom, then the room she slept in. She always kept lights on in the kitchen and living room. They were always on in the basement, too. What furniture there was, only what she needed, was pushed against the wall. There were no curtains, just shades, and she had taken off all of the closet and cabinet doors as well as the doors to each room. No way nobody could come in and hide anywhere while she was gone. Samantha was curled up like a striped yellow ball on the counter in the kitchen. The gray cat was napping in the corner.

She got Dorsey's letter and the emerald ring, pushed them down into the lining of her coat, and put it on. Instead of her heavy, fur-lined boots, she put on some that would be better for running. Two pair of socks should keep her feet from getting cold.

She took the puppy outside, hooked him to the chain by the dog house. He got along better with the dog in the yard behind her, and didn't bark unless someone came on her property. Had to keep the big dog inside, getting old and cranky, barked too much out of doors. Both dogs got along with the cats well enough.

The moon was so high it seemed almost as bright outside as in when she closed the back door and walked around to the front of the house. Lots of folks had strung Christmas lights around their houses and on bushes and trees. There was a Santa and a snowman lit up in the front yard next door. Besides that, most people kept their porch lights on all night. Outside, this much light made her nervous. Too many people could look outside and see her. Outside, she felt safer where it was dark and people were less likely to notice her. She walked fast, leaving footprints where a little snow had fallen earlier.

She didn't feel safe until she got a few blocks away to where the streets were mostly dark except for street lights. Once there she slowed down, surrounded by darkness and silence and night. There was just her night walks now. She missed having someone to talk to now that Dorsey was gone, missed having someone to cook for. Always had liked to cook.

She headed for the Cramer, same as she had ever since that lady cop told her someone else had been killed there. Bumped into him, she had, the killer, but wouldn't ever be able to tell no one who he was, never looked at him. Shoulda watched where he was going, coming up the stairs like that, turning into the hallway and almost knocking her down. Her being there musta been what kept him from killin' Dorsey that night. Stalked Dorsey, he did, comin' back till he caught her alone. And only one thing coulda made Dorsey let him in. It had to be someone she knew.

Now she kept to the dark places, knowing the streets and the alleys where she'd be safe till she got near the Cramer. Then she walked nearer the street lights where he could see her, glad when she saw his feet as she passed him standing in a doorway, listenin' till she heard his footsteps behind her.

She took off her gloves, felt the weight of the knife in her special pocket but didn't think she'd need it, took the whistle on the chain around her neck and put it in her mouth, gripping it with her teeth. She led him into the alley behind the hotel, made like she twisted her ankle, hobbled over to the dumpster. She was standing there when he came up behind her, twisted away before he could strike out at her, and grabbed his arm. She twisted his wrist until he was on his knees.

She had almost forced him to submission when she slipped on the ice and fell. She began blowing the whistle, and its shrill scream filled her ears as her head hit something hard. A loud rushing noise filled her mind. She felt like she was falling forward and wondered why, since she was already lying on the ground.

22

When the telephone rang, Marti woke up all at once. She jumped up and looked around, saw the Christmas tree lights and realized she had fallen asleep in the chair. The phone rang again and she went over to the sofa, picked up the receiver, and sat down.

"Yes." She had gone to the Cramer. Vik had too. They'd gotten their turns confused. Then she came home and sat down to look at the tree.

"Officer MacAlister?"

"Speaking."

"Sorry to wake you."

She looked at her watch, 3:15 A.M.

"This is Lincoln Prairie General. Emergency room."

Hospital. The kids were home when she got in. The other kids. George. "What is it?"

"We've got an old woman here. Won't tell us her name, says she's called Nessa."

"Nessa. Is she okay?"

"Might have a concussion. She slipped on the ice. Real obnoxious. She gave us your card and demanded that we call you."

"I'll be right there," Marti told her, wide awake.

The waiting room at the hospital was crowded. One baby was squalling, another was too lethargic to cry. Marti nodded to the uniform standing behind a man in a wheelchair who had his knee sliced open and a belt tied around his thigh to control the bleeding. Vik was slumped in a chair in the corner, eyes closed. She went over and sat next to him.

"Who called you?"

"Precinct. Hospital called there first," he said without opening his eyes.

"You know what happened?"

"No. Thought you would. She's your nut case."

Marti ignored that. "What have we got?"

"Uniform responded when someone in the alley behind the Cramer kept blowing a whistle. Found your friend, unconscious. It was that idiot rookie Burdett who damned near destroyed the scene of crime when Dorsey got offed, so I sent him back with an evidence tech just in case he's capable of learning something. They didn't find anything but signs of a struggle. Got a partial boot print that matches up with the size twelves we found back there when Doobee got killed."

He sat up. "Your friend Nessa won't talk with me so I don't know what happened to her. Burdett thought she might have been rummaging through the garbage and slipped on the ice. He actually believed she would go out looking through dumpsters with the wind chill at ten below." He shook his head. "An idiot would know better than that. He just jumps to conclusions without thinking anything through. Department could be in trouble if we don't do something about that one. We could have a whole epidemic of half-wits if Burdett ever becomes the norm."

Nessa was in the third cubicle. The curtain was open. She was propped up on the gurney, still wearing her coat. She stared at the ceiling and didn't look away when Marti came in. Marti walked around the gurney, sat in the chair near the window, and waited.

Eventually Nessa said, "Dumb folk here. Think I'm stupid just 'cause I'm crazy."

Marti stifled a yawn.

"Went looking for the man that killed Dorsey."

Marti looked at Nessa, still staring up at the ceiling, arms folded, calm. Had she managed to tangle with the killer and come away from it alive? Somehow it didn't surprise her. "Can you describe him?"

"Course not." Nessa sounded exasperated. "If I could've I wouldn't have gone to all this trouble, cold as it is. Intended to catch him for you but I fell and hit my head before I could straddle him. Your man let him get away. I told him which way the man run and that he was the killer. He say 'Sure, ma'am' and paid no attention at all. Coulda had him." Burdett had gotten Nessa riled up enough to be talkative.

"Could have got yourself killed," Marti said.

"Setting yourself up like that. Could have said something to me about it first."

"Folks know I'm crazy."

"Got nothin' to do with common sense," Marti snapped. "Just what I would have needed, another body at the Cramer Hotel."

"Nessa knows how to take care of herself."

"Don't matter. Better not be a next time for anything like this." It was a futile warning but she felt compelled to say it anyway. Nessa rarely spoke to anyone, probably didn't listen to anyone either.

"You taking good care of Dorsey's cat?" she asked.

"Was you worried about old Samantha?"

"No, I'm worried about some kids. I was just curious about what happened to the cat. Figured it was you that had it all along."

"Figured no such thing."

"You left that bag of food there, didn't you? I figured whoever did that took the cat. Anything else I should know?"

"Could be," Nessa told her, not volunteering anything else.

"They say you got a concussion," Marti said. "Course your head is kinda hard."

Nessa came close to smiling, tried to look stern instead. "Ain't nothin' but a little bump I got fallin'. Ain't no concussion or nothin' else."

"Then I'll get us some coffee," Marti said. Looked like she was in for a long night. Nessa would tell her whatever she chose to whenever she got good and ready.

"Get some of the nurses'. Nothing but slop in them machines."

Nessa was right. Marti threw the machine brew into a wastebasket and found a small lounge with a coffee pot and styrofoam cups. "You're taking it black," she said when she got back. "Too much bother to try and carry cream and sugar too."

"How I take it anyway," Nessa said. Before she could drink it a tiny nurse came in fussing about "concussion" and took Nessa's cup away. Nessa didn't protest. "Just being sociable anyway. Too early in the morning to be drinking coffee. Needs my sleep," she told Marti. "And no need trying to tell them ain't nothin' wrong with me. It's only my head. No reason why I should know if'n somethin's wrong with it. As for them kids, I been looking around for 'em too. Don't know where they could have got themselves to. Do have something else for you though."

Nessa rummaged around in her pocket, tugging at the coat until her hand was down by the hem. She came out with an envelope, then searched around some more and gave Marti a ring.

"Where'd you get this?" Marti asked.

"Belonged to Dorsey. I took it the night she got killed. Whoever did it wasn't smart enough to find where she hid it."

The ring had a large green stone. If it was an emerald it was the biggest she had ever seen. "This real?" she asked.

"Dorsey just got the pearl appraised," Nessa

told her. "She wanted to keep this. Kind of an engagement ring. Man name of Weeks gave it to her, but she wasn't s'posed to tell no one she had it. Didn't either till she showed it to me. She sold the pearl. He gave that to her to hold for him after their friend died. Then he died too and she just kept it. First of the year and she woulda been out of the Cramer. Wouldn't nobody've killed her then."

"Where'd she sell it?"

"Went into Chicago. She had to wait some while the man made sure it wasn't stolen. Got six thousand. I think it was all it was worth. Pearls are like that, more you got, more they're worth. A pair woulda got her fifteen, twenty thousand."

"She know it was valuable?"

"Not till she showed it to me."

Marti knew little about gems. She didn't ask Nessa how she came to know so much.

"Know the name of the jeweler in Chicago?"

"Can't say as I remember anything else."

"Why did you tell me about Henderson?"

"Dorsey said she needed to talk with someone by that name."

Nessa closed her eyes. Nessa had either told her as much as she knew or as much as she intended to. Marti accepted that. She looked at the envelope. Dog-eared. Postmarked Hong Kong, June. It was from Nelson Weeks, written about a month before he died.

She scanned the contents, feeling like she was trespassing and then like a voyeur as his language became sexually explicit. He closed with,

"We're going to do all the things I promised you when I come back. EarthStar's going big time and Greyson's not going to stop us this time."

Marti weighed the ring and letter in one hand. Dorsey was still an enigma. Now so was Weeks and even Bernard Greyson. No way she could fly to Colorado. She'd just have to wait until he got back in town.

She put the envelope and the ring into evidence bags, put them in her purse. She thanked Nessa. She didn't want to just leave her there all alone. But Nessa *was* alone, she reminded herself. She probably preferred it that way. Even so, she went to the nurse's station, demanded to see the doctor, found out that they wanted to keep Nessa for observation and went back to the cubicle and explained.

"Staying here's a lot better than being committed to Elgin," Nessa considered. "They gonna put me on a regular ward, right? I ain't havin' no psychotic episode. Christmas coming Tuesday. Be nice to have a turkey dinner. Was gonna cook. No need to cook much now though. Always did like messin' around in the kitchen."

Marti said she'd make sure they kept her in at least until Wednesday.

"Best bein' at home though. How my dogs and the cats gonna get fed?"

Marti volunteered.

"I'll give you my key. Get the puppy in tonight." She considered for a minute. "It's already Saturday. I got paper down, clean kitty litter. They got enough dry food and water inside to last till Tuesday night at least. I'll stay

251

here till then. They don't wanna let me out, I'm gonna call you."

That was a lot less of an argument than she expected. Maybe Nessa did want to be around other people. She had made friends with Dorsey. But Dorsey was dead. Marti asked her if she knew Dave, the young man she had met at the clinic. "Friend of Dorsey's, sort of," Marti said. "Seemed to like her a lot. Shy though. Needs motherin'."

There was a speculative expression on Nessa's face when Marti left.

23

Marti and Vik had no sooner left Nessa at Lincoln Prairie General than they received a call that John Clark had robbed an all-night quick stop. He had threatened the attendant with a knife, got the money and the keys to a Chevy Chevette. The attendant had tripped an alarm. Now Clark was at a hospital downstate in serious condition with a fractured skull. He had lost control of the car during a high-speed chase. The Chevette had gone through a divider and rolled over.

"Too bad he was wearing a seat belt," Vik complained. "Just as easy to take a tissue sample from a dead man and less cost to the state to bury him than to keep him locked up. Sure as hell hope he's the one Dorsey scratched. That and a confession and we'll be home for the holidays."

Marti felt too tired to comment. It was two days until Christmas and she was determined that her gift to herself would be a decent night's sleep.

"Too bad he didn't break his neck instead of his leg," Vik said. "We're traveling a hundred miles in the middle of the night. Perps make it damned hard for any law-abiding person to tolerate them."

"You think he's our man?" Marti asked. She wanted this to be over, wanted to have the luxury of searching for those children without the added worry of whether or not someone was after them.

"Guess we'll know soon enough," Vik mumbled.

"He almost made it to Normal, and headed west like I said he would."

"Dumb perp," Vik said. "Anyone with common sense would have kept going south."

The hospital was a sprawling two-story structure build on several acres of land. The main building was red brick and old. Additions had been added on over the years. The receptionist sat at a small mahogany desk with a brass lamp. She directed them down a hall with mauve and gray carpet to a set of elevators.

Clark's room was on the second floor at the end of a short corridor. A uniform admitted them. It was a small room with flowered wallpaper. Except for the bed, the furnishings looked like reproductions. It was more homey than any hospital room Marti had ever seen, this was a small town with well-to-do residents. But the smell was the same: Betadine and soiled bandages, whatever was coming out through various tubes. Clark might be the first criminal ever admitted here.

Clark turned his head to look at them as they entered the room. He had two black eyes, what looked to be a broken nose, and multiple cuts and contusions about the face. His eyes were little more than slits in his swollen face. One leg was in a cast, the other had been splinted. His left arm was hooked up to an I.V. He was heavier than he was the last time his police record had been updated, his flesh pale and flabby. Straight brown hair had receded a little more since the most recent mug shot was taken. It was oily and unkempt. If Clark had made advances toward Dorsey, Marti wondered what had convinced him that he wouldn't be rebuffed.

Vik spoke to the uniform. "Is he alert enough to understand if I question him?"

"Should be. Been a good four hours since they gave him anything for the pain. He's been asking for something but I figured you'd want him awake when you got here. We'll be moving him to the county jail in a couple of days."

Vik had no problems watching the guilty suffer. He went to the bed and identified himself as a detective with the force in Lincoln Prairie. With all that was wrong with him the man was probably in too much pain to consider their visit bad news.

"Want to talk with you about Lauretta Dorsey," Vik said.

"Umm."

Clark had lost his front teeth in the accident and his jaws were wired together.

Vik Mirandized him, then said, "Did you see Lauretta Dorsey the night of Friday, December eighth?"

"Mmmmm."

"Is that affirmative?"

"Mmmm." Clark said something else. Talking was difficult but not impossible. Vik bent closer to hear him, then turned to Marti.

"Let me guess," she said. "He didn't do it."

"Did you argue with her that night?" Vik asked.

"Mmmmm."

"Did you fight?"

"Unnnn."

Vik leaned over again. "She slapped him. He left."

"Left town, as a matter of fact," Marti said. "Left pretty quick, too."

"Did you cause Lauretta Dorsey any bodily injury?" Vik continued.

Clark made writing motions and Vik got a pencil and pad.

"Noise in hall," he wrote. "Went to see. Man chase kids. Dorsey dead. Got out. Fast. Didn't do it."

"Why didn't you leave the state?" Marti asked, curious.

"Look guilty," he wrote. "Not until you caught killer."

Marti conferred with Vik in the hall. They had to decide if Clark was their perp or if they'd better keep looking. They wouldn't have a tissue match sooner than Monday.

"Plenty of time to drive here after he tangled with Nessa," Vik said.

"Doesn't feel right," she told him, not caring

what he said about intuition. She didn't think she had the right man.

"Doobee weighed two-seventy. Doesn't look like Clark had the strength to kill him, much less lift him into a dumpster."

"Doesn't look anything like Doobee's father, either," Marti said.

"And how would you know what he meant by that?"

"If we take Doobee literally, he thought the man in the hall was his father. There had to be some basis in reality for him thinking that way."

"Doobee thought everyone was his father."

"No," she disagreed. "I read the diary. I don't know what triggered the association but he thought certain men were his father."

"Right, MacAlister. About fifteen hundred of them."

"Men he picked out from a crowd," she persisted. "And keep your voice down. This is a hospital."

"Intuition. Your stupid intuition. We've got facts. We don't need intuition," Vik said. "The tissue samples will tell all. Somehow I like that better than this Doobee illogic. We'll wait for the lab results."

He turned on his heel and stalked down the corridor, colliding with a nurse's aide. He kept going without any apology.

Marti shrugged as she passed the young woman.

Back in the car Vik was silent. Marti drove thirty miles before he said, "Clark was scared.

Guy doing this might not be crazy but when we meet up with him he won't be scared."

"Gut reaction?" she asked, feeling just as tired and crabby and disappointed as he was.

Vik hit the palm of his hand with his fist. "Damn, but I wanted it to be him. It's as if this guy is invisible. We don't have a name, we don't have a description, nothing. And tissue samples won't do a damned bit of good if Dorsey scratched Clark when she slapped him, but was still alive when he left. Hell, the perp is here and we can't find him."

"He's here," Marti echoed. "And so are those kids. And they're as invisible as he is. Someone must know where they are. Kids can't be getting that good." But these were. "I bet they're right under our noses."

"Best place to hide," Vik agreed.

When they got back to the precinct, Slim and Cowboy had ordered a large pizza. All of her favorites: mushrooms, pepperoni, sausage, bell pepper. No spinach or zucchini. But even when she smelled it she didn't feel hungry.

"What?" Slim said, giving her a dimpled smile. "Is that daughter of yours finally converting you? Have you sworn off junk food for life?"

She poured her seventh cup of coffee since she had picked up Vik and sat at her desk without answering him.

"Might have a little something for you," Slim cooed, putting a slice of pizza on her desk.

"I'm not hungry," she snapped.

"You know, partner," Slim said to Cowboy,

"I think that the worst case scenario is beginning to develop with the Dyspeptic Duo. His grouchiness is rubbing off on her."

"Be a real shame if that happened," Cowboy drawled. "Especially since we got a little something to pass along to her."

"What?" she asked. "What? Tell me and then leave me alone."

"Uh-oh," Slim said. "It was kinda nice having one Marti around here. Looks like we got two Viks now instead."

"What have you got?" she demanded.

"Couple of our little ladies of the evening been noticing someone hanging around downtown. Walking past the Cramer and circling around in about a two, three block radius. One's been seeing him for the past couple of days now. Other one's been noticing him for a couple of nights."

"So what?" Vik demanded. "Some bum who prefers not to spend the night at a shelter. Or some john who finds the pickings too slim."

"Do you slight our ladies of the night?" Slim asked.

"Describe him," Marti said, not even pretending to be interested.

The description matched the one Doobee had given them.

"Don't you say it, MacAlister," Vik warned. "Doobee thought everyone was his father."

"No he didn't," Slim said. "He thought guys who were tall, kinda thin and gray-haired were his father. Our ladies say that this guy looks like that."

Marti pointed at Vik. "I told you there was a type."

Slim chuckled. "Lordy, Lordy. Two grouches and they're arguing with each other."

Cowboy spit out his wad of gum. "No reason not to listen to Doobee just 'cause he wasn't all there in the head. Be about like not listening to these little ladies 'cause of the way they earn a living. Nothing wrong with Doobee's sight. Nothing wrong with theirs."

Marti thought for a minute. "He's looking for them within three blocks of the Cramer," she said. "Get the map again."

Before anyone could, a uniform came to the door. "Mrs. Greyson to see you."

Marti looked up, expecting to see Adeline. The woman in the doorway looked nothing like her. Petite, she was wearing slacks and an aqua ski cap and jacket that seemed to add highlights to ordinary brown hair. Her otherwise average looks were enhanced by her vitality. There was a vibrance in her expression, an expectation in her eyes that made her look youthful. Marti liked her before she even said a word.

She compared Frannie to Adeline and wondered why, given a choice, a man would want Adeline. Then she thought of how different Adeline looked fifteen years ago. It would have been impossible to imagine that she would age this fast and look as bad as she did now.

"The first Mrs. Greyson?" Marti said.

"Yes." The woman stepped into the room, looked at Slim and Cowboy who were wearing shoulder holsters armed with service revolvers, then at Vik's dark expression, and sat down next to Vik's desk without appearing the least bit nervous or intimidated. "I'm Frannie Greyson. I take it you've met Adeline."

Marti nodded.

Vik got up, asked Frannie if she'd like a cup of coffee.

"Decaf, please, if you have any."

"Of course we do. I'll be right back with it," Vik assured her, escaping from the squad room to begin what Marti was certain would be a long and fruitless search. Marti looked at Slim and then Cowboy and raised her eyebrows. She might be able to get more out of Frannie without them. They took the hint and closed the pizza box, made their excuses, and left.

"I hope Bernard came with you," Marti said. "We need to talk with him."

"That's why I came here. Bernard isn't in Colorado. My oldest son called you and pretended to be his father."

"Why?"

"They thought it was another one of Adeline's games. I haven't talked to Bernard for over two weeks. Before then he'd been calling me every day. When he called just before Thanksgiving he said he was going to ask Adeline for a divorce. Then about a week later he called and said that someone knew, that they were after him and he had to escape, that he'd come to Colorado as soon as it was safe."

"Didn't this sound strange?" Marti asked.

Frannie hesitated for a minute. "Everything Bernard has done for the past two years has been strange. And even before then, his behavior was odd."

"What do you think he meant when he said that someone knew?"

"I have no idea." She looked away, biting on her lower lip. "I think he might be dead. I think that for a long time she's been driving him crazy and maybe now she's killed him. I need to know. One of the reasons Bernard's been so frantic lately is that someone else has asked me to marry him. I don't know if I wanted to be married. But I would never marry Bernard again."

Frannie Greyson began wringing her hands. "I can't convince him that even if he were free, I wouldn't want him."

Marti wanted to ask a dozen questions. Instead she waited. Frannie was doing just fine without her interference.

"I gave this a lot of thought, what I would tell the police. It never occurred to me that I'd be talking with a woman. I kept thinking no, I can't say that, they'll think I'm hysterical, or I can't say that because they'll think I'm callous." She gave Marti a small smile that reached her brown eyes and added a dimension of strength to her face.

"I think I'll just be honest. I have a good life. I like everything the way it is. I cannot get Bernard to leave me alone. Adeline is a hypochondriac with a few legitimate health problems. The sicker she gets the more she wants him. Adeline has always been obsessed with Bernard. Over the years, Bernard has become just like her, only he's obsessed with me. Bernard's biggest worry is that I'm too happy."

She gnawed at her lower lip, then stared out the window. "All the time he thought he was sneaking behind my back she was calling me, describing what they did together. She sounded so smug. I think those calls almost drove me crazy. Bernard never knew, but when he did ask me for a divorce, it was those calls. As soon as he asked, I said yes. I took everything I could get. When she got him, I didn't want her to have one thing more than I had to part with. I've made some smart investments. I like my life. I don't want that to change."

Marti saw Vik in the doorway. He took one look at her and backed away.

"What happened two years ago?"

"Her arthritis got worse. That might not be one of her imaginary ailments. They traveled a lot until then. I traveled a lot. Bernard would go wherever I went, bring her along, sneak and see me. I was flattered for the first few years. It was one way that I could get even. I started calling her, telling her what Bernard and I did while she was in her hotel room alone." She stopped speaking, looked down at the floor for a minute. "Sick, wasn't it? The three of us were really sick."

She made a little fluttering movement with her hands. "Funny. My kids grew up, went off to college, two got married. I began growing up too. My life became disengaged from theirs. But Bernard. He had to come to Colorado on the least pretext. She would stay at the hotel while he visited with the family." She shook her head. "It wasn't amusing anymore. I had stopped feeling vindictive."

She paused for a minute. "I think there was something in all of this for Bernard. I don't want to even try to figure out what. But two years ago, Adeline became housebound and most of their traveling stopped. It was as if that had been some kind of a safety valve for him."

She began twisting her hands again. "It has been such a relief these past two weeks, his not calling. He had been calling me every day for months. To see where I was, who I was with, what I was doing. He would question the kids when I wasn't home. Once, I changed my phone number. He flew to Colorado to find out what was wrong."

Looking at her, Marti saw a woman who knew she had won. Too bad Bernard wasn't much of a prize, for either woman. "Why do you think he's dead?"

"I can't think of any other reason why he'd leave me in peace this long. And you mentioned that woman, Dorsey. Two of her friends died just before Bernard divorced me. You brought it all back. Bernard acted strange then, too."

She shook her head. "Well, he did arrange their military installation tours. He must have known them fairly well."

Marti heard the questions as she spoke and let her voice them.

"It was that he was so moody before they died and so . . . relaxed afterwards. It was as if his feelings were in the wrong order. He didn't feel bad about their deaths. Not even a common-place emotion like sadness that they died so young, or in such a terrible way. There was something about the band signing with a re-cording company. He was furious, kept saying Julie King couldn't do that to him. Took it very personal, their wanting to go on to recording. He had stopped them once. After she died he seemed so . . . relieved. . . . I remember thinking that he must have changed his mind about that. He seemed glad to be rid of them."

"Did you know Dorsey?" Marti said.

"No, but Adeline knew her. She called right after Dorsey was committed and said she had Bernard now." She seemed puzzled. "She said all she had to do was tell him why she didn't want him and he'd be hers forever."

Frannie was slowing down, becoming more introspective. Marti didn't rush her. "Bernard came home drunk the night before he walked out on me. He sat at the dining room table and called this Dorsey every name he could think of and then he threw up on the carpet."

"Do you have any idea of where he could be?" Marti said.

"You don't think he's dead?"

"We should probably try to find him before we decide that."

"If he isn't with her, the only other place he would be is our—his—cabin in Baraboo. She thinks he gave it to me when we got divorced. He's gone there several times in the past two years. Stays about a week. She calls me and says she has one catastrophic illness or another, and I relay the message to him. He goes home. That's what she's doing now. This time it's breast cancer and she can't have the surgery unless Bernard is with her. It's all in her head. I just can't give him the message. It felt so good to be free of him. I was so grateful for those times when he went to the cabin . . ." Her voice trailed off. "I think I'm hoping he *is* dead."

Frannie looked out of the window. The sun was still shining. "Maybe it'll snow while I'm here. That's the only thing I ever liked about this place."

Marti sat back, looked at Frannie, saw an expression of loathing flicker in her face as she rubbed the back of her hand. She understood Bernard Greyson's compulsion. As soon as this woman, any woman, didn't want him anymore he would become obsessed.

24

Adeline Greyson sat alone in the living room. It was dark outside, getting late. She didn't have any lights on. The room took on texture and shades of darkness as she sat there. The curtains lighter than the walls, the base of the lamp a fat dark globe on the table. Small noises, comforting and reassuring, made the old house unique, made it hers. Glass rattling as the wind blew against the windows, the settling and re-settling of the wood frame that she had never wanted to have sided with aluminum. The knocking in the pipes as they cooled. They should have been able to afford better, would have if it hadn't been for Frannie. Adeline felt her nails cutting into her palms and flexed her fingers.

She would rather have had a nicer home than do all of that traveling. But Bernard, there was no keeping him still. How he loved it, staying out all night in foreign cities that she didn't like. And that Frannie, following them wherever they went, calling her with lies about Bernard. She had checked his clothing and underwear and never found any sign of Frannie.

It was always so good to get back home. Bernard was always glad to escape from Frannie again. Poor man, so exhausted on the flight back, looking ten years older, face drawn, heart palpitations by the time the plane landed, then his ulcer would act up for two or three months. And so quiet, not talking to her, taking long walks in the morning, napping all afternoon, then staying up alone late at night.

At least some good came from her arthritis. It was so bad these past few years they had to stay home. Poor Bernard, always looking at those travel magazines and brochures. Getting more as fast as she threw them away. He had a dozen more trips planned. Not that she would ever allow him to go too far away without her.

Wait until she told him that Dorsey was dead. She was glad. But why was that police officer coming here? What did she want to find out? If she knew anything at all she wouldn't have to come around asking questions.

That thief, Dorsey. Calling to tell her she had just found out that a pearl Nelson Weeks had given her was real. All excited because she could afford another place to live. And going to keep the emerald ring because it had sentimental value. They were hers, not Dorsey's. Dorsey had no right to any of that jewelry. Bernard had risked his military career, his freedom, bringing jewels into the country and fencing them.

Dorsey, calling her after all these years as if she believed they had really been friends. Wanting to talk with her and Bernard about Julie King's accident and the car crash that killed her fiancé. Dorsey sounded almost sane this time, sounded almost like the old Dorsey. Almost. Who would have thought Dorsey would sound so normal after being ill for so many years and taking so much psychotropic medication?

That night, years ago, when she found out Weeks was dead, she couldn't wait to tell Dorsey and watch the laughter go away, watch her cry. But instead of the hysterics that she expected, Dorsey had just stared at her. It pushed her right over the edge, Weeks dying so soon after Julie King. Dorsey, the poor little rich girl who had always had everything she wanted and lacked the sense to appreciate it. Suddenly, Dorsey had nothing.

One visit to the psych ward a week later had been enough to convince her that Dorsey would never be normal again. Docile Dorsey was doing just as she was told. Dark circles around her eyes indicated that she was being given large doses of Thorazine. Dorsey had always been more bluster than spunk and even that was gone. As soon as Dorsey began talking in that little-girl voice about going dancing, describing the charity fetes and dinner dances her mother had given at their home, it was clear that she had gone back to a time when she thought she was safe and that she intended to stay there.

Hard to imagine Dorsey dead. She could never sit without swinging her legs or tapping her feet. Couldn't talk without her arms sweeping through the air, her hands waving. And always laughing and smiling until everyone around her was too.

Adeline reached for the shawl she kept handy, eased it around her shoulders and folded her arms beneath the soft, warm wool.

She had been glad when Weeks died. Stupid man. Thinking he could replace Julie as Bernard's mule. Thinking Bernard owed him some kind of payoff. Served him right, getting himself killed.

She had gained everything after Weeks died. Bernard was hers at last. Dorsey had told her everything she needed to know to figure out what Bernard was doing. She even knew the names of those foreigners who gave the raw gems to Julie King. She had shown Bernard the pictures of Julie wearing that jewelry and those she had taken with the telephoto lens of Bernard passing those same gems to his contact. Poor Bernard. He had panicked, begging her to marry him. He was so insistent she turned him down for a week.

All of those months she had spent figuring out how she would get him and when she did, it hadn't been the way she had planned it at all. Scary, marrying someone. Scariest thing she had ever done. But it was that or face getting old alone. And that was worse. Both of the aunts who raised her had died old maids and alone.

The furnace had kicked on, the fan whirling and hot air gusting toward her. Her arthritis had gotten much worse over the past two years, spreading inward from toes and fingers until it reached her spine. She ached almost all of the time now. One joint, or several, always hurting. It never seemed to get warm enough to penetrate the aching in her bones. When she felt the perspiration gathering in warm pools in her armpits she spread her hands in front of her. Not too stiff. She stood, a familiar dry stiffness in her knee sockets but enough mobility to get around without too much discomfort.

The phone rang. Startled, she went to the hall without stopping to turn on a light. Bernard. In her haste she knocked the receiver out of the cradle. "Bernard!" She couldn't have broken the connection. She picked up the receiver. "Bernard!"

There was no answer, but someone was on the line.

"Bernard? Is that you?"

There was a click. Puzzled, she hung up.

She went upstairs without putting on any lights. Went into her bedroom, where the blinds were still up to let in the moonlight. Her wedding pictures, several dozen, framed and hanging above the bed. Another large photo like the one downstairs hung where they could see it as they lay back on the pillows.

Her wedding. Not only had that spinster Adeline Henderson managed to get herself a husband, but she had gotten herself an officer, a wealthy and attractive man. And not somebody that no one else wanted, either. His first wife had wanted him very much, but she, Adeline Henderson, had taken him.

Bernard was a real ladies' man when he was married to Frannie. But once he married her, there was no one else. And all of them, those who had thought her too poor or too dull, had stood back in amazement as she walked off with the prize. It hadn't mattered, not once, how she'd managed to get him. And keep him. She had been happy all of these years. She had been. She was.

The neighbor's dog began barking, a distant sound but annoying. Adeline walked to the window, pulling the curtain aside. Ice patterns had formed on the panes. The dog's bark became a persistent whine. She had complained about the last dog until the woman was forced to get rid of it. She had begun complaining about this one too, but now her neighbor had smartened up, put the dog out when it got dark, let it stay out to torment her with its yelping and whining, and then took it in just before ten o'clock so there wasn't any ordinance violation. One night she was going to take Bernard's gun and go out there and shoot it.

Adeline went over to the bed and sat down. Her side of the bed was soft enough to sink into. Bernard complained that a soft mattress gave him backaches and slept with a board on his side between the mattress and box spring.

Bernard. What had that conniving, deceitful Frannie told him this time to get him to Colorado? That she was dying of something, most likely. The lengths that woman would go to to get Bernard back. And those kids of theirs. Adults now and Bernard still couldn't do enough for them. She had refused to have any. She knew it was his children's fault that he had asked her for a divorce. Poor man, he had left right after that, unable to face the pain. Good thing she had those pictures of Julie King and that fence with the jewelry. She smiled. She was the only one left who knew, besides Bernard. And the pictures were in a safe place.

Just as she got up the back door opened. Bernard. He had gotten away from that woman and come home to her. She wanted to run to the door, rush down the stairs, give him a big welcome-home hug. Instead she stood there, savoring the sound of his footsteps coming toward her. Bernard didn't like such blatant affection. She tiptoed over to the window, stood there with her back to the door, hugging herself as she listened to Bernard coming home.

She could hear her heart beating, pounding in her chest. It was so hard to just stand there, to let him come to her. The stairs creaked just a little, like they always did when he came up to bed, then the floorboards in the hallway. Creaky old house, Bernard always said, but she thought of the grunts and groans of the wind-battered old farmhouse she had grown up in and found some contentment.

She shivered as he came into the room, hugging herself tighter to keep from turning and throwing her arms around him. As he came closer she whispered his name.

25

When Marti got back to the precinct, Christmas carols were playing somewhere in the building, probably compliments of the desk sergeant. They had made the round trip to Baraboo, Wisconsin, to check out Greyson's cabin in less than four hours and come away empty.

The place smelled of recently brewed coffee and fried bacon. White fat had congealed in a frying pan. Water had to be brought in in containers and there were two, half full. The outhouse had been used. But no Greyson. Frannie Greyson was convinced that something had happened to her ex-husband. She was on her way to the town where Greyson lived. Marti suggested that she go to the local police first, not to the house. Frannie said that she would.

When they got back to Lincoln Prairie she took Sherman Avenue, slowing down as they reached the apartment building and drove past the old library. The abandoned industrial buildings were outlined unevenly against the night sky, dark against the darkness. As she looked from the library in the foreground to the collapsing buildings behind it, she had an uneasy feeling, as if she had overlooked something.

Back at the precinct, she yawned. "I'm tired as hell," she said. Her arms and shoulders and back ached.

"Me too," Vik said. "Don't think I've had a decent night's sleep this month. At least my cold's better."

Marti hoped she didn't look as bad as he did. His eyes were bloodshot and dark pouches sagged beneath them.

"Who would have thought one dead nut case in the Cramer Hotel would lead to all of this?" he said. "The night we found her I was glad we got a positive ID and there were next of kin. Didn't think there would be much more to it than that."

"Do you think Greyson's dead?" Marti said.

"I don't know enough to think anything."

"Tell me about it," she agreed. "This link between Adeline Greyson and Dorsey is all that we have. That and their connection, however tenuous, to Bernard Greyson and King's and Weeks's death." Her eyes began smarting. She rubbed them, looked in her desk drawer for some Murine, and applied the eyedrops twice. Blinking, she said, "It just seems like we'll never get to the bottom of it. Unless we talk with Greyson, or find a few new leads. Adeline sure isn't going to tell us anything."

"Meanwhile, we've got five kids to find." He ran his fingers through his hair. "God, five of them."

"Let's take one more look at your map before

275

we hit the street," she said, reaching into her drawer again. "Slim and Cowboy's little ladies of the evening say he's staying within a three-block radius of the Cramer." She marked off the area with a yellow highlighter, used a green one to mark all of the alleys.

They looked at Vik's crude squares and rectangles: the hotel, the bus station, the row of small businesses, the apartment building, the old library, and the older single-family homes. "We've been checking this area out for days but they've got to be here somewhere," Marti said. "They go into that field and somehow they lose us."

"It'll be Christmas Eve in a couple of hours," Vik said. "Someone has taken them in or they've gone to a shelter."

"There is no shelter here for kids," she reminded him.

"Well then there should be," he growled.

"Thank God they're not in what's left of those old industrial buildings," she said. "But what about that old library?"

Vik tapped his finger on the square he'd penciled in for the library. "No way to get in there. Secured. Built like a fortress. New one's nice, but you go in and everything's right there. This old one was great, laid out like a maze."

Marti shuddered, thinking about the industrial buildings. "Now it's cold and damp and infested with rodents and bugs. Yuck."

"I wonder what those people from the historical society found when they went inside," Vik said. His eyebrows came together in a thoughtful frown.

Marti thought of the dark building silhouetted against the night sky as they were driving back. The library, gray, almost bright in relief. "Wait a minute . . ." She recognized what had nagged at her before. "The roof, Vik. There wasn't any snow on the library roof. There's heat in there, has to be."

Vik called Brian and asked if the preservation people had reported to the city council on their tour yet, then asked if the building was heated. He listened for a minute, then turned to Marti. "There was no tour. This preservation business started last year when Stazak was in office. Brian's setting up a conference call with the president of the historic society."

He hung up after a few minutes. "Stazak gave them the go-ahead last year. The building was inspected and they awarded a contract for basic repairs. And the utilities were turned on. Everything was put on hold when the city council decided to redevelop that whole lakefront area. And that's where it is now, in limbo."

"And?"

"And the utilities were to be turned off but the historic society got a gas bill last month. Nobody's looked into it yet."

Marti didn't know what was causing the chill, but she got gooseflesh. "Let's go."

As she reached for her coat Vik said, "Don't get your hopes up. It's located on a major thoroughfare with high visibility. It has been secured and there are those iron bars on the outside of the windows."

"And we put a spotlight on the area when we went in and searched. Whoever's looking for them there knows that we are, too."

And the library was habitable. "What are you waiting for, Jessenovik?" She was halfway down the hall when he came out of the office.

The desk sergeant stopped them on the way out. "Dispatcher just called. Got a call from a kid requesting an ambulance."

"Right," Vik said, without breaking stride. "We get a call like that every other day."

Marti stopped. "Why is she passing this to us?"

"Said it didn't sound like a prank call. Kid hung up before she could get an address."

"Great. Put Lupe Torres on it, will you?" She hurried to catch up with Vik.

There was a metal stub in front of the library where a street light had been. The sidewalk was cracked and slanted down to the concrete stairs. Traffic was lighter on Sherman Avenue than she expected.

"Heaviest when people are going to and coming from work," Vik said. "About normal for this time of night."

The front was just as they both remembered it. The windows were too high up to access without a ladder, five-by-nine and bow shaped at the top. The plywood was four-by-eight.

They checked the front door, heavy, mahogany or oak. Padlocked and chained. They went around back, unlit flashlights in hand. The sky was clear. A full moon reflected off the snow, creating a brightness that made the old building seem darker and ominous. Weeds and bushes were dense. Dead branches cracked as they pushed their way through. Anyone inside could hear them, but without the lights they might think the noise was caused by animals.

Marti stopped and pointed to several paths where dead brown weeds had been trampled. The barred windows continued around the building. The boards looked secure.

There was a lower level not visible from the street. Small windows, more bars. One door, midway between the two levels of windows, maybe six feet from the ground. An ordinary door, one panel pushed away.

"Tell me the floor plan," she whispered, remembering he had said it was mazelike. He described the layout. Eyes closed, she pictured what Vik was saying, then repeated it back.

Six-inch squares of concrete jutted out on either side of the building as if stairs had been there once. Marti used them to climb to the door where the plywood was pushed to one side. She closed her eyes for a minute, then poked her head inside, seeing pinholes of light as her eyes adjusted to the darkness. The midway point in a narrow spiral stairwell. For a moment, a light illuminated the steps. Someone was upstairs with a flashlight. Then the light was extinguished.

She heard something, listened. Paper, someone walking on paper. Footsteps, not the scurry of rodents. She nodded to Vik, pointed to her eyes, to the flashlight, and then pointed inside so he would know someone was in there with a light. Then she stayed put while he went to their vehicle.

Burdett was one of the uniforms who responded to Vik's call for a backup unit. Vik, still at ground level, swore under his breath when he saw him. Burdett and his partner approached the rear of the building just as they had been instructed to do, quietly and without using flashlights.

The three men looked up at Marti. She shook her head so that Vik would know she hadn't heard or seen anything else, then motioned to Vik that there were winding stairs leading up and down.

Vik held up five fingers. Kids inside? She raised one hand. She didn't know. Burdett looked from one of them to the other, turned to his partner and shook his head.

Vik clasped both of his hands together, held them up. She nodded. They could get into a hostage situation. Vik whispered to the two uniforms, turned to her and pointed up. Again, she nodded. She would go upstairs with one rookie. He would go downstairs with the other. Their consultation complete, Burdett came up the footholds opposite the ones she was on. Might have known he was the one she'd get stuck with.

She crawled inside, stayed low, crouching with her back against the wall. Burdett poked his head in, closed his eyes to adjust to the darkness, then came in with her. Hugging the wall, she advanced up the curving stairs. As she rounded the corner near the top of the stairs she heard breathing, hard and even, as if whoever it was had been running, but was not out of breath.

She was sure she only heard one person, didn't know what that meant. The thought of the children made the muscles of her stomach tighten. Maybe they were too late and the children were dead. Gripping her gun in one hand and an unlit flashlight in the other, she took the last two steps to the top. A small room opening to the largest room. Light, coming from the tops of the front windows where the plywood stopped.

The small room was empty. Shelves built into one wall. Once she was in the big room she could go left to the reference room, with an even smaller room east of that. Or she could go into the big room in front of her and turn right. Then there would be one small room east, the youth section, then a second room for preschoolers to the north, and a bathroom.

She walked with a sliding motion, moving her feet just above the floor but close enough to touch anything in her way. Solid floors, no creaking. She went closer to the big room, still heard the breathing, couldn't tell where it was coming from. Slow and even. Whoever it was was waiting for her. She stayed in the small room, pressed against the wall. Peering into the room she could see rows of old bookcases, all with backing so she couldn't see between the shelves.

Burdett was breathing hard now too, scared.

Obscuring the other sound. She couldn't tell which way it was coming from. She waited. Whoever it was knew she was here, let them make the first move. Better than going into the room any sooner than she had to.

A low whistling kind of moan made her step back against Burdett. He was too close. It was only the wind finding a way to blow in. She felt Burdett's breath warm on her ear, took a step away from him. Another footstep, paper on the floor. To her right. Moving away from her. Some place among the bookcases in the big room.

A smothered *whapping* sound. Something loose. Footsteps, quick, moving further away. A dull thud. More *whaps* in uneven rhythms. Something caught in an updraft. She couldn't hear Vik or the other rookie, the walls and flooring were too solid. Made her nervous. Felt much farther away from Vik than she wanted to be.

Burdett's breathing became shallow, harsher. She could smell his sweat, his fear, felt her own armpits getting damp. There was a small noise, and Burdett jumped but kept his mouth shut. A bumping sound in the big room and to her left.

She waited, knowing where he was now, keeping her own breathing steady, but her palms were sweaty. He would move again. Paper rustled, a scurrying sound and squeaking. Mice this time. The wind made another whistling noise, shrill, like a scream.

More bumping. Someone moving, just a little, away from her, toward the small room, the youth room. There was no way out except the way they came in. She and Burdett were blocking the exit. She'd have to wait for Vik, couldn't risk being lured away.

Burdett touched her elbow. She turned, warning him to silence, shook her head. Where was Vik? What was downstairs? Another sound, louder, deliberate. Someone wanted to get out, wanted her away from the exit. Another poke from Burdett. She put the heel of her boot on his foot, pressed lightly, kept her heel there without pressing down. Burdett wanted to go into the room. Vik was right, kid wasn't thinking. Too much light coming from the tops of the windows.

Then she heard one soft click behind her. Vik signaling that he was coming alone. Burdett tried to turn around and see who it was. She increased the pressure on his foot so that he could only turn his head. Burdett cussed under his breath. She put a little more pressure on his toes. Footsteps. Vik coming up behind them.

She didn't want to take Burdett into the room with her, and didn't want to leave him to guard the opening they had come through, either. She didn't know what Vik had found downstairs, but he had left the other rookie there.

She signaled to Vik that someone was in the big room and motioned him to the opening. Then she waited. Someone walking. She peered around the corner and saw why. Wide doorway going into the youth room, plenty of space to escape once she was behind one of those bookcases. That or she'd be more of a target, if this was the perp and the perp had a gun.

She signaled to Vik that she was going in fast. Then she took her heel off Burdett's foot and pointed to the far wall, mouthing the words "cover me," then "follow," and hoping he knew what she wanted him to do. Going into the room with Burdett behind her made her feel like she was going in alone.

As she went in and flattened herself against the wall one shot exploded, loud as a cannon. She hit the floor, heard a thud as Burdett did, too. Nobody had been hit.

Feet, moving fast, a man cursing as he hit a bookcase, not deliberate this time. The bookcase fell over. She was rolling as the second shot hit the wall where she'd just been. She saw the flash, returned fire, didn't hit anyone. Her shoulder hit the side of the bookcase farthest from the youth room. She got behind it.

Burdett. She peeked around. He was in the room, along the wall separating this room from the room they came through. Perp couldn't see him. She motioned to him to stay put on the floor, praying that if he did have to fire his weapon he wouldn't hit her by mistake.

Five rows of bookcases. First one knocked over, leaning against the opposite wall. She began sliding along the floor, using her elbows to propel herself down the aisle to the north wall. Four bookcases standing. She was between the farthest two, began inching forward. Another shot. Nobody hit. Burdett didn't return fire. Another shot. Random, panicky shooting now. No targets, just fear.

She crawled to the two bookcases still standing that were closest to the youth room, into the aisle between them, waited. Listened to the wheezing. Much closer. Ragged. It wasn't Burdett. Inching forward she reached the middle of the room, stood up, and pushed the bookcase. So heavy she couldn't topple it. Bracing herself against the one behind her, she pushed again, felt it lurch forward, gave another push, and switched on her flashlight as it fell. Saw a man standing in front of her, covering his eyes.

"Police. Drop it. Now!" she yelled. The gun clattered to the floor. She noticed another light was trained on the perp. Burdett had done something right. The man was wearing a dark watchcap and a long black coat. Gray hair escaped from beneath the hat.

"Mr. Greyson," she said. He had aged, but she recognized him from his wedding picture. Keeping the light trained on his face and her weapon aimed at him she moved forward. She had to assume Burdett was covering her. That was scarier than apprehending the perp.

When she got close enough she kicked the gun away, then tucked her flashlight under her arm and took out her handcuffs.

Vik came out of the darkness and she realized he had been right there in the little room, covering her and Burdett all the while.

26

"The kids?" Marti said, as Burdett took Greyson outside.

"We found four," Vik said. "Greyson followed the other little boy up here."

Her stomach lurched. "Let's see if we can find him."

Vik insisted on going first. They went through the room with the overturned bookcase to the room with cartoon characters painted on the walls and came to a closed door.

"Bathroom," Vik said.

Heart pounding, she watched as Vik turned the knob.

A small child was huddled on the floor with his coat pulled over his head. Vik knelt down. "He's okay."

"Thank God." Her breath was ragged.

Vik pulled the coat away. "It's okay," he said. "I'm not going to hurt you."

Marti saw a thatch of black hair, looked into eyes filled with fear.

"We're police officers," she said. "You're safe now."

He looked from her to Vik. "You caught the man we saw at the hotel?"

"We've got him," Vik said. "What's your name?"

"Padgett," he whispered. He began trembling.

"How old are you?"

"Nine."

Theo's age. "You've got the bluest eyes I've ever seen," Marti said.

Vik helped him stand up.

Padgett hiccupped. "Georgie. He's sick. I went to get help. The man saw me. I tried not to let him follow me. I couldn't go downstairs 'cause he'd find them and it was dark up here." He began crying.

Marti stroked his hair. "You were very brave, Padgett. You saved your friends."

That seemed to calm him. He put his thumb in his mouth.

Marti looked at Vik.

"Georgie's sick but everyone else is okay," he said. "Sorry about you being the one to go upstairs, but I thought if they weren't all right—"

"Jessenovik . . ." He had let her go upstairs because he was more concerned about her finding five children dead than the risk of finding an armed perp alive. There was a convoluted compliment in that so she decided not to complain.

"And I'm sorry about you being up there with Burdett. I just didn't feel like being bothered with him again."

Marti took Padgett by the hand. "Let's go

downstairs and let everyone know you're okay."
She could hear an ambulance siren and wondered if Ben was on duty tonight.

The children were in a back room, huddled together around the oldest girl who was obviously pregnant.

"Are you okay, LaShawna?" Marti asked.

"How you know my name?"

"I'm a cop. I'm supposed to know who you are." No sense letting these kids think they were too smart.

Georgie was lying on a pile of coats on the floor. LaShawna cradled his head in her lap. His eyes were closed and his chest was heaving as he struggled to breathe. Marti helped him sit up. "Just for a minute," she promised.

She put her ear to his chest, then to his back. A lot of congestion. Not good. His forehead felt hot. He slumped against LaShawna.

"Georgie's awful sick," LaShawna said. "Jose and Padgett got him some medicine, but it ain't helping him enough." They waited till a lady come and say the medicine is for her little girl, but it don't seem to do Georgie much good." She looked at Georgie. Tears came to her eyes. "He's gonna be all right, ain't he?"

"The ambulance is coming now. They'll take good care of him," Marti said. "Just like you did. You're a big girl, taking care of all of these children by yourself. We'll try to help now." Seeing the fear in their eyes, she added, "And you don't have to be afraid anymore."

"Where we going?" LaShawna asked. She had

one arm around a little girl and the other child, Jose, was on the pile of coats beside Georgie.

"You're all going to the hospital. You'll be with Georgie."

"For true?" Marti nodded.

Vik came down. "Ambulance is here. Let's go, kids."

Sissy, Padgett, and Jose went right to him. It never ceased to surprise Marti the way Vik's wiry eyebrows, crooked nose, and almost unblinking winter gray stare could intimidate an adult perp but have no effect at all on children. They would trust him faster than they would trust her.

She looked up to see Ben coming down the stairs. "Please get Georgie on oxygen," she said. "I think he could use a little help with his breathing. Talk to his friends, he's been taking erythromycin for a couple of days now. Denise Stevens says to transport all of them to Lincoln Prairie General and they'll all be put in the same room." She could have hugged him when he took Georgie into his arms. Instead she said, "It's a relief to see he's in good hands."

Ben grinned. "Good to know this whole situation has been in the best of hands." To Georgie, who was barely conscious, he said, "You were a lucky little boy to have this lady looking for you." As he carried Georgie up the stairs he began explaining that the mask would make it easier for him to breathe.

Lupe helped get the children into the ambulance, exclaiming over each and chiding Jose in Spanish for giving her the slip. "Dispatch notified me," she said to Marti. "God, this feels good."

"Just like Christmas," Marti agreed.

Vik was waiting for her by their unmarked car.

"You okay?" Marti asked.

"Yeah."

"Suppose you had found them dead?" she asked quietly.

"First time I ever thought of resigning from the force."

"Then I'm glad this turned out okay." She gave him a quick hug, surprised when he hugged her back and didn't seem embarrassed. "Merry Christmas," she said.

When they got back to the precinct, Frannie Greyson was waiting. She looked pale, as if she was ill. Marti checked her watch, surprised that so much time had elapsed since they got back from Wisconsin.

"I'm sorry . . ." Marti began. She didn't want to comfort the woman because her ex-husband had been arrested for murder. "This has been rough on you."

"I think I'm okay now," Frannie said. "It's Adeline. She's dead."

"Dead?" Marti wasn't expecting that. "What did she die from?"

Frannie swallowed a few times. "She was strangled. As soon as I heard the police say that I knew he . . . he . . . must have . . . killed her." Frannie put her hands on her throat with her thumbs to the front, then shuddered. "Something he learned while he was in 'Nam, before we were stationed here. I got angry with him for showing my boys." She looked down at her hands. "Fifteen years ago I would have given anything to see that woman dead."

Marti spoke quietly. "I'm sorry to have to intrude, but there's something I need to ask you. Did Bernard know anything about electricity?"

"Of course. His father was a master electrician."

Watching her, Marti realized Greyson's first wife didn't make any connection between that and Julie King's death. After Frannie left, Marti went through her IN-basket, found the report on the emerald ring Nessa gave her. As she was reading it, Slim and Cowboy came in.

"Has the Dyspeptic Duo done it again?" Cowboy said.

Slim grinned. "The streets of Lincoln Prairie will be safe once again." He checked his watch. "One second, two seconds. There. The streets are unsafe once again."

"And," Cowboy joined in, "our heroes, though battleworn and weary, are ready to go forth once again to serve and protect."

Slim got serious. "Heard one of the kids is in pretty bad shape."

"Georgie's got pneumonia," Vik said. "I hope we found him in time."

Marti paced from her desk to the window, across to the wall. She was exhausted but still on an adrenalin high.

Cowboy slapped his hat down on his desk. "Yahoo! The big one didn't get away! Hot damn!"

"Yes!" Marti said, feeling good. "Yes!" She raised clenched fists above her head, pumping her arms up and down. "Yes! Yes! Yes, Lord! Thank you, Jesus."

"Amen!" Slim shouted.

Vik was sitting with his chin in his hands. He blinked his eyes rapidly as if that would help keep them open. "Whoopee," he said, sounding cranky.

Slim clapped his hands. "You've got a witness!"

From the hall came sounds of other hands clapping.

When it was quiet again, Cowboy said, "I still don't know what went down. Greyson's your man?"

"He's the one," Marti said. "Greyson had Julie King smuggling jewelry in from overseas. That emerald is real, worth thousands. The setting's worth seventy-five cents. It sounds like Julie was ready to get out of the smuggling business and go legit. EarthStar was to audition with a recording company. Before they could, she was dead, and Greyson knew how to fix those microphone wires. Weeks must have known something. He gave those jewels to Dorsey for safe keeping, but he didn't come to us, so he could have tried blackmail. Based on the reports, it would have been easy to slip something in his drink while he was at the Kit Kat Klub."

"Alcohol poisoning," Slim said. "We had a similar case a few years back. The wood alcohol in some moonshine. Made this kid go blind in less than fifteen minutes. He was driving at the time and rear-ended a semi at sixty-five miles an hour."

Her stomach began rumbling. The pizza boxes were gone. "You got any cookies?" she asked Vik.

He got the canister out of his drawer and passed it around. Marti looked at the cookies. They reminded her of Lenny Doobee. Her stomach growled again. She took a handful, ate three before she went on.

"I wonder if Adeline knew she was living with a killer all these years, or if she had gotten just enough out of Dorsey to convince Bernard to marry her? And poor Dorsey, finally getting her life together, and it's over. Those jewels made her the only one besides Adeline who could tie those killings to Bernard. She must have contacted Adeline after she found out what that pearl was worth. She could have begun to suspect something. Or she could have figured things out. Or maybe she hadn't even considered the possibility of foul play."

She finished off a date bar and smiled. "Premeditation," she said. "Not insanity. I like that."

It was close to five in the morning when she got home. She had the whole of Christmas Eve morning to sleep, and then she could do some last-minute shopping.

When she looked in on the kids, Joanna's clothes were on the floor right where she had stepped out of them. Marti smiled. As big a pain as Joanna could be about what they ate, it would have been unbearable if she were neat, too.

When she went into Theo's room she saw that the model airplane was completed and painted blue. She went to the bed, sat down. Theo didn't open his eyes but she had awakened him.

"Like it?" he asked.

"Very much."

"No plans. Threw them away. Almost threw the plane away. I wanted to break it."

"Why?"

"Dad wouldn't come back to help finish it."

She stroked his hair, felt it kinky and rough against her palm. "He couldn't," she said. "But he intended to."

"I know," Theo said. "I still miss him. Do you think he'd like it, too?"

"I know he would. He loved you very much."

Theo sighed, snuggled closer. "I wish we could change things."

"But we can't," she said. "We just can't."

It was a little after four when she got to the hospital. The five kids had a room to themselves. Georgie was conscious but not too alert, on oxygen and with an intravenous line. The nurse said he was responding to treatment and told her they expected to have him out of bed by tomorrow, so he could open his Christmas presents. When Marti spoke to him he gave her a small smile. She added her gifts, warm hats and scarves and mittens, to the pile of boxes that had been stacked around the base of a small Christmas tree. A collection had been taken up at the precinct and Lupe had used the money to buy them each a toy and a new winter coat. The mayor had donated boots and shoes.

The other four children were fine. The nurses had let them begin opening their gifts. Their beds were loaded with stuffed animals, dolls, doll furniture, doll clothes, trucks, board games, and hand-held electronic games.

Padgett and Jose were playing with a Nintendo. LaShawna was sitting up in bed, round with child, cuddling Sissie in one arm and a doll in the other.

Vik came in five minutes after Marti, waved in her direction as he took off his coat, and joined the boys. Giggling, they showed him how to play the Nintendo game.

"Need haircuts," LaShawna said. "All three of 'em."

Marti looked at LaShawna's hair, short strands escaping from cornrows that had been plaited a long time ago. Sissie's hair had been recently combed. Marti thought of the limitations imposed living in that cellar and offered to give them shampoos. She took her time combing, brushing, and braiding, and one of the nurses came in with barrettes shaped like buttons and bows.

Because the two girls and Georgie were orphans, related and from out of state, Denise Stevens had got waivers from Missouri and arranged placement in a Milwaukee suburb. The three of them, soon to be four, would live together in a foster home. LaShawna would participate in a special program for unwed mothers. Padgett's and Jose's futures were less certain. Denise had found homes for them, but they would become wards of the state of Illinois; a judge and DCFS would have to approve.

Before Marti left she found a rocking chair for LaShawna. Sissie was asleep on LaShawna's lap when the aide brought in snacks and Marti said her good-byes.

When Marti got home, the house smelled like Christmas. Cinnamon and nutmeg aromas rushed to meet her at the door. For a moment she thought back to other Christmases, with Momma, with Johnny. But they were gone now. She hung up her coat, then paused in the hallway. It was Christmas Eve. A feeling came over her all at once, a serenity that she hadn't felt in a long time.

When Janey woke up she was in the closet again. Something was touching her face. Feathers. Must be the woman's dress. She pushed it away. The floor was hard, and it was dark except for little cracks of light at the edges of the door. It wasn't a little closet like the one at home. Didn't smell like mothballs, either. Stank like the woman's perfume.

She couldn't hear anyone talking. Where was the woman? She began shivering and couldn't stop. Her teeth were knocking together. She pulled down a coat to cover herself. Curling up, she wished she were smaller. Too late to be scared. Should have been scared before she got on that bus in Chattanooga.

She pushed the coat away from her face, looked up at the clothes hanging above her head, then moved back until she touched the wall. Feeling around for her shoes, she grabbed one with a long, pointy heel. If that woman hit her again, at least she'd have something she could use to fight back.

This door was locked, but she had to figure out how to get away from them when they let her out again. Best to try while the woman was here alone. If she didn't get away, and the man wasn't here, the woman was gonna beat her again.

How was she gonna get back home? Never should have come here. She wanted to live with Maddie. They be just alike, her and Maddie, not smart like her other sisters. She meant to stay with Maddie in Chattanooga. Should have done that. Safe there. Baby-sat them three children for two weeks and got that money and decided she'd rather be someplace else, like a fool. Tiffany Lewis come here last year. All the way to Chicago all by herself, stayed with her auntie for a month, came home with some brand-new clothes none of her sisters got to wear first. Now she come here, she had nothing but trouble.

They were joking her, both of them. The woman joked her when she brought her here, making like she would help her find a job. Now the man would joke her too, making like he was gonna help her get back home. She would have to lie down with him and let him touch her.

A key turned in the lock and the door opened. The light was so bright she had to close her eyes. She held the toe of the shoe tightly.

"Come on outta there," the woman said.

Janey stood slowly, holding the shoe behind her.

"Come out here."

"No!"

The woman leaned into the closet, pushing the clothes out of the way, grabbing Janey's arm and pulling her into the bedroom. Janey brought her hand up and raked the heel down the side of the woman's head. The woman let go of her and cussed.

Janey dropped the shoe and ran, but the woman grabbed her by the hair. She didn't even get to the front door.

■ ■ ■

When Det. Marti MacAlister arrived at the Lakeshore Clinic, the fire was out. Some spectators were beginning to walk away, but many waited, arms folded, talking in small clusters. Children stamped their feet in the puddles of water, laughing and calling to each other as if it were a fiesta.

Marti shouldered her way through the crowd without identifying herself as a peace officer. At five ten and a hundred and sixty pounds, she was what her mother called healthy. People tended to move out of her way. It was a little after eight o'clock. Lights from emergency vehicles lit the night sky. The night was hot, even for July, and humid. Marti had changed her blouse before leaving the house and it was damp with sweat already.

She passed the yellow barricades, avoiding the hose lines from the two fire trucks that remained at the scene. It would be several hours before the building cooled down and the risk of the fire re-igniting had passed. She checked to see if her partner had arrived, but didn't see him. One ambulance was parked near the two-story building, lights out, doors closed. She walked toward it.

The odor of smoke and charred debris grew stronger as she approached. The red brick was blackened above the windows. Water ran from windows in thin streams. Shattered glass was scattered across the sidewalk.

Ben Walker, a paramedic Marti knew, was leaning against the ambulance, his face streaked with soot. His uniform was dirty. Walker was a bear of a man—not fat, just big, with the lumbering grace of a large person who was light on his feet and accustomed to his size. Marti couldn't picture him doing anything as delicate as starting an IV. His nine-year-old son, Mike, was a friend of her nine-year-old, Theo.

Ben gave her a slow smile that began in his eyes. "You're late, MacAlister. Your partner's already around back. He must not be causing too much trouble tonight. The arson investigator on this one doesn't have much patience with people telling him how to do his job."

"Little things like that don't bother Vik." She nodded toward the ambulance. "Think you've got another victim inside?"

"According to the doctor who owns the place, there shouldn't have been anyone in there."

"He still around?"

Ben nodded toward the building. "Saw him go around back. He identified one of the bodies for us. One of the receptionists."

"Dispatch says you found two females. How bad were they?"

"Smoke inhalation. One ran into the closet.

The other one was on a table in an examining room. The doors were closed and the fire didn't burn in that direction. Wouldn't surprise me if they both could have gotten out."

"Young? Old?"

"Receptionist was twenty-two. Hispanic. Her mother was here five minutes after the first units arrived. The brother showed up and they both had hysterics until he started hyperventilating and mom began complaining of chest pains. We sent them both to the hospital."

"And the other victim?"

"Black, looks to be ten, twelve years old. The clothes she was wearing seemed a little odd for a visit to the doctor, but the way they dress nowadays . . ." He shrugged. "You could have laid her out in the casket in that dress when she first put it on."

Marti looked past the barricades, at girls who flirted and boys who cajoled. Worst thing she could think of, burying a *child*.

"Does it look suspicious?"

"An arson investigator is checking it out. You can see the line of demarcation at the base of the stairs. Spread fast. Moved from the center of the building eastward. West end wasn't involved."

The front door was at the west end. "And that's where the bodies were found?"

"Right."

"Upstairs or down?"

"Downstairs was vacant."

They would have had to negotiate a flight of stairs. Maybe they could have gotten out.

"What kind of time frame have you got?"

"It was called in at 6:47. Almost half the building was involved when we got here four and a half minutes later."

"Be nice to know why the victims were in there and the doctor wasn't."

Ben grinned at her. "And I'm sure you'll find out."

Vik was in the alley, standing away from the building, talking to a tall, thin man who seemed to be ignoring him. They were almost the same height, but Vik was a bit taller at six two.

Vik had a tendency to lean over people. There was just a hint of ferocity in his face, with his beak nose bent from a break and his wiry eyebrows curling in all directions. There were dark pouches beneath his eyes that weren't caused by lack of sleep. Children would walk right up to him, but most adults found his appearance intimidating.

The other man glanced at Marti as she approached, then moved away.

"The doctor?" she asked Vik.

"Yeah. Edwards. James Edwards."

She watched him but didn't speak. In a few seconds he turned to her. "Yes?"

"Detective MacAlister." She showed him her shield.

"I certainly hope you don't want to ask questions, too. Not after this." He gestured toward the building.

He had the kind of voice she'd expect to hear if she were speaking with someone in broadcasting. Moderate tone. Perfect diction. No hint of where he came from. If she was listening to him without being able to see him, she would never guess that his skin was as smooth and as brown as the oak table in her kitchen.

"Good thing you weren't in there."

"Nobody should have been in there." He jammed his hands into his pockets. His slacks were tan, and clean.

"Why not?"

"Teresa called and said she'd be a few minutes late."

Marti waited. When he didn't volunteer anything else, she asked, "What time were you expecting her?"

"Seven, seven-fifteen."

Again she waited. "What time did you leave here today?"

As he looked at her, he seemed to be looking down his nose. He had a face she thought of as economical: narrow nose, thin lips, small, deep-set eyes. His ears stuck out a little, making him seem less stern and severe. Not talkative. At least not tonight. Shock, maybe. Perhaps grief, if he was fond of the receptionist, knew her well.

"How long did Teresa work for you?"

"Two years." He seemed almost mesmerized by the burned-out clinic.

"What time did you leave here today?" she asked again.

"Sixish."

"And when you got back?"

"The building was on fire."

"Did you call it in?" she asked.

"They were already here."

He had been away from the clinic for about fifty minutes. Not much time.

"Where did you go?"

"Is this some kind of interrogation?"

"I'm with Homicide. I have to know how the victims died, maybe why."

He took a few steps away from her. Without turning he said, "The electrical system and anything else in there that could possibly have caused this was upgraded before I moved in. I hadn't thought of that until now. How can I help you?"

"Anything unusual happen with the receptionist? Fight with the boyfriend?"

"I wouldn't know. I didn't see Teresa tonight, but she seemed fine on Tuesday. We had evening clinic two nights a week."

"What about the other victim?"

"Never saw her before. I have no idea why she was here. I can't even guess."

"And Teresa shouldn't have been here either?"

"Not that early."

"How did she get in?"

"She had a key."

"For the front or the back door?"

He seemed puzzled. "She had a key to both. I really should go to her mother. The poor woman's distraught."

Instead of leaving, he stood across from the back door and kept staring at the building.